Dear Readers,

Many years ago, when I was a kid, my father said to me, "Bill, it doesn't really matter what you do in life. What's important is to be the *best* William Johnstone you can be."

I've never forgotten those words. And now, many years and almost two hundred books later, I like to think that I am still trying to be the best William Johnstone I can be. Whether it's Ben Raines in the Ashes series, or Frank Morgan, the last gunfighter, or Smoke Jensen, our intrepid mountain man, or John Barrone and his hardworking crew keeping America safe from terrorist lowlifes in the Code Name series, I want to make each new book better than the last and deliver powerful storytelling.

Equally important, I try to create the kinds of believable characters that we can all identify with, real people who face tough challenges. When one of my creations blasts an enemy into the middle of next week, you can be damn sure he had a good reason.

As a storyteller, my job is to entertain you, my readers, and to make sure that you get plenty of enjoyment from my books for your hard-earned money. This is not a job I take lightly. And I greatly appreciate your feedback—you are my gold, and your opinions *do* count. So please keep the letters and e-mails coming.

Respectfully yours,

William W. Johnstone

WILLIAM W. JOHNSTONE

BLOOD BOND
BROTHERHOOD OF THE GUN

PINNACLE BOOKS
Kensington Publishing Corp.
http://www.kensingtonbooks.com

PINNACLE BOOKS are published by

Kensington Publishing Corp.
850 Third Avenue
New York, NY 10022

All Kensington Titles, Imprints, and Distributed Lines are
available at special quantity discounts for bulk purchases for
sales promotions, premiums, fund-raising, and educational
or institutional use. Special book excerpts or customized
printings can also be created to fit specific needs. For details,
write or phone the office of the Kensington special sales
manager: Kensington Publishing Corp., 850 Third Avenue,
New York, NY 10022, attn: Special Sales Department, Phone:
1-800-221-2647.

Pinnacle and the P logo Reg. U.S. Pat. & TM Off.

First Pinnacle Books Printing: February 2006

10 9 8 7 6 5 4 3 2

Printed in the United States of America

It is not what a lawyer tells me I *may* do; but what humanity, reason, and justice tell me I ought to do.

—Edmund Burke

Chapter 1

They were blood-brothers, bonded by the Cheyenne ritual that made them as one. And more importantly, they were Brothers of the Wolf.

Two young men, Matt Bodine and Sam August Webster Two Wolves. The two men could and had, many times, passed as having the same mother, which they did not. Both possessed the same lean hips and heavy upper torso musculature. Sam's eyes were black, Matt's were blue. Sam's hair was black, Bodine's hair was dark brown. They were the same height and very nearly the same weight.

Both wore the same type of three-stone necklace around their necks, the stones pierced by rawhide. Both were ruggedly handsome men.

Both had gone through the Cheyenne Coming of Manhood, and each would carry the scars on his chest until death turned the soulless flesh into dust.

They were both Onihomahan: Friends of the Wolf. Both revered the great Gray Wolf, and both had raised wolf cubs as boys. The Indians did not have the fear of the wolf that the white man possessed, probably because the Indians took the time to understand animal behavior. Matt had learned the white man never took the time—any animal he didn't understand he wanted to kill.

"Are we going to have to ride forever to reach Arizona?" Two Wolves asked, shifting in the saddle.

"I think we are in the territory, brother. I also think we are being followed."

Neither one of them knew it, but they were already in Arizona, having crossed the border two days back.

"You think? Hah! I have known about that for at least two hours."

"Nice of you to say something about it."

"I was waiting for you to dig the sand out of your eyes and ears and discover it yourself. You would have probably noticed something amiss just before they—whoever they might be—conked you on the head."

Matt grunted. "At least four of them, I figure. Maybe more."

"I would say four. But you're right; maybe more."

"There are Apache here," Matt said. "But there are a lot of Navajo and Zuni too. Hualapai and Kaibab are to the west of us."

"Those behind us are not Indians," Sam said. "We'd probably have never spotted an Indian." He smiled. "At least you wouldn't have," he needled his friend.

Matt silently agreed with the first part of Sam's statement. He ignored the second part. The blood-brothers were always sticking the needle into each other and had been for years. Neither took it seriously. Matt pulled his Winchester out of the boot, shucked a round into the chamber, eased the hammer down, and rode with the rifle laid across his saddle horn. Sam Two Wolves did the same.

Sam pointed to the west and Matt cut his eyes. The ruins of an ancient pueblo could be seen. "Navajo?" he asked.

Sam shrugged and gave the reply that most Indians of any tribe would. "Those who came before us."

"Let's cut straight south," Matt suggested. "Keep your eyes open for Los Gigantes Butte. We want to swing to the west of that."

"We're running low on water. This would not be a good time for us to get caught up in a trap."

"Lukachuka Creek is south and west of the butte." Then Matt remembered what a drifting cowboy had told him a long time back. "There's supposed to be a tank in the rocks just up ahead," he told Sam. "If the cowboy knew what he was talking about and it isn't dry."

"Your words are so comforting, brother."

Matt twisted in the saddle, looking behind him. Those following them were no longer trying to hide their presence. The dust trail was clearly visible. "I don't like it," he stated.

"Neither do I. Let's find that tank and find it quick."

"And full," Matt added.

It wasn't full, but there was more than enough water to fill their canteens, water the horses, fill a coffee pot, and still have enough for several days should they have to defend the place.

The tank was located high in the rocks, with graze for the horses and good cover for both man and beast.

Neither Matt nor Sam were too worried about the men following them. If anything, the men following should be worried about what would happen should they catch up with Matt and Sam. Matt's reputation as a gunhandler had begun when he was just a boy. He killed his first man at age fourteen; the bully prodding the boy into a fight. The bully had not even managed to clear leather.

Less than a year later, the bully's brothers came after Matt Bodine. They got lead in the boy, but when the smoke drifted away, Bodine was standing over their bodies, his hands filled with Colts. When he was sixteen, rustlers hit his father's ranch. Bodine's guns put two more in the ground and left two others badly wounded and wishing they had taken up farming for a living.

At seventeen, Bodine went off to live with the Cheyenne for a year. He'd been spending forbidden time with them since a boy—often for weeks at a time.

At eighteen he was riding shotgun for gold shipments. Outlaws tried twice to take the shipment. Four more men were planted in unmarked graves.

At nineteen, he began scouting for the Army.

Between the ages of nineteen and twenty-five, the guns of Matt Bodine became legend in the west. His guns as well as his fists were much-feared. Bodine knew Indian wrestling, boxing, and down and dirty, kick and stomp barroom brawling.

Bodine's mother was a school-teacher and she saw to it that the boy was very well educated.

Sam Two Wolves—a half-breed, his mother was from Vermont—did not have the name of a gunfighter, but he was still just as feared as Bodine and better educated, having been schooled at a university back east. His mother's dying wish.

Sam's father was the famed war chief, Medicine Horse, who died on Last Stand Hill during the Custer fight. Medicine Horse rode up to Custer unarmed except for a coup stick, wishing to die rather than live in disgrace.

Matt and Sam had witnessed the Custer fight, from atop a hill overlooking the valley of the Little Big Horn. And they would spend their lives trying to forget the awful sight.

"I wonder who those guys following us are, and what they want?" Matt said, his back to a rock, a cup of coffee in his hand.

"If I had a crystal ball I'd tell you," Sam replied, without opening his eyes. He was stretched out flat on his back, in the shade of a boulder.

It was the fall of the year, and it was hot. Not the blistering heat of full summer, but still hot enough to kill a man if he wasn't careful.

A bullet whined wickedly off a rock and went howling off in another direction.

Without opening his eyes or getting up from his prone position, Sam said, "Well, now we know what they want—us!"

"Yeah. But why?" Matt had taken his rifle and moved to a guarded position where he could look out over the land below them.

"I'm certain your sordid reputation has something to do with it. What would my poor mother think? Me keeping company with a notorious gunfighter?" Sam choked back laughter and rolled to his knees, picking up his rifle.

"Very funny." But Matt could not conceal his grin. "I can see it now."

"See what?"

"The inscription on our single tombstone: Here lies the Injun and the white guy!"

"Single tombstone! Ye Gods! You think I'm going to be buried with *you?*"

Matt chuckled. "If we go out together, we probably won't have much to say about it, right?"

"What a dismal thought. Brother? What are we going to do about this slight problem facing us?"

"How about us finding out what they want?"

"What are you going to do: invite them up for coffee?"

Matt ignored that. "Hey!" he shouted. "What's the matter with you guys? What's the idea of shootin' at us?"

A bullet was his reply.

Matt tried again. "I think you people got the wrong guys. We haven't done anything to you."

"Give us the gold and you can ride on!" the voice bounced around the rocks.

"Gold?" Sam said. "What gold?"

"We don't have any gold!" Matt shouted. "I told you, you got the wrong people!"

"You a damn liar. We been trailin' you two all the way from Green River. You thought you'd throwed us off when you left the fork of the Walker just inside the Territory. But I want that poke you mined out. And we'll take that woman with you, too, mister. Then you can ride on. We know she's nothin' but a stray. She ain't worth dyin' over."

Sam sat straight up, his back against the boulder. "Woman?"

"I told you to cut your hair," Matt said, grinning at him.

"Idiot! My hair is no longer than yours."

"What woman?" Matt yelled. "There's nobody up here but Sam and me."

"Have Sam sing out!"

"What do you want, you nitwit?" Sam yelled.

Silence for a few moments. "You boys show yourselves," the man yelled. "If you ain't Wellman and the girl, you can ride on out."

"You believe that, Matt?"

" 'Bout as much as I believe in fairy tales. They were going to rob those people, Sam." Raising his voice, he yelled, "Hell with you, mister. I got no reason to take the word of a damn thief."

"Here we go," Sam muttered. "Robin and his Hood strike another blow for the poor and downtrodden."

"We'll starve you out!" the outlaw yelled.

"Not likely," Matt called. "We have plenty of food."

"You'll die of thirst then!"

"No, we won't. The tank was full. But you boys are gonna get mighty thirsty if you hang around long."

Matt and Sam could hear cursing from below them.

"We'll make a deal with you!"

"I don't deal with scum."

"Then die, you bastards!"

The air around Matt and Sam was suddenly and viciously filled with howling, whining lead. Both pulled their saddles over their upper torsos to help against any flattened ricochets and let the outlaws bang away. Their horses were just below them, in a small depression, safe from any stray bullets.

They made no attempt to return the fire. The gunfire stopped and the sounds of galloping horses reached them. Both lifted up to where they could see and looked out. The outlaws were fogging it away from the rocks. Five of them, heading west.

"They must have picked up our trail at the fork, thinking it was the man and the girl," Sam said. "We took the east fork. Now those scum are heading west to pick up the trail."

Matt looked up at the sky. It would be dark in a couple of hours. "No point in taking off after them now. We might ride smack into an ambush. We'll spend the night and pick up their trail in the morning." He met Sam's eyes. "If that's all right with you, that is."

The half-breed smiled. "Oh, I think I'll tag along with you. Somebody has to watch your back trail."

Matt reached down for the blackened coffee pot and began cussing. One of the outlaw's slugs had torn the pot apart.

"Now that irritates me," Sam said. "Anybody who would deprive a man of his coffee is just no damn good!"

Chapter 2

Both men were still griping as they saddled up and rode out the next morning. Western men like their coffee and they like it often. To wake up without a pot of coffee strong enough to dissolve a horseshoe was just a lousy way to start the day.

"I get my hands on those damn thieving bums," Matt said, "I'm gonna make them wish they'd never ridden up to that tank."

"I sure would like a cup of coffee," Sam said wistfully. "Where do you suppose is the nearest town?"

"The way we're heading, there's supposed to be a trading post just built. Some guy named Hubbell built it. But it's a good ninety miles from here. Three days without coffee," he added.

Sam cussed in Cheyenne and then switched to English. He was very graphic in both languages.

They crossed Lukachuka Creek and made camp in Chinle Valley. They did not push their horses or themselves, for this was rugged country and they wanted to spare their horses.

The tracks of the outlaws were easy to follow and from the way they were traveling, the thieves were also taking it easy, not wanting to come up with a lame horse and be set afoot in this country.

They reached the trading post during the late afternoon of the third day. A number of horses were tied at the hitchrails in front of the long and low building. The place appeared to be full of customers. Odd for this sparsely populated land.

Matt and Sam reined up in back of the building. Both men slipped the hammer thongs from their guns as soon as their boots touched the ground.

Sam took one look at the hoof-chewed ground around the hitchrails and said, "Those are our people, all right. See the chipped out place on that shoe?"

"Yeah. Come on. I want a drink first and then we'll see about settling up for a new coffee pot."

The adobe and stone post bore the scars of many Indian attacks. The wooden support posts of the porch roof was embedded with arrow heads. Sam Two Wolves looked at the broken shank of one.

"Apache," he said.

"Yeah. They have attacked as far north as the middle of Utah Territory; they back off when they get into Ute country." He stepped up to the porch and grinned. "They might not serve you in here, you know?"

"I hope they try that," his blood-brother replied, a dangerous glint in his dark eyes.

The bartender didn't even blink when Matt and Sam ordered whiskey with a beer chaser. But he, along with everyone else in the dark barroom, did notice the tied down twin guns of the strangers.

Two Wolves and Bodine took their drinks to the far end of the bar, where their backs would be facing a wall and they could get a good look at everybody in the place.

It wasn't a pleasant view.

"Did you ever see so many ugly people gathered in one place in all your life?" Sam said, raising his voice so all could hear.

The buzz of conversation stopped abruptly and both men could feel the hot burn of very unfriendly eyes swing toward them.

"For a fact," Matt said. "If a beauty contest was held in this place, nobody would win."

"You got a fat mouth," a voice came from out of the smoky murk of the room.

"Who owns that horse with the Four-V brand?" Matt asked, knowing full well that somebody had used a running iron to make the brand, probably out of a double-W.

"I do," the same voice replied. "If it's any of your damn business. Which it ain't."

"You owe us a coffee pot," Matt told him.

"Huh?" A chair was pushed back and boot heels and jingling spurs moved closer to the bar. "I don't owe you nothin', mister. But I just might decide to give you a skint head if you don't shut your mouth."

"The only thing you're going to give me is a new coffee pot. Now buy it from the man, set it on the bar, shut your big mouth and set your butt back in the chair you just vacated."

The outlaw yelled out a violent oath and lumbered toward the bar, heading straight for Matt, his big hands balled into fists. Sam stepped aside, his hands by his side, so he could watch the crowd and grab iron if anybody tried to interfere.

Matt opened the dance with a short, straight right fist to the man's mouth. The blow knocked the outlaw spinning. He crashed into a table and sent beer mugs and cards and poker chips flying. He bounced to his boots and charged Bodine, screaming filth at him.

Bodine stuck out one boot and tripped the outlaw. He slammed into the bar, belly-high, and knocked the wind out of himself and a plank out of the bar just as Bodine slugged him twice above the kidney, with a left and right, bringing a squall of pain.

The outlaw staggered and turned, his eyes filled with pain and confusion.

Bodine hammered him twice in the face with a left and right combination and then drove his fist into the man's belly. As the burly outlaw slowly sank to his knees, Bodine grabbed him behind the head and brought his knee up, all in one fast, practiced movement. Knee connected with nose and nose got flattened.

Bodine turned his back to the man and faced the bartender as the outlaw fell on the floor, blood pouring from his broken nose. "Fill up the beer mug, friend. I just worked up a thirst."

"You just worked yourself up for a killing, is what you just done," a voice spoke from the murky depths of the barroom. "That there is Ray Porter, the Idaho gunslick, and this room is filled with his men. What do you think about that, hotshot?"

Bodine drained half his beer, set the mug on the bar— when Porter had crashed into it he had knocked it somewhat askew, spilling all the drinks that were there—and looked at the room full of gunslicks.

"Three days ago, me and my buddy here," he jerked a thumb toward Sam, "was ridin' south, just north of the Los Gigantes Buttes, when we decided to camp near a tank. This jerk," he pointed to the unconscious gunhand from Idaho Territory, "and four other jerks started shooting at us. They gave it up after about an hour, but not before they shot up my coffee pot. Now, I'm fixin' to get a couple of dollars out of this hombre's pocket and buy me a new coffee pot. And if anybody feels like they want to stop me' just come on. Now, does anybody want to start this dance?"

"That just plumb breaks my heart," a man said, pushing his chair back and standing up, his hand close to the butts of his guns. "But I tell you what you should have done, mister. You should have carried two coffee pots. But it don't matter no more. 'Cause you ain't gonna be needin' 'em after today."

He grabbed for his guns and Bodine cleared leather, cocked, and shot him just as the man's hands gripped the butts and he began his lift. The slug took the man directly in the center of the chest, piercing the heart. He was dead as he hit the floor.

"Jesus H. Christ!" a man whispered hoarsely. "He's as fast as Smoke Jensen."

"What's your name, buddy?" another asked.

"Matt Bodine. And this is my brother, Sam Two Wolves."

Someone sighed in the crowd. Another cleared his throat nervously. Another man cussed softly; cussing his bad luck to be in the same room with Matt Bodine and Sam Two Wolves with both of them on the warpath. Still another slowly stood up, his hands in plain sight and walked to the door. "I'm gone," he said, and put his hand on the batwings. Just before he stepped outside, he said, "I'll be takin' me a bath and a shave out back."

Another man stood up, walking carefully. "Tell that boy to fill another tub, Harry. I feel the need for a soak myself. I'll get my extra set of longjohns from the saddlebags and join you in a minute." He walked to the batwings and the both of them were gone.

"A man shouldn't oughta plug another man's coffee pot," a gunhand said. "Hard enough rollin' out on a cold mornin' with coffee waitin'. Plumb discouragin' without it. You hep yourself to some greenbacks from Porter, Matt. He owes you a coffee pot."

"Thank you." Matt knelt down and pulled a wad from Porter's pocket. He took two dollars and handed them to the barkeep. "One coffee pot, please."

"Yes, sir, Mister Bodine. I'll be back in a jiffy. Will there be anything else, sir?"

"Coffee, beans, flour, and bacon. We'll settle up when I leave."

"Yes, sir!"

"And grind the coffee coarse," Sam told him. "We like it stout."

"Yes, sir, Mister Two Wolves."

Matt turned to face the crowd. "One of you tell Porter that we're riding to join up with the man and the girl that Porter wants to rob. Tell him if I see his ugly face again, I'll kill him on the spot, no questions asked."

"My back was getting sort of itchy riding away from that place, brother," Sam said.

"I do know the feeling. And I don't think my words changed any minds back there."

"No. They'll be coming after the man and the girl, whether we're along or not. They smell gold. Some of Porter's men must have linked up with him back at that trading post."

"Yeah. You ever heard of a gunfighter named Porter?"

"No. I think he's probably more thief and outlaw than gunslick. But I did see Don Bradley back there."

"So did I. And I have to wonder about that. He's too good with a gun to be mixed up with a small-timer like Porter. Last I heard, Don was getting top dollar for his skills. Who else did you see? I didn't have much time for eyeballing."

"Bob Doyle is the only other one that I knew. I saw three or four young punks with fancy rigs. I guess they're out to make a reputation."

"What they'll probably get is an unmarked grave. Let's play a hunch, Sam. Let's make a guess that Wellman and the girl deliberately took the west fork of Walker Creek to throw off Porter and his men. You with me?"

"Yes. Then they headed straight south. You know this country, Matt; I don't. Where are they going?"

"I don't know," Bodine admitted. "Green River is a long way from here. They were heading straight south all the way until they took the west fork. Two people, a man and a woman—maybe just a girl—heading straight into Apache country. Why, Sam?"

"And carrying gold. A lot of gold, I would guess." He shrugged his shoulders. "I don't know the why of it. But there's one way to find out."

"Catch up with them and ask."

"That's it."

"You game?"

"That goes without asking."

The two young men turned their horses and headed south. They pointed their horses' noses toward one of the most dangerous places left on the American continent: the great rugged mountains and the inhospitable deserts and the fierce warriors who inhabited that land. It was called Apache country.

Chapter 3

They made camp the first night at the northern tip of Wide Ruin Wash. It had been slow and careful going, always checking their back trail and keeping a close watch left, right, and in front of them. Bodine had been through this country several times, but he was far from being expertly knowledgable of this still hostile land.

This land did contain a lot of friendly Indians, mostly Navaho and Zuni, with most of them being peaceful farmers of the land. But the Apache roamed all over the territory, and they hated the white man with a passion unequalled anywhere. One thing Bodine and Sam knew for a fact: they would not allow themselves to be taken alive by the Apache.

Skilled torturers, the Apache could make a rendezvous with the Grim Reaper seem a joyous occasion.

They found a small but heavily armed wagon train on the northern edge of the Painted Desert and stopped for coffee and to listen for any information those in the train might have about a man and a woman traveling alone.

Starting on their second cup—the coffee was strong enough to dissolve nails—Bodine and Sam perked their ears up when a man said, "Fool's mission. That's what them two is on."

"I'll sure agree with that," another man piped up. Damned if I'd be headin' south of Horsehead Crossing with anything less than the Army with me."

Horsehead Crossing would soon be renamed Holbrook.

It was a small settlement on the Little Colorado. About thirty-five miles to the northwest, another small town was springing up. In a few more years it would be named Winslow.

"There ain't nothin' left of that little girl noways," the wagonmaster stuck his opinion in. "And who'd want anything to do with a girl after the Injuns got done with her."

Sam hid his smile behind his tin cup; only Matt noticed the curving of his lips. Both men knew that Indians loved children—of any color—and raised them well, if harshly, when judged against white standards.

If it was a boy, he had a rougher time of it—among many tribes—but if he was spunky enough, he could make it.

"How's the coffee, boys?" a man asked.

"Good," Bodine said with a grin, holding out his cup. "We'll have another."

The man returned the grin and refilled their cups.

"We left a town over in New Mexico Territory. What was left of it," one of the men around the fire added. "What wasn't dryin' up and blowin' away was saddlin' up or hitchin' up and ridin' away. Fool place to build a town anyways."

"You boys lookin' for work?"

"No, we got us a little poke from workin' up in Wyoming and thought we'd just see the country; thought it best to head south for the winter, though."

"Well, don't head too much farther south. The 'Paches is on the move. We just heard about them raidin' a ranch over yonder way," he waved his hand toward the west, " 'bout a month ago and kilt ever'body there; feller and his wife and three hands. It was awful what them savages done to them.

Death was a merciful thing. Kidnapped a little girl and took her God knows where. Another bunch come through here last week and raided another ranch. Kilt all them folks, too. It's a sorry time, boys."

"You were talking about someone on a fool's mission," Sam said. "Relatives of the child who was taken from the ranch?"

"You betcha. Couple of fools is what they is. The girl's grandfather and some woman he picked up along the way who lost an older brother to the 'Paches some twelve years back. She admitted she was only eight or so when they snatched him, and didn't think she'd be able to recognize him. Now, ain't that about the dumbest thing you ever heard of? The brother would be more 'un twenty years old now accordin' to her—and if he's alive, he's nothin' but a gawd-damn Injun by now. Probably can't even speak English no more."

Then it came to Matt. Wellman. *Dick* Wellman? If so, the famed old mountain man would be pushing seventy hard. But if it was Dick Wellman, seventy years old or not, he would still be a ring-dang-doodle to fool with.

Matt turned to Sam and winked at him. "That must be those tracks we keep seein' ahead of us. Three-four days old."

Before Sam could reply, the wagonmaster said, "You bet it is, boys. That old man and that girl is a headin' straight south. They think the girl is being held somewheres in the vicinity of the Gila Mountains." He shuddered. "That's Chappo's country. And if there ever was a bad one, Chappo is it."

He would get no argument there. Chappo's bunch were as savage as they come. Chappo's Apache name was unpronounceable to whites, so somewhere down the line, so the story went, an army lieutenant had nicknamed him Chappo. It stuck.

Tending to their horses, Sam said, "I just put it together, Matt. *Dick* Wellman?"

"Yeah. Me, too. Dick Wellman. That's a hard man, brother. That mountain man might be old, but he's still tough as nails and meaner than a silver-tip." He shook his head. "But for the life of me, I can't imagine him taking a girl into Apache country."

"Chappo's country," Sam mused. "We'd best find us another pack horse at the post and lay in the supplies . . . especially .44 rounds."

"You're reading my mind, brother."

They pulled out at dawn the next morning. At supper, they had told the people what they were going to do.

Everyone in the train turned out to see them off.

"You boys is young and mighty brave," the wagonmaster called out. "But goin' up agin Chappo and his bunch is a stupid thing to do. I wish you'd think about it."

Matt and Sam lifted their hands in acknowledgement of the warning and rode out of the protection of the wagon train.

They rode through the stillness of the Painted Desert, and it was a sight that neither of them had ever seen before and would never forget. They both found it a lonely and foreboding place, and they marveled at the fallen stone trees and wondered how old they were; how long they had lain in this brooding land?

They picked their way through the silent land, gradually cutting west; they had to resupply at Horsehead Crossing.

"We're close to them," Sam said, drinking the last of his coffee and watching the sun sink slowly behind the horizon. The rays of the dying sun painted multi-colored hues over the stark landscape.

"Those horse-droppings we looked at pretty well confirm

we're not more than a few miles behind them. Two riders and a packhorse, and the packhorse is not heavily loaded."

"Apaches have no use for gold, brother. If Wellman is carrying several sacks of gold, he isn't planning on buying his granddaughter's freedom from Chappo. Somebody else is involved in this."

"Maybe Chappo is raiding the ranches and kidnapping the kids for someone else."

"For example? . . ."

"Who knows? To sell into slavery, maybe. Or maybe if the kids are young enough, to sell to people who want kids but can't have children of their own. Or maybe there is a darker side to all of this; if you know what I mean."

"Yes. I do. However, I would prefer not to think about that. It's too disgusting for words."

"But possible."

"Oh, yes."

"I think, brother, we need to catch up with Wellman tomorrow and find out what he thinks."

"What about Wellman?" the cold voice came out of the darkness. It was followed by the hammer on a Winchester being eared back.

"Ten more ought to do it," the man said, looking at the frightened little girl. "Ten pretty little girls just like this one."

"That'll give us twenty-five we can ship down to Captain Morgan. I'll get word to Chappo."

"Tell him to hurry up. Tell him I'll give him ten rifles and a case of ammunition for each girl he brings me."

"That ought to prod him into action. Uh, Lake, some of the boys was wonderin' if maybe, ah, they could . . . you know?" He jerked a thumb toward the girl.

"No!" the word was explosive coming out of Lake's mouth. "And I'll kill any man who touches one. Morgan says the Arab sheiks demand the girls to be pure and blonde and not over ten years old. You make damn sure the men understand that."

"Yes, sir, Lake. Anything you say."

"We're gettin' big money for these kids, Mavern. And it's sure better than robbing banks and rustling beeves. So let's don't screw it up."

"Yes, sir, Lake. Ain't none of the kids been touched. Some of the boys was just askin' is all."

"You make certain they understand, Mavern. And they'd better understand."

"I'll shore do it, Lake. Count on me."

Lake lit a long thin Mexican cigar. He fixed his one steady eye on the man. The other eye was an off-color pale blue and it drooped and was cock-eyed. He'd been kicked by a horse on the side of the face some years back, breaking his cheekbone and jaw and he'd never had it set properly. He took a long drag from the cigar and blew a fat smoke ring. It drifted gently toward the other outlaw. "Oh, I do, Mavern. I do for a fact."

Mavern left the room and Lake muttered, "About as far as I can see you, that is."

Both Sam and Matt were startled and highly irritated. And they both immediately froze where they were. For someone to have slipped up on them meant that the person was very, very good, and probably very, very dangerous.

And Matt had a good idea who it was holding the rifle on them. "Wellman?"

"Maybe."

"I'm Matt Bodine. This is my brother, Sam Two Wolves."

"Bodine, huh? The Wyoming gunslick?"

"I've used my guns, yes. I've never hired them out."

"Two Wolves, son of Medicine Horse?"

"That is correct."

"Knowed him. Good man. Sorry business what took place in the Rosebuds. Custer was a fool. You got airy coffee left in that pot?"

"Probably a cup. It ought to still be hot."

"Pour me some. I'm coming in."

The old mountain man moved as silently as a wraith. He grinned at Matt and Sam and began poking around in the coals, adding twigs to build up the fire. Then he tossed a couple of sticks onto it.

"Don't y'all worry none. Ain't no 'Paches around, boys. Not no more. But you was right in killin' this fire 'fore dark come. You smelled the dust, hey?"

"Yes, sir," Sam said.

"They was 'Paches, all right. But they veered off to the west. Probably gonna raid some Hopis and steal their horses. They long gone now." He lifted cagey old eyes toward Matt. "You been on my backtrail now for some few days. You mind tellin' me what's goin' on?"

Matt leveled with him, starting with Porter trying to kill them. He ended with their suspicions about someone other than Chappo being involved in the kidnapping.

Wellman grunted. "There ain't much to Porter. He's a thief, a murderer, a two-bit bank robber, a bully, a coward, and an all around no-good. He comes traipsin' down this-away we'll just blow him out of the saddle and let the buzzards eat him."

"Can I come in now, Mister Wellman?" a woman's voice called from out in the dusk. "It's cold out here!"

"Come on in, Laurie. Bring the horses in with you, child."

First thing that popped into Matt's head was that Laurie was anything but a child. Looking at Sam, he got the impression his brother felt the same way.

Blonde hair and blue eyes, and a little bitty thing; maybe five feet tall. All dressed up in men's britches; both jeans and shirt poked out in all the right places, for sure.

Both Matt and Sam got to their boots when she walked up to the fire and shook the coffee pot. It was empty; Wellman had drained it. She tossed the pot to Matt and plopped down on the ground.

"Well, make some more!" she said. "Don't just stand there lookin' like a jackass!"

Chapter 4

The old mountain man cackled at Matt's expression and laughed out loud and slapped his knee when Matt tossed the coffee pot back to Laurie and said, "You want some coffee, you make it yourself, or learn how to ask in a nice way."

Laurie hung a cussing on him, using words he had never heard a woman use.

"Hee, hee, hee!" Wellman cackled. "She's shore a salty one, ain't she, boys? I come up on her in Utah. She was totin' a rifle nearabouts as big as she is and ridin' a wall-eyed geldin' with the meanest look I ever did see in a horse."

"You should have left her up there," Matt said.

Laurie stuck out her tongue at him.

"Make some coffee, girl," Wellman said. "And act nice."

"Why should I?" she challenged him.

" 'Cause I got me a notion these boys been followin' us so's they can throw in with us." He looked at Matt. "Is my notion correct, boy?"

"Yes."

"Why would you want to do that?" Laurie asked, glaring at him across the small fire. "You don't know us. How do we know you aren't outlaws? And if you're not up to no good, why are you out here in the middle of this Godforsaken place?"

Wellman laughed at that but otherwise remained silent. He was enjoying the verbal confrontation.

Sam took up the question. "We're not outlaws, Miss. Both of us own large ranches up in Wyoming. Profitable operations. Both of us lost . . . people we cared for during the Custer fight. We needed to get away from that area for a time. That's why we're out here."

"You got Injun blood in you, don't you?" she asked.

"Yes. My father was Cheyenne and my mother was white."

"I don't like Injuns," she said flatly.

"That is certainly your prerogative. However misguided. If you know me and don't like me, I can understand that. If you don't know me and don't like me, that's ignorance on your part."

"I ain't ignorant. But you talk funny," she said.

"Educated," Wellman told her. "Medicine Horse sent him to a fancy college back east so's he could learn all them big words. Medicine Horse was a fine man, Laurie. And from what I can gather, so is Two Wolves."

"Who?" she looked at him.

"Sam. That's his Injun name. Two Wolves. And Bodine ain't no outlaw, girl. He's a gunslinger who always fights on the side of the law or the good and just."

"Robin and his Hood," Sam muttered. "Bringing justice to the wild frontier."

"You 'bout half smart-aleck, ain't you?" Laurie cut her eyes to Sam.

"So I have been told, Miss." He jerked a thumb toward Matt. "Usually by him."

"And if someone else tells you? . . ." Wellman asked, a twinkle in his eyes.

"Sam has his own graveyards," Matt said.

Laurie shut up and concentrated on making the coffee.

"Outlaw by the name of Lake is bankrollin' Chappo," Wellman said. "Chappo and his braves case out a ranch for young blonde girls. Ten years old or under. This has been goin' on for about a year and I don't guess anybody other than me has put it all together. Or if they did, they ain't done nothin' about it."

"They sell them into slavery?" Sam asked.

"Worser than that. One shipload went to South America. Another went to the A-rabs. That's where the next ship will be headin', too."

No one wanted to verbalize what the young girls were being sold into, but all knew.

"There are disagreeable people among all races," Sam said with a sigh of frustration.

"That ain't exactly the way I'd say it," Wellman told him. "But that'll do for the time bein'."

"Lake," Matt said. "The bank robber?"

"That's him. Bank robber among other things. He's filth more'un anything else. Got him an army of about fifty or so men that's just as bad or worser than he is. Got him a place somewheres down in the Patagonias. Right close to the Mexican border. It's an old fort. Build to withstand damn near any army."

So the Gila Mountains story had been a ruse on Wellman's part. "Have you ever seen it?'

"Several times. Last time was about twenty-five years ago. The Mexican Army built it outta adobe and rock. Walls twelve-fifteen feet high and two-three feet thick. They was gonna protect the town nearby. But the town never did amount to nothin' so the soldiers left. The girls is taken by wagon over to a little town on the Gulf of California, where the Coyote runs into the Gulf. They're loaded on ship there."

"The ship's captain?" Sam asked.

"Morgan. Run slave ships back when that was a boomin' business. He's a pirate, among other things."

"The name of the ship?" Matt asked.

Wellman spat into the fire. *"The Virgin Princess."*

Laurie might sometimes have the disposition of a hyena and the mouth of a painted-up hurdy-gurdy girl, but Matt would give her good marks for cooking. He admitted that reluctantly.

She fried up bacon and then cut up potatoes and a little bit of onion and red peppers. She'd made pan bread in another skillet and served up a good breakfast. But her coffee was a tad weak for the men. However, no one had yet mentioned that to her, since none of the three felt up to receiving a good cussing this early in the morning . . . especially after such a good breakfast.

Sam, the ever-diplomat, said, "This is an excellent breakfast, Miss Laurie."

"Thank you, Sam," she smiled at him. "Please drop the Miss. Just Laurie."

Wellman winced and Sam gave his blood-brother a dirty look when Matt said, "Coffee's weak."

Laurie gave him a bleak look and then proceeded to tell Matt where he could put his coffee cup, full or empty, and if there was room—and according to her verbiage, there was probably ample space—his saddle, his guns, and his boots as well, including the spurs.

"Laurie and I will share the duties of cooking," Sam jumped in before Matt could unload on her. "She can continue preparing these excellent meals and I shall make the coffee. If that's all right with you, Laurie?"

"That's fine, Sam," she said with a tight smile. "You're too nice a person to have taken up with the likes of him!" She glared at Matt.

Matt smiled at her. "I'm so looking forward to traveling with you over all the miles yet ahead of us, Laurie. I've always wanted to learn more about the seamy side of life."

Laurie smiled very sweetly at him. "No doubt," she said. "Since probably the only romance you've ever had is when you kissed your horse!"

Wellman and Sam were still laughing as they saddled up and rode south. Wellman took the point and Matt brought up the rear, Sam, Laurie, and the packhorses between them. It promised to be a very exciting trip—in more ways than one.

The small band turned more west than south, keeping the Puerco to the south of them. They stopped and cooked supper several hours before sunset. Then they moved on several miles before making a cold camp for the night.

Matt and Laurie had little to say to one another and did their best to avoid each other. Much to the relief of Sam and Wellman.

"We'll be in Horsehead Crossing in a couple of days," Wellman said the next morning. "We can resupply there and rest for a day. Prowl around and see if we can pick up any information. And my bones is tellin' me we got someone on our backtrail."

"They're laying back," Matt said, pouring another cup of coffee. "It's probably that bunch we met back at the trading post. Porter and his gang." He lifted his eyes to look at Laurie. "Porter wants you, Laurie. He called you a stray."

"I know him. I been on my own since I was fourteen. Cooking in two bit towns; drifting while I looked for my brother."

"Your brother is probably all Apache by now," Matt told her, a gentleness in his voice. "And I don't mean that in an ugly way."

"I know you don't," Laurie replied. "And I realize that if he's still alive, he no longer thinks of himself as white. He was just a boy when they took him. I was eight years old. That was almost thirteen years ago, I don't have to see him, or even get close to him. I just want to know if he's still alive. Indian or white. He's the only family I have except for some cousins back east that I've never seen. Do you understand, Matt? Any of you?"

Matt slowly nodded his head. "I think we all understand, Laurie." He held out his hand. "Truce?"

She took his hand. Her hand was not lady-soft, but rough and callused. Matt could sense the strength in her flowing through her hand. The young woman had done a lot of hard work in her life, making her way alone in a predominately man's world.

"Truce, Matt." She grinned impishly. "But you wouldn't know a good cup of coffee if it was poured on you!"

Laurie and Sam were hitting it off well, and both Matt and the old mountain man were glad to see it. Sam was usually very stand-offish around women, and Wellman had said that Laurie just flat-out didn't trust men.

"Maybe some good will come out of this fool's errand after all," Wellman said.

"You think this is a fool's mission?"

"In a way. Even if we find that old fort—and it's sorta fuzzy in my mind exactly where it is—how the hell are three men and a child gonna fight our way in and get the girls out?"

"Laurie is no child, Dick," Matt reminded him.

"Maybe not to you. But she is to me."

"If you don't think there's a chance, why did you start out?"

"I'm seventy year old, boy. I've took a lot of lead in my time, and three arrowheads. One's still in me. And it's done moved. It ain't where it was all these years. I done been to three doctors. They all say the same things: They can't operate 'cause they don't know where it is, and that I could drop dead any time if the arrowhead hits some vitals. Or be paralyzed if it lodges next to my backbone. Death's all right. Not bein' able to walk or ride ain't. 'Sides, this girl them crud tooken is a favorite of mine. And she ain't my granddaughter; she's my great-granddaughter." He grinned, exposing a pretty good mouthful of teeth for his age and the time. "I married young." He turned around, twisting in the saddle and that move saved his life as a bullet wuffed past his head, followed by the boom of a rifle.

"Sam!" Wellman yelled, pointing. "Head for the rocks to your left."

"Why there?" Matt shouted, over the pounding of hooves as they raced up the canyon.

"I know this area. They's water and good graze behind them rocks."

If they could get to it, both men were thinking as they spurred their horses.

Then there was no more time for hollered conversation— only survival, as the lead began bouncing off the rock walls of the canyon, whining and singing wickedly. Whoever it was shooting at them were in positions above them, at the top of the canyon walls.

When they reached the protective covering of the rocks, Matt saw blood on Sam's face. Sam shook his head. "Piece of rock hit me. I'm all right. Who are they, Matt? Did you see anything?"

"Nothing. But if they were Apaches they wouldn't have screwed up the ambush. Porter and his bunch, probably." He looked around. "Hold down the place. I'm going to look for water."

As he inspected the flat among the rocks, he knew they had lucked out. It would take an army, storming the place, to get to them.

Now if there was just water.

He crawled up into the rocks, his Winchester cradled in his arms and dragging his canteen by the strap. Being careful not to expose himself, Matt found a notch and peeked out. He grinned at what he saw. Across from him and some feet below his position, on the lip of the canyon wall, he could plainly see several men squatted down behind rocks.

Matt leveled his rifle, sighted in, and shot one through the head. He shifted the muzzle and got another in the belly just as the man jumped up to run for better cover. The outlaw squalled and fell headfirst over the lip of the wall, screaming on the short trip down. He landed on the hard-pack below and did not move. Matt scooted back a few feet, and continued his search for water.

He found the tank high up in the rocks, and it was in a shady location and full. Matt drank deeply of the coolness and made up his mind that if they did not have to use any of the water, they would not. They would leave it for the birds and bees and small animals who depended on it being there.

Matt found himself a comfortable spot with a good view and settled in. Sooner or later one of the outlaws would get careless and expose himself. It would be his last careless act.

Matt Bodine pulled a piece of jerky out of his pocket and chewed on it slowly, savoring the juices. He had plenty of time.

Looking down from his high perch, Matt could see the others in the party settling down in secure positions; the horses had been placed behind boulders and Laurie was with them, calming them down, whispering to them. Matt didn't want to give away his new position just yet, so he waited and watched.

"Wellman!" the shout split the quiet after the brief gunfight.

"What'd you want, punk?" the old mountain man called out.

"The gold and the woman. Give 'em up and you can ride on."

"Go to hell!"

Matt knew the mountain man would die before giving

Laurie to that bunch of crud. He listened to them cuss each other back and forth across the canyon trail.

"We got water and graze, Wellman. So we'll just wait you out."

Graze was the problem, Matt silently pondered. They had a few hatfuls of corn for the horses, and that was it when it came to feed. They had water for the animals, but no natural graze except for a few stubby plants that were defying odds by growing amid the rocks. Matt didn't even know what they were. Whatever they were, they wouldn't last long.

"Well, now," Matt muttered to the sky and the rocks, as he thumbed back the hammer on his Winchester, "I reckon I'll just open this dance and see how they like the tune."

Chapter 5

Matt searched carefully until he found a target. And he had to look twice to make sure it was what he thought it was. One of Porter's men had part of his boot exposed; the front part. Matt sighted in, took up slack on the trigger, and let the rifle fire itself.

Wild, painful screaming followed the booming of the Winchester.

"Oh, Jesus Christ!" the man yelled. "He blowed my toes off. Oh, God, it hurts."

The outlaws on the other side of the canyon opened fire, but they hit nothing except air and rocks.

Midday passed with only a few shots being fired from the other side of the canyon. The shots drew no blood from those positioned safely in the rocks. The outlaws cursed and called out wild and obscene suggestions about what they were going to do with Laurie when they grabbed her. Sam carefully sighted on one man and shot him through the kneecap. His screaming put an end to the obscenity-shouting for a time.

About four o'clock, the shadows beginning to purple and lengthen, Porter and his bunch gave it up with a final shouted threat and rattled their hocks out of there. Matt stayed in his position and watched them ride out, first to the west, then cutting south. Two men were riding tied in their saddles.

"It looks like they're riding toward Horsehead Crossing!" he called from above the others. "I'm coming down."

Matt scrambled down and joined the others.

"How many of them?" Wellman asked.

"I'd say a good twenty still sitting their saddles and able to fight. Let's bury those we dropped."

"Hell with them," the mountain man nixed that idea. "They knowed what they was gettin' into when they jumped us. Leave 'em for the varmits to eat on. I'll not have a part in buryin' heathen."

Matt and Sam took the dead mens' guns and ammunition and caved in part of the canyon wall over their bodies. Dick Wellman would have no part in the burying. He stayed in the shade on the other side of the canyon with Laurie. The mountain man was hard as nails and true to his unwritten and uncompromising code.

They rode out of the canyon with about an hour of daylight left them. Dick took the point, heading them west and a little south. The route would take them to Horsehead Crossing. Dick's plan was to cross the river and recross to come in south of the town.

At this point in time, Horsehead Crossing was wild and woolly and full of fleas and was no place for a pilgrim. It was calming down a bit at a time, but was still filled with rough men and few women; fewer still were ladies.

All of them expected to run into Porter and his gang in Horsehead Crossing. And by the set of Wellman's jaw, he was going to push the point when he caught up with them. There was a mean look in the old mountain man's eyes, and he rode with his Winchester across his saddle horn.

"We got enough to worry about with what's ahead of us," he said. "Damned if I want to keep lookin' over my shoulder for both 'Paches and Porter's crew. When we catch up with them, I ain't gonna be no Christian about it: I'm goin' in shootin,' boys."

And Matt and Sam knew he meant every word of it. Wellman was riding with gunsmoke in his thoughts.

Mountain men followed their own strange moral code, seldom paying the slightest bit of attention to the changing times and the written laws of men. Many a tale has been spun over campfires from the Pacific Ocean to the Mississippi River about the antics and the bravery and the cold nerve of mountain men . . . and the blood that was spilled when one crossed a mountain man.

"Should be interesting when we reach Horsehead Crossing," Sam whispered to Matt.

"Very," his blood brother agreed.

Horsehead Crossing in the mid-1870's was a wide-open, anything-goes-town. Shootings were common and the town marshal stayed out of it unless it was a back-shooting. Then he would have to get involved, however reluctantly.

Just outside of the town—but not too far out, for this was Apache country—the quartet passed several hardscrabble farm and ranch houses. From all appearances, the families who occupied those ratty-looking dwellings were just barely hanging on, for most settlers came West with more ambition than money.

Matt was the first to spot the river and the first to let his horse dip its nose into the waters.

"Horsehead Crossin's just a few miles yonder," Wellman said, pointing. "There ain't no point in shilly-shallyin' around this, boys. We'll ride in, stable our horses, put Miss Laurie up in the hotel, if they is one, and then we'll go huntin' Porter and the rest of them no-goods. That all right with you-all?"

"Not to me, it isn't!" Laurie said. "You're not about to

stick me in some flea-bag while you go off and have all the fun. *I'm* the one they said all those awful things about, remember? I got just as much right to have a part in this as any of you—maybe more. And I can shoot just as good as any of you. Maybe better with a rifle." She stuck out her chin and glared at them, one at a time.

Laurie had a Winchester .44 stuck in her saddle boot, and Wellman had told Matt and Sam that the little lady knew how to use it, and would not hesitate to do so.

"Suits me," Matt said. "But what are you going to do if we have to go inside a saloon?"

"Go right in there with you!"

Wellman bit off a chew of tobacco from a plug and shook his head. "The world shore is changin'," he said sorrowfully. "Wimmin ridin' astride and wearin' men's britches. Next thing you know they'll be gettin' the vote."

"And won't that be a glorious day?" Laurie said with a smile, her teeth very white against her tanned face. Most town and city ladies of that day avoided the sun, in order to maintain a white, unmarred complexion.

Wellman grunted and swung back into the saddle, pointing his horse's nose toward Horsehead Crossing and a showdown with the Porter gang.

The quartet rode in using the back streets of the small town, swinging in at a livery stable. Dismounting, they beat the trail dust from their clothing with their hats and washed their faces in a horse trough. Then they checked their guns, wiping the action clean and loading up the usually kept empty chamber under the hammer. Laurie levered a round into her Winchester and shoved another round into the tube, bringing the full load up to eighteen.

The man who ran the stable was standing back, in the shade of the huge barn, eyeballing the group nervously. "You, ah, boys and, ah . . . lady," he was looking at Laurie's attire, especially the jeans she filled out quite well, "want me to look after your horses?" he finally got up enough courage to inquire.

"Yeah," Wellman told him. "Rub them down good and give them all the grain they want to eat. Watch that brown gelding the lady rode in on. He's a bad one. Kick the snot out of you or bite your arm off."

"Yes, sir." He looked at Laurie's gelding, who was looking all wall-eyed at him. "How about them pack horses?"

"The same treatment," Sam told him.

"Big bunch of sorry-lookin' hombres ride in here some hours ago?" Wellman asked. "Some of them shot up?"

"Yes, sir." The livery man's adam's apple bobbed up and down and his eyes were jumpy under the brim of his hat. "They shore did. They all stayin' over to the hotel. But they in the saloon now. That one." He pointed up the street.

"You got law here?" Bodine asked.

"Yes, sir. Sort of. There ain't much county law, howsomever. But we got us a town marshal. That's his office yonder." Again, he pointed.

"He in?"

"Oh, yes, sir! He ain't left the office since them hardcases hit town. Takes all his meals inside the jail."

"They some rowdy, huh?" Wellman asked.

"You could say that."

"You ain't seen us, partner," the mountain man told him. "You keep your butt right here, seeing to them horses of ours, you hear?"

"Yes, sir! I'm a-fixin' to start curryin' and feedin' right now."

The livery man got to his work, doing his best to remain deaf, dumb, and blind.

"I got an idea," Matt said.

"Let's hear it."

"Let's go see the marshal."

"What for?"

"Let's see if he'll deputize us."

"I don't need no badge to stomp on a snake," Wellman said. "I ain't never toted no badge in my life and damned if I intend to start now. I saddle my own horses."

"It was just an idea," Matt said with a shrug. He could tell that Wellman was hot under the collar and operating with a full head of steam.

Just how hot the mountain man was became very evident as they began walking up the street. A young dandy with shiny guns tied down low stepped out of the saloon and froze when he spotted the quartet.

"That one of them?" Wellman asked.

"Yes," Sam said.

"Hey, punk!" Wellman called. "Drag iron, you little weasel!"

The dandy grabbed for his guns and Wellman leveled his Winchester and shot him in the chest, spinning him around. The kid would die screaming with one arm hanging over a hitchrail. He had not cleared leather.

"One less," the mountain man growled. "Now let's go clean out a snake-pit."

Up and down the main street of town, shutters were being banged shut and secured, curtains drawn, and people getting off the dusty street. Men were rushing out to grab the reins of saddle horses and pulling wagons out of the line of fire. In less than a minute the wide street was void of life. A strange silence quickly settled over the little town.

The batwings of the saloon slammed open and two gunnies stepped out to see what all the noise was about. They saw the dying, now weakly-whimpering dandy, his blood staining the dirt beneath him, his own guns still in leather. The two gunslicks yelled back into the saloon, cussed, and grabbed for their pistols.

The quartet opened up with Winchesters. The two outlaws never had a chance. A deadly fusillade of .44 slugs tore into them, knocking them spinning and jerking to the rough and warped boardwalk. One caught a spur between boards and fell awkwardly, smashing through a front window into the saloon.

"I'm going in the back of the saloon," Matt said. "Don't shoot me," he added.

"Don't get in the way," Sam told him with a grin.

"Good huntin'," Wellman said tersely, and kept on walking.

"What the hell-fire's a-goin' on?" the shouted question came from behind the walls of the combination jail and marshal's office located just across the street from the saloon.

"We're snake-huntin'!" Wellman yelled. "You want to come out and join us?"

"Hell, no! You boys just hunt on!" the invisible marshal shouted. "And then get gone out of my town so's I won't have to arrest you."

Sam laughed at that remark.

"That'll be the damn day when the likes of you arrests me," Wellman muttered, and stepped up onto the boardwalk, presenting less of a target to those in the saloon. The outlaws had busted out the remaining windows and were shooting wildly and in all directions, hitting nothing except air and boards. "You stay behind me, Laurie. Sam? You with us?"

"Right here. I have an idea, Wellman: let's wait until Bodine comes in the back shooting and we'll hit the front at the same time. More or less," he added.

"I'm goin' in right now," Wellman said. "Lead, follow, or get the hell out of the way." He was gone in a bowlegged lope up the street.

"The man does have a mind of his own, doesn't he?" Sam muttered.

"You just noticed?" Laurie asked. Then she was gone in a feminine run after Wellman.

"I keep asking myself," Sam muttered, running up the boardwalk after Wellman and Laurie, "how does a nice Indian boy like me get himself in so much damn trouble!"

Chapter 6

Bodine leaned his rifle up against a wall and rounded the corner of the saloon with both hands filled with Colts. He ran right into a gunny running out toward the alley he'd just left. The outlaw's hands were also filled pistols. It was point-blank range and Matt was the first to fire. The slugs struck the rowdy in the belly, doubling him over and dropping him to the ground, just as two more ran out the back door and around the other side of the building before Matt could fire.

Bodine let them go and stepped into the darkness of the storeroom just as he heard Dick Wellman screaming like a puma as he ran into the saloon, tearing one batwing off its hinges. The screaming alone probably scared the pants off of half a dozen of the outlaws.

Matt heard running feet on the outside stairs and knew that some of Porter's men—probably including Porter—were getting away. He put that out of his mind and opened the door to the saloon.

Wellman was standing to the left of the batwings, Laurie to the right, and Sam was crouched in the center of the broken batwings.

The three of them had turned the barroom into a smoky hell. Moaning men lay writhing in pain on the floor, sprawled across tables and hanging one-handed and dying on the upper bar rail.

The two barkeeps had hit the floor behind the long bar and were hugging the sawdust.

"Don't leave me out of this, boys!" Bodine called, and a gunny turned, his face filled with fear and fury and a curse on his lips.

He pointed a pistol at Bodine and Matt shot him through the brisket with his right hand Colt just as another got to his knees, blood leaking from a shoulder wound, and leveled his pistol at Sam. Bodine finished what someone else had started.

Laurie leveled her rifle and plugged one right between the eyes.

Then it was over. An eerie silence fell like a shroud over the gunsmoke-filled room, broken only by the moaning of the wounded.

Matt began walking through the bloody sprawl. None of the high-priced guns he and Sam had seen back at the trading post were down and dying. And neither was Porter.

"You see that yeller-bellied Porter?" Wellman asked, shoving .44's into his Winchester.

"No. But I did see some men leaving out the back door and then heard some others running down the outside steps."

"That figures. That was Porter and some of the other ones with him. And Porter was in the lead. Bet on it. The man's a coward."

Matt looked over at Laurie. The young woman's face was flushed, but other than that she appeared calm. She'll do to ride the river with, Matt thought. She's got more than her share of cold nerve.

Laurie met his gaze and for a very brief moment the two stood staring at each other, silent messages passing between them. Laurie's face flushed even deeper crimson and she finally turned away.

The bartenders had gotten up off the floor behind the bar and were looking at the carnage. One shifted his eyes to Matt. "I know you!" he cried out. "You're Matt Bodine, the Wyoming gunfighter."

The bartender pointed at Sam. "And you must be Sam Two Wolves."

"Right on both counts," Wellman said, stepping up to the bar. "Gimme a rye."

The marshal stepped gingerly into the barroom and pulled up short at the wreckage, both human and to the saloon. "Lord, have mercy!" he said in a shocked tone. "I ain't never seen nothing to match this."

"Then you should have been with me at that trading post up on the Platte back in '39," Wellman said. "Or maybe it was '40. I disremember 'xactly."

"You're Dick Wellman," the marshal said, a hushed and reverent tone to the statement.

"Yeah. And stop interruptin'. Me and some others brought our pelts in to sell. Bunch of hardcases got it into their heads they was gonna steal them. I think the body count was forty-five when we got through. Looked like we'd been slaughterin' hogs." He downed his rye and gestured for a refill. "Step up here, marshal. Have a drink, son."

The marshal was at least fifty years old. "I got to write a report on this!"

"Oh, hell, marshal," Wellman told him. "Just say the punks got into a squabble among theyselves. That'd be the easiest way to tell it."

Several badly shot-up would be gunhands started moaning and hollering on the barroom floor. Wellman looked at them in disgust. "Either drag them crybabies outta here or kick 'em in the head. If somebody don't do something with 'em I'm a-fixin' to shoot the both of them—again."

"Here, now!" the voice came from the shattered batwings. A man in a black suit, white shirt, and high starched collar stood there, a leather bag in one hand. "They'll be none of that."

"Howdy, Doc," the marshal greeted him. He waved at the bloody scene. "Looks like you got your work cut out for you."

"Help me, Doc," a duded up young dandy moaned from the floor. "I'm hurt awful bad."

The doctor moved toward the young man with holes in his belly.

"You shoulda stayed to home with your momma and helped your daddy slop the hogs, boy," Wellman told him bluntly, not one note of pity in his voice.

The young dandy hollered once, drummed his boot heels on the floor, coughed up blood, and then died.

Bodine and Sam moved to the bar. Laurie stood at the far end of the bar. "Two beers for us," Matt told a barkeep. "And whatever the lady wants."

"Lemonade," Laurie told him.

"You ain't even 'posed to be in here!" the barkeep told her.

"You better give her some lemonade and shut your mouth," Wellman said. "I'm tellin' you now, you don't want to make her mad."

The barkeep poured a glass of lemonade and slid it down the bar toward Laurie.

Matt moved toward one gunhand who appeared to be suffering only flesh wounds. He jerked him off the floor and sat him down not too gently in a chair.

"Where'd Porter and the others go, punk? And give me straight answers and give them to me fast."

"Here, now!" the doctor protested. "You can't treat a wounded man like that."

"That's Matt Bodine, Doc," a barkeep said.

The doctor shut his mouth and tended to a patient; but he was angry and his face showed it.

"I ain't got no idee, Bodine," the gunhand moaned the words. His left arm had been shattered just below the elbow by a .44 slug and hung useless by his side. "And that's the truth. But they ain't gonna give up on gettin' that gold and the girl. He'll just get some more men and keep right on followin' y'all."

"And you?"

"I'm out of it. Soon as I can ride, I'm headin' back to Nebraska. Didn't none of us count on you and the breed throwin' in with Wellman."

"Why did Bradley and Doyle and those other top guns join up with trash like Porter?"

The outlaw's face mirrored his inner struggle. He sighed and decided to level with Bodine. "Money. They's good money to be had in slavin'. Porter and the others—me included—was on our way down to meet with Lake; see if we couldn't get in on some of the action he's got goin' for himself."

"Gawdamn filth," Wellman cussed him from the bar. "Them's scared little girls they's kidnappin' and sellin' into bondage. Ain't you got no morals atall? I oughtta kill you where you sit."

The wounded gunny started sweating. "They ain't nothin' but nester trash!" he said. "Who cares what happens to them?"

"You call my little girl nester trash?" Wellman snarled, turning from the bar. Matt backed away from the gunny, sensing what was about to happen.

The gunny spat on the floor.

Wellman kicked a pistol toward the man. It came to a stop by the man's boots.

"Pick it up, you heathen," Wellman told him. "And you can tell the devil I give you a better break than you and your kind is givin' them little girls."

The outlaw hesitated.

"Pick it up, scum!" Wellman shouted.

The gunny grabbed for the Colt. He closed his fingers around the butt and jacked back the hammer, leveling the muzzle at Wellman's belly.

Wellman's rifle was lying on the bar. The old mountain man smiled grimly and drew his Colt, cocking and firing with a decades-practiced swift deadliness. The longbarreled .44 roared smoke and belched flame, the slug taking the slave-trader between the eyes, knocking him backward and dumping him on the floor.

Matt jerked another wounded man from the floor and sat him in a chair. "The fort where Lake and his men do their business; where is it?"

The gunny soiled himself; the stench of him filled the beery, gunsmoke-acrid closeness of the saloon. "It's down on the border, just south of Miller Peak. It's between the Huachucas and the Patagonias. And that's the truth, Bodine. I swear to God it is."

"I oughtta shoot you for even speakin' God's name," Wellman growled.

The marshal looked like he was about to wet his long handles.

The barkeeps were getting ready to once more hit the floor.

Laurie sipped her lemonade and looked at the wounded man through cold eyes. Sam took a long swig of beer and stifled a belch.

"I don't know nothin' else!" the gunslick hollered " 'Ceptin' Porter and them is gonna raid some ranches on the way down and grab some more kids for barter."

"A lot of ranches between here and there," Wellman muttered. "Bound to be some more kids grabbed." He turned from the bar, his eyes savage, burning with frontier justice. "I'll git a rope from my hoss. We'll hang him and them others still alive."

When the doctor straightened up from tending a patient who had been laid on a billiard table across the room by some citizens of the town, there was a gun in his hand, the hammer back.

"There'll be no lynchings in this town," he warned the mountain man.

"That there's Dick Wellman, Doc," the marshal warned.

"I don't give a damn who he is!" The doctor's eyes touched the three men and Laurie. "Now you people listen to me. These men are my patients. Officially so. You interfere and I'll have the territorial governor sign warrants for your arrest. Now go on about your business—somewhere other than this saloon."

Wellman glared at the doctor for a moment, then slowly relaxed, leaning back against the bar. "All right, Doc. I won't cause you no more trouble. And that's my word on it. You can put that hogleg away and go on about patching these crud up." He turned his back to the doctor and picked up his glass of rye.

"I think I'll check in at the hotel," Laurie said. "I've been looking forward to a nice hot bath for a week."

"Let's all go check in," Matt suggested. "I think the doctor would work easier without us looking over his shoulder."

"Thank you, Mister Bodine." The doctor lowered the pistol, looked at it strangely, and then laid it beside the outlaw and returned to his ministering of the wounded.

When the searchers were gone, the marshal shook his head at the doctor's bravery. "I don't think I'd a had the nerve to do what you done, Doc."

The doctor smiled and picked up the pistol. "Just between you and me, Martin, the damn gun was empty!"

Chapter 7

The few residents who ventured out after the shooting gave the four of them a wide berth as they walked toward the town's only hotel for a bath and a change of clothes. After cleaning up, they stayed together and ate a quiet supper in a cafe and went to bed early. They slept soundly, for the rowdies in town had pulled in their horns and walked lightly that evening.

They had resupplied before they had supper, so long before first light the four of them were saddled up and ready to ride. Little had been said, since nothing was open where they might get a cup of coffee. They planned to ride until dawn, then make coffee and fry some bacon.

Laurie broke the silence as they were putting the little town behind them. "Why did we practically buy out the store, Dick?"

" 'Cause they ain't nothin' where we're goin', child. And I mean nothin'. Not until we slide over to the west a tad and resupply at Tucson—if we take a notion to do that. If not, we got enough to make the border. You boys know anything at all about this country?"

Neither Bodine nor Sam knew anything firsthand about it; only what they had garnered around campfires and barrooms.

"She's wild and beautiful," Wellman told them. " 'Specially where we's heading for now. The Muggyowns. That's what us oldtimers call it. Proper name is the Mogollon Rim. She's rugged, any way you want to cut it. 'Pache country. When we get past the Muggyowns and cross the San Carlos, we'll hit the desert. And people, if you ain't never crossed a desert, you all in for a shock. It's a livin' hell."

"Is there water where we're going?" Laurie asked.

"Oh, yeah. We'll cross Silver Creek today and make night camp on the edge of the Rim. Ten-twelve miles from the beginnin's of the Muggyowns. Watch your hair, people. And whatever happens, save a bullet for Laurie. You don't want her to get tooken alive by the 'Paches. If they overrun us, put a bullet in her head and then shoot yourselves. Better that than bein' tortured for days by them 'Paches. And I ain't jokin' you none a bit. I killed a friend of mine down on the San Carlos back in . . . oh, round about '60, I reckon it was. He begged me to and I done it. Must have been a good three hundred and fifty yard shot, but I put 'er true and ended his misery. Made them savages hot, too. They was lookin' for a couple days sport with Del. They chased me for a week after that. I can get along with most Injuns. Lived with 'em for years. But I hate a gawddam 'Pache worser than I do anythin' else on the face of this earth." He spat on the ground. "Makes my mouth hurt just talkin' about 'em."

"It's beautiful," Laurie said.

They were looking down on the Mogollon Rim, after having spent the night at what was left of an old trading post near a lake. Dick had told them that the same man had rebuilt the post four times before finally giving up and pulling out.

"No business?" Laurie had asked.

"Gawddam 'Paches," Dick told her, then spat on the ground. "That man made the best whiskey in the territory, too. Never will forgive them heathens for running him out of the country."

Bodine knew that Sam would not take offense at the mountain man's remarks, and his blood brother did not. His father, Medicine Horse, had not been a savage or a heathen, having been educated in the east; but Sam was just as proud of his Indian side as of his white side. He knew the Indian way of life, as wandering nomads, living off the land and fighting and stealing horses from other tribes—more for sport than need—was very nearly over. All over the West, tribes were being placed on reservations, making the land safe for settlers. And the Apache would eventually lose his battle with progress, just as other tribes had lost and were losing.

In reflective moments, among very close friends, Sam would admit that.

"We'll camp here," Wellman said, looking around him, his eyes alive with the fires of old memories "And post guards come the night. This is old Big Rump's country. Or was. I don't know if old Wah-Poo-Eta is still alive, or not. I hope to hell he ain't."

"Big Rump?" Laurie questioned.

"Tonto Apache chief. He's the one took Del alive and was torturing him. The man I kilt to ease his misery. Old Wah-Poo-Eta had him a rear-end looked like the caboose on a train. But mean as a rattlesnake. They's a road the military uses, called the Crook Road. We'll come up on it down south a ways; cross it on our way down. It runs from Fort Apache up to Camp Verde. We might run into some soldier boys and if we do, don't tell them nothin' about what we're fixin' to do."

"Why?" Laurie asked. "Wouldn't they help?"

"Nope. Doubtful, at best. At the worst, they might try to

stop us. 'Sides, they got their hands full fightin' the 'Paches. Rustle up some grub and coffee. I'm gonna take me a look-see around. I'll be back in a couple of hours. If I ain't back then, don't come a-foggin' into the timber lookin' for me. I might mistook you for a Injun and shoot you." He picked up his rifle and slipped into the timber, moving as silently as a ghost.

Wellman came back hours later, long after dark, walking up to Sam, who was taking the second shift at watch, from ten to two in the morning.

" 'Paches all around us, boy," Wellman said. "White Mountain Apaches." He shook the coffee pot and poured a cupful of the strong brew, then tossed dirt over the dying coals. "Jerky for breakfast. No fires. We'll pull out of here first light and head southwest. Salt River Canyon's about a three-four day ride from here. Through some of the most rugged country you ever seen in all your borned days. If we get through it with our hair, it'll be a miracle. 'Cause something's done stirred up the Injuns."

Bodine had been listening to them talk. He slipped out of his blankets and joined Wellman and Sam. "Chappo and his bunch?"

"Could be. I got me a hunch they's out lookin' for more little girls to swap to that worthless scum down on the border."

"How far down to this canyon you mentioned?"

"Nearabout a hundred miles. White Mountain Lake is just to the north of us. Long Lake is just to the east of us. We'll cross the rim of the Muggyowns mid-mornin' and be hard in 'Pache country. Indee'll be all around us?"

"Indee?" Bodine questioned.

"The People," Sam told him. "I once read that if the Army had not wrongly attacked a village back in '69, killing women and children, the White Mountain Apaches probably would not be on the warpath today."

"Maybe," Wellman admitted with a grunt. "And maybe not. But the chief, Minjarez, don't like white men. Never has. Him and me, we're about the same age."

"You know him?" Bodine asked.

"I know him," Wellman replied. "And I don't trust him no further than I could throw you. And he don't like me worth a damn."

"Why?" Sam asked.

Wellman grinned. " 'Cause I shot him back in '50, that's why!" He laughed softly. "And to make matters worse, I shot him in the butt!"

Bodine pulled the lonely and cold last shift, the dog watch, and roused the others an hour before dawn. They chewed on some hardtack washed down with water from their canteens and broke camp just as the sun was turning the eastern sky a gray-silver.

"Let's ride," Wellman said, swinging into the saddle. "Rifles across the saddle horn, people. You see anything suspicious, you sing out. For the next hundred miles, stayin' alive is somethin' we gonna have to work at."

The sun broke through just as the four of them crossed the rim and the dew was still shining like broken diamonds on the varied ferns and grasses. Ponderosa pines grew tall and thick and lush, standing like silent sentries all around them.

"This is the most beautiful country I have ever seen," Laurie put into words what the others were feeling.

"Enjoy it while it lasts," Wellman tossed the words over his shoulder. "When we hit the desert you'll think you died and went to hell. The rim drops off sharp a few miles ahead. They's a crick at the dropoff. We'll pull up there and fix some breakfast. I want some coffee."

Matt gathered enough dead wood for a cook-fire and Sam

built a hat-sized fire under the low-hanging limbs of an oak, so what little smoke there was from the dead limbs would dissipate through the limbs. Wellman used his Bowie knife to slice the bacon—he liked it thick—while Laurie peeled the potatoes and got the skillet hot. Sam made the coffee.

"Gonna be cold tonight," Wellman said, sucking on a welcome cup of steaming coffee. "Might even get below freezin'. What month is it, anyways?"

"October, I think," Laurie told him.

"Time does get by a person, don't it? Twenty-five years since I been down this way, I'd guess." He took a plate from Laurie and began shoveling it in.

The howl of a wolf floated across the stillness of the morning under the rim. Wellman noticed as both Matt and Sam lifted their heads and quickly cut their eyes to one another.

"Onihomahan, eh?" he asked.

"Yes," Sam said.

"What's that mean?" Laurie asked.

"Friends of the wolf," Matt told her.

"They scare me," she admitted.

"No reason for them to," Sam said with a smile. "My father said he has never known of a healthy, full-grown wolf to launch an unprovoked attack against a human being. And I'll bet Dick has never heard of such an attack, have you, Dick?"

The old mountain man grinned. "I had a hunch you'd get me into this soon's I brung it up. No, cain't say as I ever heard of any such attack. But that don't mean I'm gonna pet one."

"You see, Laurie," Matt explained, pouring another cup of coffee, "if a person is going to live in harmony with the animals, you best try to understand them. Now, I don't know if anybody's ever gonna understand a grizzly bear. I've had them charge me—thank goodness I was in the saddle—and I've gone back later and tried to figure out what I did to provoke the charge. Most of the time it was because I was near the bear's cache of food. But there have been times when there wasn't any reason. He or she just didn't like the man scent and wanted to kill. A grizzly is just unpredictable." He cut his eyes to Dick. "You agree with that, Dick?"

"Yep. But do carry on, son. Hell, I ain't been out in the wilderness but sixty year. You might learn me something."

Matt knew the mountain man was only kidding with him, and did not take umbrage at the remark. He turned his head and an arrow whizzed by his nose, so close he could feel the wind of its passage. Had he not turned his head, the arrow would have gone right through his skull.

Wellman went one way, Sam went another, and Bodine threw his arms around Laurie and together they went rolling into the brush. Before the shaft of the arrow had stopped quivering, the campsite was deserted.

Matt was very conscious of the heat of the woman next to him. The abrupt contact with her had shown him there wasn't any artificial stuffin' sticking out; only what God gave her—which was more than sufficient.

He slowly released her and went belly down, drawing his Colts. His rifle was by his bedroll. Cautiously, using only his eyes and not moving his head, he surveyed the campsite.

"Why didn't they shoot us instead of using arrows?" Laurie whispered.

"Might be of a different tribe and at war with the White Mountain Apache," Matt returned the whisper. "Could be Chappo's bunch and they don't want the others to know they're in this area. And it could be they don't have guns."

"Victorio's bunch," Wellman called from across the small clearing. "Look at that arrow."

Matt looked. He could tell Sioux and Cheyenne and Crow and Arapaho and many of the Plains' Indians arrows, but he knew very little about the Apaches. And from Dick's hiding place, he wondered how the old man could tell the difference in the arrow.

But he didn't think this was the time or place to question the statement.

A sudden cry of anguish cut the stillness and shattered the beauty of the forest. The cry ended in a moaning burble and silence once more prevailed for a few seconds.

"They're young," Sam's voice floated out of the timber. "Just boys."

"You got 'im?" Wellman asked.

"I got him."

Screaming, a young brave, probably in his late teens, leaped out of hiding and charged across the clearing, a knife in his hand. Bodine, Sam, and Wellman fired together. The brave was stopped in mid-stride as the slugs hit him in the side, the chest, and the back, flinging him to the ground.

All heard a faint rustling sound, then the sounds of several running, moccasin-clad feet, the running sounds growing fainter, finally fading away.

But the men were all experienced fighters, and none of them moved or talked for fifteen minutes. Wellman broke the silence.

"They're gone," he announced.

"How can he tell?" Laurie whispered.

"The smell," Bodine told her. "We all have a different odor. We smell different to an Indian."

"Let's pack it up and get gone," Wellman said, stepping out from his hiding place. "We was lucky that time. Let's be about ten miles gone from this place afore them 'Paches find help and come back."

Ten minutes later they were in the saddle and riding.

Chapter 8

The four of them crossed Carrizo Creek and spent the night in a cold camp, not even chancing a small fire to cook with. At first light, they pulled out, with Wellman taking them more south than west, angling toward Salt River Canyon, the old mountain man remembering trails he'd traveled a quarter of a century back.

The country was slowly beginning to change from rugged timber and high lonesome to a slightly more arid terrain. Once they came close enough to see a huge mountain lion, watching them silently from its perch atop a rock. The big cat made no hostile moves toward them, but its muscles remained taut and its unblinking eyes never left them as they rode past, staying well out of leaping range of the mountain cat.

"When we get some farther south," Wellman said, "the 'Paches up here is gonna seem tame. Chappo's got to have the blessin's of Gokhlayeh to be doin' what he's doin'."

"Who?" Bodine asked.

"Gokhlayeh. One Who Yawns. And Big Mouth With Bad Breath—that's what I named him—don't like me not one little bit. I met him back when he was just a youngster; maybe twenty years old, or so. He didn't have much say back then, but then he left for a time, made him a name, and became a subchief. Made a name for hisself by turnin' tricky and becomin' poison mean. A few years back, the Mimbres cut a deal with him to recruit warriors. They picked the right man. He gathered together the worst bunch of savages in New Mexico and Arizona. They unholy terrors, is what they is."

"I never heard of any warrior-chief named Gokhlayeh," Sam said.

Some Mexican soldier hung a nickname on him and it stuck," Wellman replied. "Now he's known as Geronimo."

At the Salt River, the four of them rested and tried to relax. They did rest, but their relaxation was a tense one, knowing they were surrounded by Apaches. But they did manage to bathe and wash their clothes and have several hot meals. Then Matt remembered something that a drifting cowboy had told him just before he and Sam pulled out of Wyoming and started drifting south.

"I heard there was a little town, no more than a trading post, really, down near the foothills of the Pinal Mounains," Matt said. "The cowboy who told me about it was drunk at the time and wasn't too sure about the name. He said somebody named it Glob."

"Somebody must have a glob for a brain to put a post smack in the middle of 'Pache country," Wellman stated. "But it's worth a try. Somewheres along the way I done lost my chewin' tobacco. And I do like a chaw occasional." He spat into the fire. "Wherebouts in the Pinals is this Glob place?"

"He told me it was between the Pinals and the Apache Mountains."

"That'd be about thirty-five or forty miles from here.

We'll give her a shot then. Stay between Jackson Butte and Chromo Butte. It's rough country but they's water and good cover. And we'll be caught up with the Tontos to the west and the White Mountain 'Paches to the east. Anybody object to pullin' out in the mornin'?"

No one did.

The name of the two-building town was not Glob—it was Globe. And as the bartender told them, this wasn't the original location of the town. It all started out on Ramboz Peak as a mining town. It was moved here 'cause it was a better location.

"Do tell?" Wellman said. "Gimme a rye. History lessons make me awful dry."

Beer for Bodine and Sam, lemonade for Laurie, who was making the barkeep nervous just by being in the bar side of the trading post.

"Thought we might have some peace around here with old Cochise dyin'," the barkeep said. "But 'twasn't to be. Things is damn near as bad as they was."

"Chappo get up this way much?" Sam asked.

The barkeep actually shuddered at the mention of his name. "That one is the worst of the worse. He just raided a ranch west of here night before last. Killed the man and woman and tortured their teenage son to death. Kidnapped a little girl. Poor thing."

"Victorio?" Bodine asked.

"Victorio is talkin' peace among the Mimbres. But if the Army tries to move him from New Mexico to San Carlos, they'll be war. Bet on it."

"The Chiricahua reservation still going?" Sam asked.

"Not after it was found that Geronimo and his cutthroats was just usin' it for sanctuary between raids. That, and them killin's last March prompted the Army to close it. They moved 'em all over to San Carlos. Which didn't make us around here too damn happy."

Bodine knew that the San Carlos reservation was a barren wasteland of a hell-hole for the Apache. Some five thousand square miles of mostly low-lying land, populated by lizards and rattlesnakes and having terrible sandstorms, all of which made for miserable living conditions for the Apache. The vegetation was mostly cactus and mesquite and a few sorry-looking cottonwoods along the river banks. The government never gave the Apache enough food to live on. A weekly allotment of flour and beef never was enough to last more than four days. Then they went hungry. The Indians were constantly being short-changed on the beef, usually with the reservation officials being bought off to look the other way.

To make matters worse, of the five thousand Apaches who were forced onto the San Carlos reservation, there were represented some eight tribes, some of them longtime haters of the other. All in all, it was not a pleasant existence.

The government, in its efforts to transform nomadic warriors into fammers—something they did not succeed in doing—turned the reservation, for a time, into no more than a prison farm.

Bodine looked toward the south. "It must be awful for those young girls down there."

"I 'spect." Wellman fell silent for a moment and all knew he had something heavy on his mind. The old mountain man looked first at Laurie, then for several hard and lingering seconds at Bodine and Sam. "You all better know this now: If I git inside that slave factory down yonder, I ain't takin' no prisoners. If I git close enough to take a prisoner for information, I'll skin him alive if I think he knows anything that would be a help to us. Anybody who would kidnap young girls to sell into bondage—and we all growed up people, we know what's in store for them girl children—don't deserve to live. Regardless of whether they's Injun or white or

Chinapeople; don't make no difference to me. If any of you feel like you ain't got the stomach for it, now's the time to say so. Tucson ain't but a hop and a skip from where we is. You can go there and get out of my business."

"Suppose some of them want to surrender, Dick?" Sam asked.

"They got a problem," Wellman said flatly.

Laurie tried to put it in perspective. "Here we sit, four of us, talking about facing fifty or a hundred gunhands, and discussing their possible surrender. Who do we think we are?"

Reservation policy also called for the Apache to govern himself. This was confusing to them because the Apache had no system that was even close to that of the white man. And to further complicate matters, the Apache thought the white man's laws were stupid.

But so hated were the Apaches that their plight went unnoticed by the settlers whose philosophy was, "To hell with them, they got what they deserved."

From the outset, it was a culture-clash of laws and rules from a more or less civilized society meeting a centuries-old, and to the whites, barbaric way of life.

The Apaches were bound to lose.

"Where you folks headin'?" the barkeep asked.

"South," Wellman told him.

He looked at Laurie and shook his head and sighed. "Rough country between here and there."

"Yeah. I been there afore," the old mountain man said. He jerked a thumb at Laurie. "Is there a place for her to sleep decent and safe for a night or two?"

"I got a room in the back she could use. She'll be safe there."

" 'preciate it. We'll sleep in the livery with our horses. You got ready-cooked grub here?"

"Shore do. Got beef and beans and potatoes."

"You get it. We'll shore eat it."

The four of them stayed in Globe for two days, relaxing and listening for any news that might come their way concerning Chappo and his band or Porter and his men.

They learned that Chappo was likely to strike anywhere in the territory. His band numbered less than a hundred. And of the eight tribes of Apaches, only a couple would have anything at all to do with Chappo, and they were Victorio and Nana. Loco, Chato, Alchesay, and Eskaminzin would have nothing to do with the renegade Chappo; although, as one Globe resident said, that was probably due to some personal dislike more than a moral stand against Chappo's viciousness and cruelty.

Of Porter and his men, they learned that a large group of riders had been seen heading south out of the Mescal Mountains, following the San Pedro.

"That's probably Porter," Bodine said, studying a crudely drawn map of southern Arizona. "He'll probably veer to the southwest somewhere down here around the Little Dragoons and head for the Huachucas."

"That miner said a large group of riders," Sam pointed out. "That means that Porter's picked up some more trash."

Bodine nodded and Wellman said, "You two pick up a spare canteen, boys. As soon as we leave the Pinals, we'll be ridin' into a land filled with low-class people and damn little water."

"That pretty well sums up hell, Dick," Matt said with a grin.

"If it's any worser, I shore don't want to go there," the old mountain man said grimly.

They left Globe, heading south, at the best possible time of the year. Had it been summer, the conditions would have been very nearly intolerable for man and horse. They rode during the pre-dawn hours and the early morning, holing up by noon and resting during the hottest part of the day. At night they listened to the yap of the desert fox and lonely calls of coyote and once they heard the wavering howl of the wolf.

They rode through the Tortilla Mountains, past Crozier Peak to the west and Holy Joe Peak far to the east. They picked their way through a maze of ancient saguaro, some of the giant cactus more than a hundred and fifty years old, standing fifty-feet high and weighing ten tons; many of them with thirty to forty huge arms.

"Injuns eat them red fruits up there on the cactus," Wellman pointed out. "They ain't bad, but I wouldn't want a steady diet of 'em."

"How do those birds nest in there without getting killed on the thorns?" Laurie asked.

"Don't ask me, child," Wellman replied. "Just another one of God's wonders, is all I can say. They's rats out here in this hell that don't never take a drink of water, so I've been told. I don't know how they do that, either."

"What's that up ahead?" Sam asked, wiping the sweat from his forehead.

"Them's the Santa Catalina Mountains. And they's a pretty sight for these eyes."

"Water?" Bodine asked.

"You betcha, boy."

In actual distance they had traveled about seventy five miles. But their clothes were crusty with dried sweat and dust. Their eyes were red-rimmed from the intense sun and baked land and from staring hard for any sign of hostiles.

"We been lucky," Wellman summed up the journey from Globe to the Santa Catalinas.

The four of them dismounted from their weary horses to stand and gaze at the abrupt and most welcome transformation. They were looking at beautiful grassy meadows and forests of ponderosa pine, and they could hear the sound of falling water far in the distance.

"Seven Falls," Wellman told them.

"It sounds delicious," Laurie said.

"I never heared it put quite like that," Wellman spoke with a grin. "But you pegged it right." He pointed. "Yonder's a crick, girl. You go bathe and such and I'll hold a gun on these two to keep them from sneakin' a peek."

"Oh, they wouldn't do that, Dick!"

Bodine and Sam just grinned.

"You two do smell a whole lot better," Wellman remarked, after Bodine and Sam returned from a bath in the cold waters of the creek. "I was about ready to ask Laurie if she had any toilet water to pour on you boys."

"You're a fine one to talk," Sam came back at him. "I thought I was in the company of a skunk riding up here alongside you."

Wellman cackled with good humor, knowing that Sam spoke the truth. He had soaped off about five pounds of trail dust.

Laurie was a short distance away, sitting on the rocks below Seven Falls, enjoying the beauty and the peacefulness of the scenery.

"I 'spect we best plan on gettin' to the fort in the Huachucas," Wellman said. "We might get lucky and get some more lead into Porter's bunch along the way."

"Army fort?" Bodine looked at Wellman.

"Yeah. It's always undermanned, so I was told. They won't give us any trouble."

"And how far away is that?" Sam asked.

"I'd guess a good hundred and thirty-forty miles from where we're luxuriatin'. We'll stay in the mountains for several days. I know the trails. They'll be desert for a spell, 'tween the Rincon and the Whitstone Mountains—the Empire Mountains is grim, but I know where the tinajas is, or was—then we'll have another spell down to the Huachucas."

"What's a tinajas?" Laurie asked, walking up to join them.

"Natural stone tanks high up in the rocks that hold water. This is a good time of year for them to have water, too. Summer can get kind of grim."

"There any towns between here and there?" Bodine posed the question.

"Not that I know of. There used to a tradin' post some few miles south and west of the Little Dragoons. Might be a town there now. But the way the 'Paches raid and burn, I wouldn't count on it."

"When do you want to leave, Dick?"

"We'll get a good rest this afternoon and tonight. Pull out in the morning."

"People with right on their side, Laurie," Matt told her. "Lawman over in Texas once said that you can't stop a man who knows he's right and just keeps on coming."

"Or a woman," she replied sweetly, but with edged steel in the words.

Chapter 9

They left at dawn, skirting Mount Lemmon and riding south, out of the Santa Catalinas and toward the Rincon Mountains. Twice they saw sign of Apaches, but if the Indians saw them, and that was quite likely, the braves decided not to attack the riders. Perhaps it was the way they sat their saddles, or maybe it was the set of their jaws or the hard look on their faces. The Indians did not fight to take losses, and one look at the four people riding south would tell a seasoned warrior that much blood would be spilled fighting these people. Or perhaps the Apache just did not feel like making war; perhaps the signs were not right. Or as Dick put it, " 'Paches are notional folks. Ever'thing's got to be just right for them to attack. They got to sit and palaver for a time."

They left the coolness of the forests and rode into the near barrenness. There was water, but one had to know where to find it.

They cut slightly east and found the trading post just west of the San Pedro river. They had not been bothered by the Apache.

"We're about twenty-five miles from the Huachucas," Wellman told them. "And would you just take a look at them horses at the hitchrail."

Bodine and Sam had already noticed them. They belonged to some of Porter's men; some of the same horses the men had seen following the ambush in the canyon and again at Horsehead Crossing.

Bodine and Wellman and Sam checked their guns, wiping the dust from them and loading the cylinders up full. Laurie pulled her rifle from the boot.

"Let's go clean out a snake pit," Wellman said, and took the lead riding up behind the trading post.

The place could be called a town, if one wanted to stretch the meaning of that word. There were six buildings and one bumpy, rutted road running east and west.

"Ain't progress grand?" Wellman said, swinging down from the saddle. "Place has done become a regular metropolis since I last seed it. Let's go reduce the population, folks."

"You just hold on a minute, Dick," Bodine told him quietly.

The mountain man wheeled around and stared at the much younger man.

"We don't know who might be in there. And I'm not goin' in shootin' until I do know. We were lucky back up north in that no innocent person got killed. We might not be so lucky this time around. There might even be some law in this burg; a man with more guts than that old man back at the Crossing."

"So?" Wellman challenged. Mountain men would walk up to the devil and spit in his eye just to see what he'd do. They were a breed such as the nation had never seen before and with their passing as progress caught up with them, would most likely never see again.

"We're down here to try and rescue some kidnapped girls, not get thrown in the pokey because we didn't use our heads."

Wellman glared hard at Bodine for a moment, then grinned.

"All right, boy. You run this show, then. What do you think we ought to do?"

"Why, hell, Dick—go in a have a drink, what else?"

Wellman laughed.

"Laurie, you go in the store door of the building, cover us from that side."

The blonde nodded and walked toward the mercantile side of the huge building. Matt noticed that it was a pleasure watching her walk away. He put that pleasant thought out of his mind and loosened his guns in leather. The three men walked toward the saloon side, stood for a moment staring into the much darker interior, so their eyes would more quickly adjust once inside, and pushed open the batwings.

The hubbub of conversation ceased abruptly when the men entered. The three men walked quickly to the bar and fanned out, backs to the bar, staring at the roomful of rowdies who were giving them dark looks of hate.

Porter was not among them, and neither were the top guns Sam and Bodine had seen up north.

But several of the outlaws were still wearing dirty bandages from wounds suffered during the ambush in the canyon.

Wellman smiled at the crowd of a dozen or so. The old man was anxious to drag iron and the crowd of gunnies could sense it. "Where's that pig you call a boss? What's his name? I disremember right off."

"Potty, isn't it?" Sam said.

"Yeah. Something like that," Bodine picked it up. "Or maybe it was pooty."

The saloon quickly emptied of anyone not associated with the Porter Gang.

"He's around," a rough-looking outlaw said. "Which is more than you're gonna be for very long, old man."

Wellman laughed at him. "You think you're gonna be the one to cash my chips in, punk?"

"I might be," the man replied.

"Then stand up and do it!"

But the outlaw only smiled. "Some other time, Wellman. We got more important things to do than fool around some old has-been like you."

Wellman laid a cussin' on the man, calling him everything profane he could think of . . . which after fifty years in the high dangerous lonesome of the mountains, was quite a lot.

Still the man would not stand and fight. And none of his friends showed any inclination to mix it up with Wellman.

Wellman fell silent, having run out of cuss words.

Sam began moving his hands, speaking in sign language. Wellman and Bodine both laughed. Sam ended by making a kissing sound with his lips.

The gunny got the message, loud and clear. He flushed a deep red and jumped to his feet, his hands hovering over the butts of his guns. "Don't you be callin' me no sissy-boy, you damn half-breed!"

Sam smiled at him. "I just did."

"Then, draw, you greasy savage!"

Sam drew, smoothly and swiftly. He was not as fast as Bodine—few men were—but Sam was just as good a shot. He put his first round in the man's belly, the second round dead-centering him in the chest.

None of the other gunnies would stand and draw. They watched as their dying compadre collapsed to the floor.

"Whole damn bunch is yeller!" Wellman snorted.

"No," Bodine said, his eyes not leaving the gunhands seated around the tables. "I'd guess they're under orders not to mix it up with us."

"Still makes 'em yeller."

One of Porter's men stood up, slowly, his hands in plain sight. "We'll be leavin' now," he said. "See you boys around, I 'magine."

"What about him?" Bodine said, pointing to the dead man.

The gunslick shrugged. "The breed shot him, let the breed bury him."

"I just can't figure it," Wellman said.

The four of them had left the tiny hamlet about an hour after the barroom shooting. They had resupplied and pulled out while they still had several hours of good light left them.

"I cussed all them rowdies back yonder," Wellman continued his musings. "Called them boys things I wouldn't call a skunk. And they still wouldn't fight."

"They've got something in mind for us, that's for sure," Sam said. "But what is it?"

"And where was Porter and the rest of his gunfighters?" Laurie asked.

"This Lake person down on the border has fifty or so men in his gang. Porter has twenty-five or so," Bodine said. "What better way to get rid of us than for them to join forces and just wait for us to ride in there. So let's don't give them that opportunity. Dick, do you know a way in other than straight south?"

"Shore. We can either cut east and circle back, comin' in through below the Huachucas, or we can head west and circle back and come in thataway."

"Which way would you suggest?"

"Parker Canyon. We'll ride south and a tad west. They'll be expectin' us to come straight in from the Huachucas. This might throw 'em off a bit and give us just a little edge."

"What happens," Laurie tossed out the question, "if we get down there and the girls are already gone?"

Wellman bit off a chew from a plug of tobacco. "I'll track them girls right up to and then through the gates of hell if I have to." He chewed and spat. "And kill any man who gets in my way."

* * *

"It was a dark and bloody ground when Cochise was roaming these hills and mountains," Wellman said, twisting in the saddle.

They were riding south, keeping Sonoita Creek to the west of them. Just a few miles to the east, numerous silver camps were still operating, although many were even now ghost towns; Mowry being one of them.

They began angling toward the southeast, traveling through the Patagonia Mountains and into the San Rafael Valley country. A few people still lived in and around the old mining camp of Mowry and they decided to stop there and see if they might learn anything.

"They might be a few folks still hangin' on at Washington Camp," Wellman said. "That's a few miles south. We don't learn nothin' here, we'll wander down thataway."

The saloon was still open and doing business, so they wandered in and bellied up to the bar, the bartender, wiping his hands on a dirty apron front, gave Laurie a sideways glance but other than that had no comment about her being in the saloon.

"Rye," Wellman said. Bodine and Sam opted for beer, and Laurie ordered her usual lemonade.

"Ain't got no lemonade, Miss," the bartender said. "Rye whiskey, mescal, or beer. That's it."

"Beer," she told him, eyeballing the dirt and grime of the place. "Wash the mug before you pour it. And dry it with a clean cloth."

Muttering, the barkeep walked off, but he washed all the mugs and managed to find a clean enough looking rag.

"San Rafael Cattle Company still in operation?" Wellman asked, after a sip of rye.

The barkeep brightened up. "Shore is. You from this part of the country?"

"Came through once or twice. I'll come right out and say it, and if you repeat it, I'll give you up to Green River."

The bartender was an old hand; he knew that remark meant this grizzled old man was probably one of the last of the breed called mountain men. "Up to Green River," meant taking a Green River knife up the hilt—in his belly!

"Ask your questions. I ain't a man who repeats things ifn I'm told not to."

"That old Mex fort south of here . . . who's livin' in it now?"

The barkeep sighed. Shook his head. "The one down on the Santa Cruz?"

"Don't give me no damn useless tongue-waggin'. There ain't but one Mex fort around here."

"Awright, awright! Keep your pants on. Outlaw name of Lake took it over about a year ago, I reckon. Maybe longer than that. Got hisself a regular army down there. Fifty-sixty hardcases."

"Does business with Chappo, too, don't he?"

"So I been told."

"Just how much have you been told?"

The barkeep looked a little green around the mouth. "I got to live around here, mister. So I reckon I done said enough."

Wellman moved swiftly for a man his age. He snaked a hand across the bar, grabbed the smaller man by the throat, and began shaking him like a dog with a rabbit. "The name's Dick Wellman. And this here is Matt Bodine and Sam Two Wolves. The lady's name is Miss Laurie. And you're gonna tell me everything you know or I'll just squeeze the life right out of you."

The barkeep's eyes were bugged out like a frog and he gurgled and choked and nodded his head. Wellman dropped him to the floor behind the bar. The barkeep came up with a sawed-off shotgun in his hands. Matt slapped him in the face with a beer mug, shattering the mug and not doing the man's front teeth a bit of good; they bounced around on the floor like yellowed chips of stone. The bar keep hit the floor, out cold.

Wellman finished his rye and said, "Laurie, you rumble around in the back and locate the kitchen. See you can't fix some grub for us. Sam, you tie the barkeep to a chair. I got me a notion that when I tell him what I'm gonna do if he don't start jabberin', he's gonna start bumpin' his gums faster than we can listen."

Chapter 10

"You wouldn't do that to me!" the barkeep hollered, his eyes all walled back in his head as he looked at Wellman's longbladed knife. "I'm a white man!"

"You're scum, is what you is. All the time knowin' about them poor scared children down yonder and not doin' nothin' about it."

"What could I do?" the barkeep almost screamed the question. "There ain't fifteen people left in this town and half of them is drunk most of the time."

"What you can do right now is tell me everything you know about the fort. And, mister . . . you better tell me the truth."

"I cain't do that!" the barkeep yelled. "Lake and them others will kill me."

Wellman laid the big blade against the side of the barkeep's face. The smile on the old mountain man's face was not a pleasant curving of the lips. "I'll wager they'll kill you a whole lot quicker than I will."

The man started talking.

* * * *

When the four of them rode out of the dying and crumbling town the next morning, they left behind them a barkeep who would probably have difficulty sleeping for all his remaining time on earth.

Wellman had not physically hurt the man; but mentally he had scarred him forever. The barkeep had taken a long look into those hard eyes of the mountain man, felt the cold steel of the knife against his face, and decided that baring his soul would probably be a very wise thing to do, and so he did.

They rode down through Washington Camp, and there they veered more to the southeast, toward the border with Mexico. They took their time, staying alert, for this was Chappo's country. And while Chappo's followers were few, no Apache ever lived who could match their fighting skills and cruelty with prisoners.

Laurie spotted the piece of gingham and called out. Matt left the saddle and retrieved the brightly-colored fabric that had snagged on a low branch.

"I don't think it's been here long," he said, handing the cloth to Wellman while Sam walked the area, looking for signs.

"It hasn't," Sam said. "These tracks are not more than twenty-four hours old."

"Poor scared little child," Wellman muttered, his callused fingers rubbing the cloth. "A man's got to be crapsorry to be involved in anything like stealin' children to sell into bondage."

No one among them could dispute that.

"How far away from the fort are we?" Laurie asked.

"Not more than five miles," Wellman told, pointing. "Yonder's the Santa Cruz a-twistin'. We best get off this trail and make camp. Then I'll go prowlin' some to get the feel of the place agin." He looked over at Matt. "If I don't come back—and they's a chance I might not—my little girl's name is Jenny. Purty little thing. You get her out of there. I want you all to stay put. If I ain't back in two days, that'll mean I done seen the elephant. Then it'll be time for y'all to come a-foggin'. You be careful, child," he said to Laurie, then nodded at Sam and Bodine. "You boys take 'er easy." Then he swung into the saddle and was gone.

"Do we chance a fire?" Laurie asked.

"No," Matt said quickly. "Apaches would smell the smoke for miles. We'll just have to settle for a cold camp."

Wellman left his horse well-concealed about two miles from the fort and pulled off his boots, slipping moccasins on his feet. He would go it on foot from this point. He had watered his horse and there was enough water left in the small pool and enough graze for a couple of days. If he didn't come back, the horse would jerk its picket pin and be gone.

Wellman made his way cautiously through the timber and the brush. He was in rolling hills country, brown now with winter not far off. He had it in his mind that the old fort was in Mexico, set just south of the border, on the east side of the Santa Cruz. And the barkeep had said that Lake was probably paying off some corrupt Mexican officials—he thought they were Army officers—in order to stay in business. So that meant that not only were they facing anywhere from seventy-five to a hundred gunslicks and assorted trash; but that they might be looking at Mexican soldiers, as well.

Wellman knew that in Sonora, Mexico, at this point in time, the Army, for the most part, was controlled by the rich land-owners; a baron-peasant type of government, and it was corrupt to the core, the boots of the government grinding the peasant's face into the dirt.

"Well, soldier-boys," Wellman muttered, "you best be out on patrol when we get there, 'cause a bullet don't give a damn who it hits."

It took him several hours to reach a vantage point overlooking the fort . . . and it was a depressing sight in that the place looked awesome, at first glance, seemingly impossible to breach. But Wellman knew there was a way; he just had to come up with it.

The fort had been built in a clearing taking up about a hundred or so acres. The fort itself was huge, with several two-story buildings set inside high thick walls.

"Shore didn't remember the place as bein' this big," Wellman whispered to himself. "But there it is, so let's see if we can't figure a way to get in, get the kids, and get out!"

He memorized the layout and watched what activity there was going on inside the compound. He concluded that the biggest building was the headquarters and probably where Lake lived and the kids were being held. Then he suddenly grinned, an idea popping into his head.

It might work, he thought. And then he brightened as he watched a number of young kids, all girls, being escorted out into the yard of the walled compound, under heavy guard. Relief filled the man. They were still being held in the fort!

"I'll stay here with Laurie," Wellman told the others. "Matt, you and Sam beat it back to that mining camp we come through and buy all the dynamite they'll let you have. Don't forget caps and fuses. We're gonna have to blast our way into that place."

"Did you see any soldiers?" Sam asked.

"No. And I hope it stays that way."

"We'll leave now," Matt said. "There's several hours of good light left. With any kind of luck, we'll be back late tomorrow afternoon."

"Ride careful, boys," the mountain man cautioned them. "I didn't see no sign of Chappo's band, but that bunch is like rattlesnakes: it's when you don't see them that you got to worry."

* * *

Bodine and Sam lucked out at their first stop.

"I'm packin' it in," the miner said, disgust in his voice. "Pullin' out. I'll sell you boys the whole kit and caboodle cheap and throw in a pack horse. How's that sound to you?"

They bought all his dynamite, plus some other supplies, both sides thinking they had a good deal. The equipment was loaded on the pack horse, and the blood-brothers were back with Wellman and Laurie hours before they were due to return.

Wellman chuckled with dark humor as he eyeballed the equipment. "This'll damn sure get their attention. Let's start riggin' the sticks for throwin'. Four to a bunch. You bought some bindertwine, too. Good. Let's get to it, people. The sooner we can get this done and grab them kids, the sooner we can build a fire and we can all have a cup of coffee."

They were rolled out and packed up an hour before dawn. And it was cold in the pre-dawn, all of them wishing for a warm fire and a hot cup of coffee. They had to settle for jerky and a drink of water.

And they longed for a hot bath, for they were all getting gamy.

"We have to take into consideration that once we hit the place, Lake and the others might take the kids and run," Sam said. He had studied a crude map of Mexico the day before. "If that's the case, they'll probably head straight west, toward the Gulf of California. Dick, you said the ship would dock where the Coyote runs into the Gulf?"

"That's my understandin'."

"You know anything about that country?"

"Not much. Just that it's hot and dry. That's desert country."

"We'll just play it by ear," Matt said. "Everybody ready to go?"

They were ready, their faces clearly showing the tension in the pre-dawn.

"Let's ride."

They all had spare pistols, taken from dead outlaws who had faced them along their journey, plus the spare pistol that each always carried. The spares were loaded up full and tucked behind their belts.

It would be Laurie's job, once they had blown the massive gates, to stay with the horses. Wellman would gather up and hold horses for the kids to ride. Bodine and Sam would breach the headquarters building and locate and lead the kids out. But as Wellman had pointed out, all that was subject to quick change.

The sky was sodden with low-hanging clouds as they pulled out. Before they had gone a mile, it began to rain, the drops fat and cold, and while all silently cursed the discomfort as they struggled into dark slickers, they all said a silent prayer, for the rain would cover any sounds they might make. The pre-bunched dynamite had been well covered against rain the night before.

The ghostly falling drops made the silent trek even more grim. For this was a spooky place even under the best of conditions. It was high-up country, a place of crags and upthrusting cliffs, and the rain was producing sudden and fast-flowing little streams.

The rain poured and turned into a violent but, fortunately for them, a short-lived storm, with zigzagging lightning cutting the dark sky and crashing thunder that made conversation impossible. The winds tore limbs from trees and blocked the narrow trail, oftentimes forcing them to seek another route. It became so dark that one had difficulty seeing the other in front of them.

Still they rode on, knowing that the storm would keep those in the fort inside and hopefully, unaware of the searchers until it was too late. They bunched up so no one would get lost in the storm.

Finally, the storm abated, the winds calmed, and the rain

was reduced to a drizzle. The skies remained dark; night in the midst of dawn.

Finally they came to the little hollow where Wellman had left his horse that day he studied the fort. "She lies right over that ridge," he said. "We're right on top of 'er, people. I've seen it. You people crawl on up yonder and take you a good looksee at what we're up agin. I'll stay with the horses."

The faces of the three mirrored their shock at initially viewing the fortress, for at first glance, it seemed impregnable. But then Bodine shifted positions and worked his way around to where he could see the rear of the fort and began to size it up with a warrior's eyes. A dangerous smile creased his lips.

He rejoined the others. "I took me a good look at the rear of the fort," he whispered, although whispering was not necessary. "The big building, what Wellman called the headquarters, butts right up against the wall. I guess they never expected any attack from the south, 'cause there's all sorts of crap been allowed to gather back there. Rocks and crates and what-have-you."

He paused, glanced over at Sam, and grinned at his blood brother.

"Let me guess," Sam said. "You're going in the back way while we create a diversion for you in the front."

He did not pose it as a question.

"You got part of it right. Let's get back to Dick and lay it out for him."

"Boy, have you lost your mind!" Wellman said. "That there's a suicide stunt. I'm agin it."

"Think about it," Bodine urged. "With any kind of luck at all, I can get in there, get the kids out over the wall, and be gone while you three are creating a diversion. Just as soon as the last girl is clear, I'll light the fuses on enough explosives to bring down that whole damn building and stun everybody in that place for five minutes. I got to play it by ear, Dick. But I think it'll work."

The old mountain man bit off a hunk of plug tobacco and chewed for a moment. Finally, he nodded his head. "All right, boy. I admire your courage. But what kind of high sign are you gonna give us so's we'll know you're clear?"

Matt grinned. "Oh, you'll know, Dick. When that whole building blows up, that's your cue."

"You just can't be subtle about anything, can you?" Sam needled him.

Bodine grinned at him. "I'll leave my rifles here and take a full pack of dynamite. That'll give you and Dick eight fully loaded Winchesters. One of you here, the other about a hundred yards over yonder. There's a narrow wash just behind the rear wall. The kids will be running up that to the back of this rise we're on. Laurie, I want you to be where the wash peters out and meets this rise."

"There ain't gonna be no horses for the kids," Wellman pointed out.

"That's right. We'll have to rope the kids together so they don't get separated and hoof it back to that mining camp where we bought the dynamite. We can pick up wagons there."

"Rear guard?" Sam asked.

Bodine shook his head. "No. At least not right off. When we get clear, you and Laurie go on with the kids and me and Dick will lay back with rifles and discourage any who might want to follow."

Dick grinned. "Now that, I'm lookin' forward to."

Bodine took off his spurs and stowed them in a saddle bag. He filled a huge pack with explosives and struggled into the heavy pack. "I'm gone," he said, then disappeared into the mist.

Chapter 11

While the others moved into position, Bodine slipped into the narrow ending of the wash and began making his way toward the rear of the old fort. The water was about ankle deep but running off rapidly; he could see the water-line marks that had been cut during heavier downpours. The wash would not be a safe place to be during any storm. Bodine glanced up at the leaden-looking sky and hoped any further rain would hold off for another hour, at least.

He started to lean against the north side of the cut to catch his breath then thought better of it when he heard the agitated buzz of a rattler who had sought refuge in a small hole just above the waterline. Bodine moved a few yards farther on and let Mister Rattler alone.

Catching his breath—the pack weighed close to a hundred pounds—Bodine moved on. With only a few hundred feet to go before reaching the spot where he had planned to climb out, the walls of the arroyo were now several feet over his head. But he could see where a spot had caved out of the north side; he would have to climb out there. From there, it would be only a dozen yards to the wall surrounding the old fort.

Reaching the jumble of rocks, Bodine climbed up carefully and looked over the top. So far, so good. He could see no one walking a guard mount along the inner wall. He found a good grip and heaved himself up, scrambling quickly to the wall and hugging it for a moment, listening.

He could hear nothing.

Bodine tied one end of a rope around a boulder and looped the remainder around his chest. He climbed up on the pile of rocks and trash by the wall, muttered a prayer in both English and Cheyenne—one of the Great Spirits might be listening—and grabbed hold of the top of the wall. He heaved himself over the wall and landed heavily on the other side, quickly drawing both Colts and looking around him.

Nothing.

He looked up at the one window that faced the wall and the arroyo beyond. It was barred; he had seen that from the rise, and had come prepared for it.

Several faces appeared at the bars; frightened young faces. Bodine put a finger to his lips, silently warning them to be quiet. The girls nodded their heads.

Slipping out of the heavy pack, Bodine jumped up and grabbed hold of the bars, muscling himself up, bringing himself eye-level with the sill, and looking into the cavernous room. There was no glass in the window.

"Are you guarded?" Bodine whispered.

"From the outside," a girl returned the whisper.

"Do they check on you very often?"

"No, sir. Who are you?"

"A man who's come to get you out of this place. Just stay put and tell the others not to make any more noise than you normally make. Hang on, girls, I'll be right back."

Bodine dropped to the ground and ran to the corner of the building where he had seen a bench. He dragged it back to the window. From the pack, he took out a flat piece of metal he'd bought from the miner, climbed up on the bench, and began working at the bolts that held the bars in place. The adobe was old and the bolts were rusty, still it took him precious minutes to pry several loose.

He tugged at the bars and winced when one bolt make a sharp grinding sound as it came loose. He paused for a moment, listening. If anyone heard the sound, they did not think it important enough to investigate.

He could understand why there was no one back here guarding the windows. The way the bars were positioned, there was no way the children could have pried loose the bars from the inside.

Bodine put the bench back where it had been, muscled the pack up to the kids—it was all several of them could do to pull it in, even with him pushing from beneath—and with the rope still looped around his chest, jumped up, grabbed the edge of the protruding sill, and crawled through the pried-open bars. Once inside, he re-positioned the bars so they would look, at a glance, as though they were undisturbed. He let the rope dangle down the side of the building. Building and rope were almost the same color.

"Stay quiet, girls," he cautioned them. "I've got about ten minutes' work to do, and then we'll get gone from this place." He counted the girls and bit back a groan of dismay. Twenty-five of them. All of them scared and trembling.

Bodine went to a dirty, fly-specked window that faced out into the yard. He could see nobody moving about. The rain had begun, falling in a dull drizzle.

"Have you been fed this morning?"

"About thirty minutes ago, sir."

"Will they pick up the bowls?"

"No, sir. Not until dinnertime."

"How many men are inside the compound?"

"I'd guess they's between seventy-five and a hundred of

them, sir. A big new bunch rode in about three days ago. Somebody named Porter."

"Where do they keep their horses?" Bodine was working as he whispered, unpacking the explosives.

"Some of them are kept in the stable inside the walls," another girl whispered. "But most of them are kept in a corral on the east side of the fort."

Bodine could not have seen the east side and the corral from the rise, due to the two-story building he was now in. "Guarded?"

"I don't think so, sir. They've got a deal worked out with the Apaches so's the Injuns don't swipe their ponies."

"Chappo?"

"Yes, sir."

"Any of you girls ever ridden astride?"

They all grinned impishly at him.

"Bareback?"

The grins widened.

It might work, Bodine thought. It just might work. "Anybody here named Jenny?"

"Me, sir," a girl whispered.

"Your grandpa Dick Wellman is over yonder on the ridge. You girls do as I tell you, and you'll soon be out of here."

"What's your name, sir?" Jenny asked.

"Matt Bodine."

Everybody from the Canadian Rockies to the Mexican border had heard of Matt Bodine. He was almost as famous as Smoke Jensen, although the two had never crossed trails . . . yet.

Like Jensen, Bodine had never sought the name of gunfighter. And like Jensen, neither Sam Two Wolves or Matt Bodine had ever hired out their guns.

Matt laid out enough explosives to ensure the total destruction of the two story building the girls had been held prisoner in, and anything that might be close to the structure.

He had placed charges beneath support beams and posts, against the walls at stress points, and would lay the final charge against the front door. He began cutting the fuses, guessing at the time of each fuse. That done, he moved to the window and pulled the rope taut, securing his end around a support post. He pushed the bars away from the window and motioned for the girls to gather at the window.

"Use the rope one at a time, hand over hand, kids," he told them. "Drop down to the other side of the wall and stay close to it. Jenny, your grandfather says you've got nerve. You think you and three or four other girls can slip around to the corral and steal some horses?"

She grinned at him. "Yes, sir!"

"OK. Follow the arroyo around and get the horses. Two apiece and lead them around to this wall. We don't have time for saddles. Grab a handful of bridles if you can find them, if not, you know how to grab onto a mane. Walk them around here and keep them quiet. When I give the word, swing on and follow this arroyo to where you'll see a lady waiting for you. Her name is Laurie. She'll lead you over the rise and to safety. You understand?"

"Yes, sir."

"OK, Jenny. You first. Go!"

As the last girl was hand-to-handing it across to the wall and dropping out of sight, Matt saw the first of the horses being led up the wash. Then he heard the sound of a key being fumbled into a padlock. He moved quickly to the door, picking up the flat bar on his way over.

"All right, girls," the man spoke before he had the door open. "You pretties got to take a bath, you all leaving in the . . ."

His words hung in his throat as he stood open-mouthed, staring at the vastness of the empty room. He turned to yell just in time to catch the flat bar in the center of his forehead. He hit the floor, his forehead caved in from the force of the blow.

Matt closed the door and ran to the window. "Walk your horses out of here!" he called in a hoarse whisper. "Be quiet and move!"

The girls, riding two to a horse, began moving up the wash. "Just a little more time, Lord," Matt pleaded. He stood by the window and counted them. Jenny was on a pony by herself and was out of sight. When he counted twenty-five, he slipped into his considerably lighter pack and ran back to the door and lit the fuse, then moved swiftly around the room, lighting fuses. When the last one was sputtering, Bodine was across the rope and over the wall in two heartbeats and running up the wash.

"They're gettin' away!" he heard the screaming from behind him.

Matt turned, drawing a Colt and earing back the hammer as he did so. The man was on the second floor of the building he had just left, leveling a rifle in Bodine's direction. Bodine snapped off a shot that missed, but drove the man back inside the building.

Then the charges blew.

The walls blew out on all four sides. The roof caved in and a huge cloud of dust rose into the air, so great the rain took several moments to clear it. The shock of the explosion trembled the earth and collapsed the water tower inside the compound, sending hundreds of gallons of water in a minor tidal wave over the ground.

Bodine ran for the ridge and scrambled up just as Wellman and Sam opened up with rifles from their high-up vantage point.

"Lousy place to build a fort in the first place," Bodine panted the words, throwing himself down beside Dick.

"There ain't nobody come out of that rubble, Matt," Dick told him, tossing him a rifle. "I seen one man blowed clear out a window and high up in the air—out of the second story. I hope to hell it was Lake."

"Yeah, me, too," Matt said, checking the Winchester. "But for right now, let's get gone!"

Wellman and Sam took the lead, the kids in the middle, and Matt and Laurie bringing up the rear. The going was very slow, for the rain had picked up and the kids kept falling off the wet backs of the horses. Wellman left the trail and plunged them into the brush.

"We got to make the mining camp," he called over his shoulder. "This way is longer, but it's smoother ridin' for the young'uns."

The kids were game, Matt would give them that. Not a one cried or complained during the tortuous ride. When one fell off, she just scrambled right back on again without a word and kept on going.

It was no more than ten miles—over some of the roughest country in the southeast—to the first of the many mining camps that dotted that part of the territory along the Mexican border, but it seemed to be taking them forever to reach it.

And none of them could understand why it seemed that no one from the fort was pursuing them.

Finally, Wellman was forced to call a halt. The horses needed a break and the weather had turned from bad to just plain lousy.

Jenny stayed close to her grandpa as Matt searched for dry wood and Sam built a fire under an overhang. Jenny started brewing coffee in every container they had. The kids were given hardtack and jerky to chew on.

"I think those at the fort have circled and are waiting for us between here and the mining camp," Bodine said, gulping at the tin cup of coffee Laurie handed him. "They'd guess that we have to get the kids to some sort of civilization, and that's the closest inhabited area. And they also know that none of us—including the kids—can be allowed to live.

Working with the Apaches would be bad enough in the minds of settlers, but stealing kids to sell into bondage would be putting a noose around all their necks. They have to get rid of us. They don't have a choice in the matter."

"They've killed other kids," a little girl told them. "I've seen them do it," she added.

"There we have it," Sam said. "These people are the lowest of the low. I don't think we can afford to go busting up into that mining camp. Lake and his people may have beat us there—that would account for no one hot after us—and taken over the place."

"Or lying in wait just outside the camp," Matt said.

"I was grabbed from my folks' farm just across the border from Nogales, Mexico," one girl spoke up. "We could head there."

"How many people live around there, girl?" Wellman asked.

"Not many," she admitted.

"Enough to fight off maybe fifty or seventy-five hardcases like them back at the fort?"

She shook her head. "No, sir."

"Then that's out," Dick said. "Folks livin' along the border got enough grief without us bringin' more to their doorsteps."

"They're expecting us to head west or north," Matt spoke quietly, his words just audible over the steady fall of rain. "They won't be expecting us to backtrack and head east."

"Yeah," Wellman said. "Right back through their own territory. Half a dozen or so miles east of the fort, we can cut north, ride through the Huachucas, and head for the Army fort."

"Let's get the jump on them, then," Laurie said. "Let's go!"

Chapter 12

They backtracked, heading into the San Rafael Valley area, the steady fall of rain muffling their horses' hoofbeats and helping to wash away their tracks. Sam stayed a mile or so ahead of the column, scouting the terrain for outlaws and Apaches; for sure Lake would have gotten word to Chappo and the guerrilla chieftain and his band would be looking for them.

Just before night began wrapping the land in its cloak, Sam found a blow-down: several acres of storm-fallen trees, thick with underbrush. Working swiftly, they all pitched in to weave together a crude shelter for themselves and the horses and made ready for the night.

They chanced a fire; a necessity, for they couldn't afford to let any of the kids come down with pneumonia. They found plenty of dry wood, buried beneath underbrush and fallen trees, and the fires were built under overhangs, so the smoke would vanish through the limbs.

Laurie put together a stew, of sorts, and that just about finished what supplies they had left.

"We can't risk a shot bringing down any game," Matt

said. "Sam and me will make some traps and see if we can't snare us some rabbits. Sam's got his bow; maybe we'll get lucky and he can bag an antelope or javelina. If not, we're going to be traveling with mighty empty bellies."

"But we'll be alive," a little girl said solemnly, her eyes wide and frightened.

The traps set during the night got them a few rabbits and Wellman brought in three big rattlesnakes.

"What are you going to do with those!" Laurie said, disgust in her voice.

"Eat 'em," the old mountain man said. "They's right tasty meat; tastes like the white meat of chicken." He began skinning the snakes, cutting away the edible parts, and wrapping them in leaves, tossing them on the coals to bake.

"Won't be long," Wellman said. "I cut 'em sliver-thin so's they'll bake quick. We're gonna have a long pull today, with precious little time to rest. Eat up and let's git gone."

They crossed the west fork of the Santa Cruz and headed northeast, toward Parker Canyon. "Probably the best fish you ever stuck in your mouth," Wellman told them. "Fish practically jump on the hook. I was always told that 'Paches don't eat fish, so the lake'll be full. We can lay low there and bake enough fish to take us on into where the soldier boys is." He grinned. "Then you children can be safe."

The rain stopped and it turned hot as they moved into scrub-oak country, mixed with gray-green needled Chihuahua pine, manzanita, cedar, Mexican piñon pine, and Arizona sycamore. It was rolling hill country, perfect for an ambush. Little of the storm they had endured in the mountains had reached this part of the country, and the horses kicked up dust as the survivors rode on.

Sam caught a glimpse of antelope and headed off toward them, his bow ready. The antelope were elusive and he failed to get a shot, but he did bag two wild turkeys. Not much for twenty-nine people, but the meat filled at least a small corner of their stomachs.

Twice during that day they spotted dust in the distance and both times they quickly went into whatever cover was available to them. The first dust was to the north and it bypassed them, traveling east to west. The second dust was caused by a roaming band of Apaches and the Apaches were looking for trouble with all senses working overtime.

They reined up, sat their ponies for a few seconds, and then wheeled about and were gone in a drum of hooves and a cloud of dust. A few seconds later, not a sign of them could be seen.

"They didn't spot us," Wellman said. "But they sensed something was wrong. They'll be comin' for us. And when they do, it'll be as sneaky as a ghost."

"How far are we from the canyon?" Laurie asked.

Wellman spat. "Too damn far. How many did you count in that bunch, Matt?"

"About a dozen."

Wellman cursed. "That's a bunch of them savages. War party. Travelin' light, too. Damn people will ride a good horse to death and then eat it. I hate anybody who'd mistreat a horse."

"Is there anything about an Apache you like, Dick?" Sam asked softly.

"Yeah," Wellman said, rolling his chew and spitting. "I like 'em when they're dead!"

Matt saw a bush move ever so slightly about three hundred yards out. It might have been the breeze rustling through it, or it might be an Apache moving closer, utilizing every bit of cover he could find, and they were experts at that.

Matt could let him come closer while he pondered their

situation. The location wasn't that bad. The four of them were on a rise, the highest point around. The girls and the horses behind them in a depression, where they had stopped to take cover when they spotted the second dust. But they would have to very carefully ration water, making sure the horses got enough in case they had to make a run for it. If this was Chappo's band, so they'd been told up at the Crossing, Chappo didn't pay the slightest bit of attention to Indian superstition; he'd just as soon fight at night as during the day. Might call him an Indian atheist. Among other things.

Matt looked at the bush again. It had moved, just as he had suspected it would. It was maybe five feet closer than before. He pointed that out to the others.

"We'll keep an eye on it," Sam said. "When it gets well into range, we'll all have a shot at it."

"Jenny," Wellman called. "Get that short-barreled carbine outta my saddle boot and join Miss Laurie. I taught you how to shoot, girl. Make them all count."

Four of the other girls called out that they could shoot and had done so during other Indian raids on their farms and ranches.

"Get them armed, Laurie," Matt called to the other side of the knoll.

The kids began scrambling for the spare rifles and pistols.

"A game bunch of kids," Sam pointed out, his eyes on a slight movement in a clump of brush below him. "The future of this country, and I think it's in pretty good hands."

"That's put right good," Wellman said. "Plumb poetic. Now why don't you shoot that 'Pache that's slipping up over yonder by that clump of manzanita just to the left of that sycamore? I would, but you're in the way."

Sam suspected it was a little more than that: Wellman wanted to see if a half-breed would shoot another Indian. He should have known better; Plains Indians never did have much use for the desert tribes.

Sam waited until the Apache made another move, and gave him a .44 round in the brisket, knocking him spinning. The Apache tried to lunge back into cover. The second .44 round from Sam's Winchester stopped him from moving . . . ever again.

Sam locked eyes with the old mountain man. "You satisfied, now?"

Wellman grinned. "I ain't got no idee what in the world you're jabberin' about."

"Right," Sam said drily.

"That one behind the bush is about two hundred yards off," Matt pointed out.

"Let's take him out," Wellman said, adjusting the rear sight on his long-barreled .44-.40. "You boys dust him out and I'll nail him."

Sam and Bodine fired as one. The slugs must have stung the Apache, for he rolled to one side and tried to fling himself into deeper cover. Wellman dropped him with one well-placed shot. The warrior did not move.

"Now!" they heard Laurie shout, and the air was filled with rifle and pistol fire for a few seconds. "Good work, girls!" Laurie said.

"What'd you get, girl?" Wellman called, after the firing had subsided.

"Two dead and two wounded," she called calmly. "Jenny got one of the dead."

"They'll pull out," Sam stated, the Indian in him surfacing. "Their medicine is bad. Regardless of what we were told about Chappo, he's still an Apache. Four dead and two wounded have cut his band by half. Indians don't fight to take those kind of losses. But they'll be tailing us all the way to the fort, you can bet on that; just waiting for a chance to take one or two of us out."

"Let's ride," Matt said.

The Apache must have thought that his medicine was not

just bad, but awful. They followed the group for several hours that day, then dropped back and headed southwest, toward the border.

"Smoke." Matt pointed to several thin lines of smoke rising from the southeast. "Something's up that's made them edgy."

Sam sat his saddle and watched them go, then rode up onto a ridge to get a better look and to make sure it was not a ruse. It was not; the Apaches were indeed leaving. Just a few minutes later they all found out the reason why as a patrol of cavalry rode into view.

"Captain Gibbs," the officer in charge introduced himself. Although he knew the answer to the question, he asked, "May I inquire as to why you people are out in the middle of Apache country with these children?"

Quickly, Bodine explained.

"And you are?"

"Matt Bodine. Sam Two Wolves. Dick Wellman. That's Jenny, Dick's granddaughter. And this is Laurie. She was looking for her brother."

Several of the troopers shifted nervously in their saddles. They knew their captain's orders and none of them liked it. They liked even less the fact that Sam Two Wolves had shifted his horse and the muzzle of his Winchester was now pointed directly at Sergeant Larsen's belly. Miss Laurie's rifle was carelessly laid across her saddle horn, the muzzle aimed at Lieutenant Packard's stomach. Wellman's rifle was laid across the saddle horn, the muzzle pointed straight at a trooper's belly. Bodine held the reins in his left hand, his right hand near the butt of a Colt. If the captain tried to carry out his orders, a lot of people were going to die.

Captain Gibbs noticed all that, and also noticed that several of the young girls were armed. He had his orders, but sometimes out in the field one had to put common sense into play. Gibbs knew he was dead, cooling meat if he tried to arrest the four adults for violating the territory of Mexico, destroying a fort, and killing several Mexican nationals with explosives. He had twenty-five men with him. Ten would die in a matter of seconds. And if the adults started shooting, so would the armed girls; and who among them was going to shoot a child?

He sighed heavily. "Mister Bodine, I have a bit of a problem here. The government of Mexico has demanded your arrest for violating their sovereign territory, for murder, and for destroying an army post. Mister Lake claims that he bought the children from Chappo out of the goodness of his heart, to prevent them from being placed in the hands of slavetraders . . ."

"He's a liar!" Jenny lashed out at the captain, startling the army officer. "Him and Chappo have a deal worked out, and all of us here will swear to that."

The Captain really did not know what to do. However, he had other cards to play, but not at this time.

Bodine said, "How do we know you're really U.S. Cavalry? Those uniforms may be stolen; you may be part of Lake's gang for all we know."

"Matt," a trooper spoke from the mounted line of blue uniforms. "I'm from the Sweetwater. Jim Harris. My daddy had the Rocking V until that winter two years ago wiped us out. We've met several times."

Bodine stared at him. Nodded his head. "Yeah. I remember you, Jim. You know about your father?"

"Got word several months ago. Ma wrote me. She's gone back to Kansas to live with her sister."

"I know Sergeant Larsen, Matt," Wellman said. "Met him years ago in Utah Territory. They's soldier boys, all right."

"So what do we do?" Matt tossed the question out.

"My suggestion is," the captain said, "we ride to the

canyon and make camp, let these young ladies have a proper bath and a hot meal, and discuss this matter like civilized men."

"And women?" Laurie put her two cents into it.

"Right," Gibbs said, looking at the muzzle of her Winchester, which had shifted and was now pointing at his belly. The muzzle silently spoke volumes. "By all means, Miss."

"Y'all head on out," Wellman told them. "We'll take the drag. Someone's got to keep an eye out behind you."

"That's very considerate of you," Gibbs said.

"Think nothin' of it," Wellman responded politely. "We're only too happy to hep out the Army."

It was at times like these, Gibbs thought, as he took the lead at the head of the column, that he wished he'd followed his mother's wishes to become a carriage maker.

Chapter 13

The girls splashed and hollered and had a good time flouncing around in the cold waters of the lake at the canyon while their freshly washed clothing dried on makeshift lines. The men, their backs to the young ladies, talked over coffee.

"Of course we know that Lake and Porter are filth," Gibbs said. "And liars. We know all about Captain Morgan and his odious business. But since he never puts in at any American port, there is very little the government can do about it. But Mexico, more specifically the state of Sonora, has lodged an official protest with our government—concerning your actions. So what do you suggest we do about it?"

"Ignore it," Matt said. "Hell, Captain, the kids were kidnapped and being held against their will while certain officials down there were being paid off to turn their backs to it."

"Can you prove that?"

"You know I can't."

"Then the government, our government, has no choice but to press on with the charges against you."

"You know what all this is, don't you, Matt, Sam?" Wellman said. "It's all a crock of bull-crap!"

Gibbs stiffened. "I beg your pardon, sir?"

"Oh, blow it out your back-flap, Captain!" Wellman snapped at him. "You think I rode into this mess blind? I sent a hundred wires off seeking information afore I started out down here. Our government receives fifty or sixty protests a month from the Mexican government . . . for one thing or another. They been doin' it ever since the Alamo fell—forty damn years ago. And all of a sudden you gonna single us out for charges? Crap! Git to the bottom line, soldier-boy."

Matt was confused for a moment, studying Gibbs's flushed face. Then pieces started falling into place. He hoped he was wrong . . .

Matt said, "The bottom line is this: Chappo, Lake, and Porter, right, Captain?"

Sam looked at his blood brother. "Have I missed something along the way?"

"Let me put it this way: Our government isn't above turning its back to some unlawful act if its interests are served in the process, right, Captain?"

"I didn't come up with this idea, Bodine. And I don't like it."

"Do your men know about it?"

"No. That's why I could say nothing about it out in the field."

"Lake and Porter would be as easy as breathing," Matt said. "So it has to be Chappo."

"Certain . . . ah . . . rewards will be given in return for his death."

"I don't need rewards," Matt told him bluntly. "I own a very large ranch up in Wyoming; as does Sam. But I can't speak for either Sam nor Wellman."

"I struck a rich vein years ago," Wellman said. "I got enough to live on for five lifetimes." He then proceeded to tell the captain where he could stick his rewards.

"I have an idea," Sam said. All eyes swung toward him.

"Let the money go to Laurie. You can't raise Jenny, Dick. But Laurie could, with some financial help."

"I just told you I got gold a-plenty," Dick said peevishly. "But that ain't a bad idea of yourn."

"You know, Captain," Sam spoke the words softly, "if we don't agree with this, all we'd have to do is contact some reporter and public sentiment would turn against the Army."

"I realize that. However, there is a small matter of a shooting up at the Crossing still to be resolved . . ."

Matt held up a hand. "Enough, Captain. You've got a lot of green troopers, don't you?"

"More than seventy-five percent of them, yes."

"All right. Sam is half-Cheyenne, I was practically raised by the Cheyenne, and Wellman is an experienced Indian fighter. The feeling is that a very small band of highly seasoned men could probably do more than a large force of basically untrained troops, right?"

"Yes."

"Well, why didn't you just ask us to do it?" Sam stated. "That's what gripes me. Why all this elaborate scheming?"

Gibbs smiled, thinly. "You ever been around a bunch of high-ranking officers, Sam?"

"Fortunately, no."

"For your sake, try to keep it that way."

They rode to the fort in the Huachucas and rested. Over a lot of protestations from the both of them, Dick sent Laurie and Jenny back to his small spread on the Utah-Idaho border and told them both to stay put. He had hands on the ranch; they would be taken care of. He then found himself a lawyer and had a will drawn up, changing his old will, leaving everything he had to Laurie and Jenny. They liked each other, they had each other, and that was about it as far as family went for either of them. Families or friends of the other girls were notified that they were still alive.

"You act like you're not coming back from this foray, Dick," Sam observed.

"Don't 'spect I will, Two Wolves. Don't know as I want to. Been in some pain lately. Arrowhead's moved, I reckon. I told Laurie we'd look for her brother. If we don't find him, and I pray we don't, you tell her we did and that he's dead, boys."

"That would be the best thing," Matt agreed. "Where do we start in this quest? Anybody got any ideas?"

Sam shrugged. "I'm just along for the ride. I've always enjoyed risking my life on quixotic ventures."

Wellman shook his head. "I wintered with a feller once that read Shakespeare. You and him would have hit it right off. Where to start? Well, let's take the hard part first and tackle Chappo. Porter and Lake is gonna be easy. Chappo is gonna be a grizzly, I'm thinkin'."

"I made the list of supplies you requested, Matt," Sam said. "Dick and I agreed with it, but there is a question we both raised: are we going on an extended expedition?"

"We just might. I've spoken with some Army scouts and they've shed some light on why Chappo's been so hard to catch. When he gets too hot here in the Territory, he and his people hightail it down into the Sierra De La Madera mountains."

"The Sierra Madres," Dick said, almost in a whisper. "I always wanted to see them mountains. Never got around to it. It fits. Chappo would have him a rancheria down there. All tucked away in the mountains where he could relax and hide." He grinned as he and Sam exchanged glances and smiles. "Now I see why you got all that dynamite."

"Yeah," Matt said, and all three of them started laughing.

* * *

They would leave their horses at the fort. Hopefully they would come out of this alive to pick them up later. Then the three of them chose big, tough, horses of a light brown color, to better fit with the land they would be riding into. They all bought—at the Army's expense, which irritated the commanding officer at the fort—new clothing, all tan and brown, right from their boots to their hats.

They picked their pack horses carefully, choosing only those who appeared to have an even temperament and lots of staying power.

The three of them spent several hours putting together the dynamite, from two and three sticks wrapped together for throwing, to the wrapping and tying together of massive amounts that could bring down the side of a mountain.

Then came the early morning hours when everything that could be done was concluded. They had not made plans to pull out that day; they just got up, looked at each other, rolled their blankets in their ground sheets, then walked toward the stables.

After saddling up, loading up, and tying down, they strolled over to the mess hall for a cup of coffee. Captain Gibbs was standing on the porch, having a smoke in the pre-dawn hours.

"I thought today would be the day," the officer said, then walked inside with the trio and took a seat at a table.

Over breakfast, Sam said, "It goes without saying that if we get down in Mexico and get in trouble, we'd probably better not hold our breaths waiting for the cavalry to come charging to our rescue."

Gibbs nodded his head in agreement. "We received word late last evening that Laurie and Jenny have arrived safely at your ranch, Mister Wellman."

"That's the biggest load off my mind," Wellman said. "They both got 'em a home now."

"What route are you taking?" Gibbs asked.

"Straight down," Matt told him. "Right through the Huachucas. We'll tackle Chappo first."

"Misters Lake and Porter seem to have disappeared."

"They ain't gone far. As long as they's gold or silver bein' mined out of them mountains, crud like them two will be hangin' around lookin' to steal it."

The hunters finished their coffee and stood up as one. "See you," Sam told the captain. The trio walked outside, swung into their saddles, and put the post behind them with still an hour to go before the dawning.

"Chappo'll get word of this," Wellman said, as dawn touched the country with light, chasing away the purple shadows and bringing the land to new life. "You can bet he's got people back at the post feedin' information to him. I ain't never seen it fail yet, and I done a lot of scoutin' for the Army in my time."

"I've been thinking that he might take this as a personal affront," Sam said. "The three of us being sent in to take him—when whole armies could not—might seem very arrogant to Chappo."

"He'll have heard of the three of us," Wellman replied. "And he'll respect us for what we've done. It'll make him a tad cautious. But he'll still be out to take us, alive if possible, to torture us for as long as he can, to see if we die well."

"They've been singing songs around the fires for those we killed back on the ridge a couple of weeks ago," Matt said. "Fueling the hate they feel for us. I keep going over supplies in my head, wondering if we've forgotten anything."

"No," Sam said. "I don't think so. There is no magic potion to keep us alive."

Wellman tapped the side of his head and then lifted his Winchester. "Our eyes, our brains, and our guns. That's the best magic I know of."

The Apache seemed to have vanished from the mountains. The three of them rode out of the Huachucas and into the timbered country south of Miller Peak without seeing a single sign of the Apache.

It was Bodine who spotted the challenge, hanging from a tree limb along the trail. Three wooden Apache-carved dolls, two of them with tiny necklaces around their necks, the third one a bearded old man in buckskins. The feet of the dolls had been burned.

"Tellin' us what he's gonna do to us when he catches up with us, or we catch up with him," Wellman said. "Told you he'd know we was comin' after him."

"I got a hunch," Bodine said.

"Lay your cards out," Wellman told him.

"Let's go visit the ruins of an old Mexican fort."

"Real sneaky like?" the old mountain man said with a wide grin.

"Yeah."

"That might be something Chappo would do," Sam agreed. "He'd know we're not just after him, but also Porter and Lake. He just might have some warriors lying in wait for us."

They angled toward the southwest, once more crossing the west fork of the Santa Cruz and staying with it, following it down on the west side toward the border. They rode with rifles across their saddlehorns, always searching for sign of the Apaches, but seeing nothing. And the absence of the Apaches made them more and more certain that they were riding toward an ambush at the old fort.

"But not by Chappo," Matt spoke, when they were only a few miles from the fort.

They all reined up.

"What'd you mean?" Wellman asked. "Who the hell else would it be?"

"Who has more reason to hate us than Chappo?"

Wellman and Sam glanced at each other and spoke as one. "Lake and Porter!"

"That's right. This just came to me: Chappo might have warned them that if they didn't stop us, he would no longer insure their safety plus his cooperation."

"A nice way of saying he'd kill them on the spot," Sam said, straightening in the saddle to give some relief to his back. Since leaving the fort they had all been riding with tension heavy on them.

"Lake and Porter ain't gonna be there," Wellman said sourly. "One's just as yeller as the other. They'll leave some flunkies behind to do their work. Let 'em sit there and sweat. We'll go deal with Chappo and get that over with."

They pointed their horses' noses south, by-passing the fort; if they ever got back this way alive, they'd tend to Lake and Porter.

That evening, after they had stopped to build a fire and eat, then moved on several miles before bedding down for the night, Wellman spoke from his blankets. "What'd you think about it, Sam? How come the white man and the Injun can't get along?"

Sam sighed then said, "Well, there was and is right and wrong on both sides. Indians didn't own the land like the white man thinks he does. And Indians never stayed long in one spot. My father's people drifted around, hunting and living off wild plants."

Sam almost never spoke of *his people*. It was always *his father's people*.

"The white man came looking to settle in one spot and farm or ranch. They built permanent shelters. The Indian couldn't understand that. There were some white men who wanted to live in peace with the Indian, and some Indians who wanted peace with the white man. But not enough of each on either side. Stealing horses was a game for the Indians. The whites took it much more seriously. And," he said with a sigh, "when an Indian makes war, he goes by the philosophy that little whites grow up to be big whites and therefore will cause trouble when they grow up so why not kill them now? And that, of course, is something the white people could not accept. My father could never accept it either. Medicine Horse was a fair man. But look where that got him," he added bitterly.

"The Indian wars were something my father's people were born to lose. There were too few Indians and too many white people. But my friend, hear this: if all the Indian tribes would have united under one leader, instead of fighting each other all the time, the westward progress of the white man would have halted at the Big Muddy. And you can believe that."

"Oh, I believe it," Wellman said. Then he chuckled.

"What's so funny?" Sam asked, rising up in his blankets.

"What you just said about all the tribes comin' together. That's what I told your dad back some thirty years ago." He spat out his chew of tobacco, pulled his blankets up over his head, and went to sleep.

Chapter 14

None of them knew much about the desert south of the border. Only what they had either read or heard. But they all knew that when a man left a trail, in the woods or the desert, he'd better have a destination in mind, for his life is on the line every moment, waking or sleeping. And nowhere was that more pronounced than when in Apache country . . . especially when Chappo was around.

"I hope that Army scout knew what he was talking about when he told us about water down in this part of the country," Matt said.

"He did," Wellman replied. "Bill Lewis knows this country as good or better than any white man alive."

"Although he didn't say so," Sam said, "I got the impression he'd led some raids down here."

"Shore has. Deserts are alike in a lot of ways. I been all over the Mojave, the Great Salt Lake Desert, and all over Nevada Territory. You boys know the mountains and the plains. I do too, but I'm older and was always fiddle-footed. Two things you got to keep in mind out here: water and survival. The two is one and the same. You got to be either headin' for water, or know where some is if you have to leave out from the way you planned to head first-off."

Sam shook his head at the old man's grammar, but knew enough to grasp and retain the wisdom of his words.

"You boys know how it is with water," Wellman continued. "If you don't know where it is, you got to know what to look for to find it . . . and that's something you've both been taught. Boys, I don't know exactly what happened up yonder in Montana with Custer and with your daddy, Sam, but I got me a suspicious feelin' you boys do—you was probably watchin' from a rise. That's why you both took off, leavin' successful ranches behind you. So you're gonna wander for a few years, try to forget the horror of it. That's fine. You know about the mountains and the plains, so I'll teach you about the desert.

"You ain't got much leeway for mistakes out here. But the desert is not your enemy, and it isn't your friend. It's neutral. They's water out here that is generally known, and they's water out here that's known, for the most part, only by the animals . . . and the 'Paches." He smiled. "And by a few Army scouts and old codgers like me. You got to work with the desert, boys; don't never try to fight it. 'Cause you won't win."

The three of them rode toward a hot, dry unwavering finger of hell, as they headed for the Sierra Madres and Chappo.

Dick suddenly held out a hand and reined up. Matt and Sam smelled it seconds after the old mountain man. Dust, and a lot of it.

"No band of Apaches would be travelin' like that," Dick said. "I think, boys, we's about to come nose to nose with a Mex army patrol."

Sam pointed to the heat-wavering distance. "More than a patrol. It looks like half the Mexican army coming our way. We'd better get our stories straight, and we'd better do it quickly."

"Buenas tardes, señors," the officer who rode at the head of the large column greeted the trio.

"Afternoon, sir," Matt said, noting the small pleasure on the man's face as he called him sir.

Matt guessed at about a hundred troops, all well-armed and well-supplied, and from the looks of them, all seasoned veterans. Matt decided to take a chance.

"Has war been declared, sir?"

The officer looked puzzled. "War, *señor?* What do you mean?"

"This is Arizona Territory, sir. If you're not at war with the United States, then you are violating border treaties."

The officer smiled. "No, no, *señor.* It is not we who are in violation, but you. This is Mexico."

Matt stubbornly shook his head. "No, sir. That miner back yonder in the Huachucas who sold us the claim we're ridin' toward, said to follow the Santa Cruz, keepin' it to the west of us, for about ten miles and then we'd come up on our claim."

The officer and several others laughed aloud. The officer shook his head. "I am afraid, sir, that you have been misled. You are not from this area, I take it?"

"No, sir. We're all from Wyoming."

"Ahh! I see. That explains the confusion. I regret to inform you, *señors,* that you are in Mexico, the state of Sonora. You are welcome to visit here, of course; we are a very hospitable people. But I am sorry to say that you cannot own land here."

Wellman had caught on fast. "Why that sorry . . ." Then he proceeded to hang a cussin' on the non-existent miner.

The Mexican soldiers listened with awe on their faces as Wellman expertly traced the miner's history back to the caves. Several of them cheered and applauded when he finished.

The officer smiled his approval. "I do not know whether I would like to be present when you men find the miner who swindled you. But I must warn you that you are in grave danger riding in this area."

"Why is that, sir?" Sam asked.

"Chappo and his band of renegades have left their stronghold in the Sierra De La Maderas and are heading back to Arizona Territory."

"Lord have mercy!" Wellman said, putting a hand over his heart. "It's a miracle we still have our hair. What do you figure we should do, General?"

"I am not a general, sir, but thank you for the promotion. Perhaps someday. But for now I am Major Luis de Carrillo. The border is not far. Perhaps you would like to ride with us to the border?"

"Why, that's right kind of you, Major," Dick smiled. "We'll take you up on that. And maybe while's we're riding you could sorta brief us on this Chappo person. We've heard some wild tales about him."

"But of course. I can assure you gentlemen, they are not tales. The man is a monster!"

They parted company at the border. All of them finding the Mexicans friendly and open and good compadres to ride with.

At the border, Major Carrillo called Matt to one side and told him where Chappo was hiding. He smiled and added, "I hope your hunting is as skillful as your acting, Mister Bodine."

Matt met the man's dark eyes; they were twinkling with good humor. "You knew all along?"

"But of course. It saddens me that certain people in our government—yours and mine—are so corrupt. There are many good, decent people on both sides of the border. For my part, there has been an abrupt shift in the offices of the governor of this state. We were riding to put the slave-traders at the old fort out of business. *Permanente.* I was looking forward to placing the outlaws, Lake and Porter, in front of a firing squad, under my personal command."

"And Captain Morgan?"

"We will find him. And if our navy finds him at sea, the *Virgin Princess* will be boarded and Captain Morgan will be hanged."

Matt stuck out his hand and the major took it. "Good luck to you, Major."

"And the same to you, Matt Bodine."

"One question, Major?"

"Of course."

"This rancheria of Chappo's . . . will there be women and children there?"

"I can answer that quickly and truthfully. No. The warriors leave their families at a reservation." Again, he smiled, his eyes flashing with silent laughter. "You may use the dynamite you have under the canvas with complete abandon."

The gunfighter and the soldier shared a laugh and then went their separate ways.

"Well, I'll just be dipped!" Wellman said. "So he knowed who we was all along."

"They all did. I think with Major Carrillo south of the border, Chappo will not return to Mexico. I don't think I'd want the major hunting me."

"That's the feeling I got," Sam said. "You noticed those troops under his command were all tough, older men; probably with a lot of experience behind them."

"Yeah. So I think Chappo's going to be fighting a last ditch war. He knows his days are numbered, so he's going to be striking like a mad rattler, hitting anything he can whenever he can."

"Let's go get him," Wellman said.

"There isn't but one hitch in that," Matt said.

Both Wellman and Sam looked at him.

"He's moved."

They swung into their saddles and pulled out, after both Wellman and Sam did some fancy cussing. Wellman settled down after a moment and said, "I know the Dos Cabezas and the Chiricahua Mountains. Chappo might be in the Dos Cabezas, but I tend to doubt it. He's in Cochise's old stomping grounds; I'd bet on that. He might even have picked up some of the old boy's braves. Either way, them ranges ain't for no pilgrims to wander in."

"Major Carrillo told me something he'd heard from one of his generals," Matt said. "It summed up how many of the American soldiers feel about this part of the country and the Apaches. He said that General Sherman, back around '70, he thought it was, wrote to the Secretary of War and said, 'We had one war with Mexico to take Arizona, and we should have another to make her take it back!' "

Wellman chuckled. "I don't doubt that a bit. Don't git me wrong, Sam; I ain't bad-mouthed the Plains Injuns none at all. But when it comes to great fighters and just being low-down mean, the Apache tops the list."

"That's the first time I ever heard you come close to paying the Apache a compliment. Even a left-handed one."

"They're the greatest guerrilla fighters that ever lived," Wellman told them.

They were riding out into the flat, desert country, angling to the north and east, heading for the Chiricahua Mountains.

"Even out here," Wellman waved his hand. "In the open, they could be twenty-thirty 'Paches hidin' not ten yards away and most folks would never see them until it was too late. They can take a mouthful of water and run thirty-forty miles a day. We'll be lucky to do that on horseback." He smiled, but it was void of any humor. "Mayhaps, Sam, I dislike 'em so much because I'm so much like 'em."

Wellman took the lead, leaving Sam and Bodine to scratch their heads and wonder about that last remark.

They rode into the Mule Mountains and pulled up in

Bisbee late one afternoon. The town was just getting started and made up of three or four wooden frame buildings and dozens of tents of all sizes and description, and the mining town was wild and woolly.

They stabled their horses and secured a guard for their supplies for as long as they would be gone. Then made arrangements with the stable owner to sleep in the loft that night.

Both Bodine and Sam thought Wellman was going to hit the man when he charged them a dollar apiece to sleep in the loft. But Wellman chewed his chaw savagely for a moment, glared at the man, and then forked over the dollar (it was the Army's money anyway) and the men went off to find a saloon and have a drink.

Wellman brightened up considerably when Sam pointed out some, by this time, awfully familiar horses, all of them wearing Triple-V brands.

"Well, now," he chuckled. "This could get right interestin'. We might be able to catch one of them no-goods and see if he'd like a choice."

"What do you mean?" Sam asked.

"Tell us where Chappo is or get skinned alive."

"I see what you mean about being so much like the Apache."

"Somewhat, but they's a difference. I believe the only way we'll ever stop outlawin' is to get rid of the outlaws. I never shot a man—Injun or white—that wasn't tryin' to do harm to me or one of mine, family or friends. I never stole nothin' in my life—except some feminine affections, now and then," he said with a twinkle of remembrance in his eyes and a smile on his lips. "And I see the same qualities in you boys that I got in me. If I didn't, I wouldn't have nothin' to do with you."

Both the young men grinned and Sam asked, "What's the drill this time?"

Bodine stopped a man, a miner from the looks of him, and asked, "Is there law in this town, mister?"

"Only what you're carryin' on your hip, buddy." He hurried on his way.

"Guess that answers one question," Wellman said, removing the hammer-thong from his long barreled Colt, slipping it up and down in leather a couple of times. "I got me a powerful thirst for some rye with a beer chaser. I do hope none of them scum in yonder start shootin' afore I can cut the dust outta my throat."

"And once you've done that, then you'll start shooting, right?" Sam questioned.

"Why, heavens no, boy!" the old mountain man replied, doing his best to put a hurt look on his face. "I'm just a peaceful old man a-livin' out his last days on earth, in harmony with all of God's creatures."

"I just had to ask, didn't I?" Sam questioned, shaking his head as they stepped up on the freshly-milled and laid boardwalk.

Bodine pushed open the batwings and the three of them walked inside.

The half dozen outlaws recognized them immediately and one dropped his hand to his gun. Another caught the man's arm, preventing him from opening the fight.

Bodine, Sam, and Wellman all saw the movement and filed it away for later reference. The movement didn't make any sense. The three of them were temporarily limited in vision due to just stepping into the murk of the saloon from the bright sunlight. Now would have been a perfect time to take them out—or to try to take them out.

"Rye and a beer for me," Wellman said, bellying up to the bar.

Sam and Bodine ordered a beer.

The outlaws left the long bar and walked to the rear of the room, carrying their drinks with them.

"What's goin' on," Wellman muttered, lifting his shot glass and taking a sip.

Sam looked, amazement spreading across his face. "They've taken seats with their backs toward us. Everyone of them."

"They know that we're looking for Chappo; they probably knew that two days after we agreed to it." Bodine was thoughtful for a moment. "Perhaps Porter and Lake figure the easiest way to deal with us is to let us go on in after Chappo. The three of us against several hundred of Chappo's Apaches is not the best of odds any way you want to look at it."

"With us out of the way, they wouldn't have to keep looking over their shoulders," Sam added.

The men were speaking in low tones, so they could not be overheard.

"What now?" Wellman said. "They's too damn many miners in here to just haul 'er out and let 'er bang."

"And if we goaded them into a fight, in front of this many witnesses, even though we probably wouldn't go to trial for it, it'd be a black mark against us," Bodine said. He took a swig of beer.

"Hell with it." Wellman knocked back his rye and swallowed half his beer. "I'm hungry. Let's go get something to eat."

Chapter 15

While they were eating in a tent cafe, the three of them watched as the outlaws left the saloon, mounted up, and rode out. The gunslicks and outlaws headed west, but all knew that didn't mean a thing, since they could and probably would change directions as soon as they reached the edge of town.

"They'll get up in the Mules and make camp so's they can watch us," Wellman said, forking a huge piece of apple pie into his mouth. "See which way we leave out. Them's part of the bunch that held my Jenny. I've a notion to follow 'em and just shoot 'em out of the saddle like the hydrophoby skunks they is."

Several men seated close enough to hear what was being said eyeballed the trio and then got up and moved to a table across the canvas-covered room. It took only one look for the miners to know that these were men who would brook no nonsense.

The trio finished their meal, had another cup of coffee, then returned to the stable. Bisbee was an hour behind them at dawn.

To the north and west of them, the prospector Ed

Schieffelin was digging in the earth in his search for silver. Soon the town of Tombstone would be born.

The land the three men rode across alternated from near-barren desert to shady glens invitingly placed under canyon recesses. It was a land perfectly suited for ambush. There were ranchers in this section of the territory, but they lived behind walled fortresses, with enough cowboys on the pay-roll to make up a small army. For the most part, those ranches were south of where the trio rode.

Bodine called a halt after making fifteen miles that first day out of Bisbee. They fixed their evening meal, carefully put out the fire, and moved on several miles before bedding down for the night. They were in Apache country, but the next day would put them smack in the middle of Chappo's country, on the edge of the lonely and dangerous Chiricahua Mountains.

The morning dawned hot. An hour's ride, with Wellman at the point, brought them to a spring where they watered their horses and filled up their canteens and then cooked breakfast, all the time keeping a wary eye out for trouble. All of them felt as though a hundred hostile eyes were on them. And as Wellman put it, "They probably is."

"Then why don't they attack?" Bodine asked, his nerves stretched tight, as were the nerves of all three of them.

"They might think we're crazy," Sam conjectured. "Just three men riding into the heart of Chappo's territory. Chappo himself might think we're crazy for doing this."

"Worked for me one time," Wellman said. "Up on the plains. Utes had me fair and square. I started babblin' and singin' and preachin' and a-droolin' at the mouth. Then I sat down on the bank of a crick and started eatin' mud. That done it. Them Utes high-tailed it out of there. They didn't want no truck with no crazy person. Chappo probably does think we're all nuts; but that ain't gonna cut us much slack. Not for very long. We got six fine horses between us and it's a mighty curious thing in his mind what we got tied under the canvas on them packhorses. I 'spect they been watchin' us since late yesterday. Some of 'em's bound to make a move at us today."

They headed out, riding single-file, with no one talking and with all senses working hard.

With few exceptions, the time for hot meals was done. From this point on, it would be cold biscuits and jerky, washed down with lukewarm water from their canteens.

They were abruptly into the mountain range, almost without warning, and the attack came without warning, as they all knew it would. Had not Bodine been watching his horse's ears, they would have been dead men.

The ears came up and Bodine felt the animal tense between his legs. "Here they come!" he yelled, and put the spurs to the horse.

Sam, who had just taken the point from Wellman, led them into a draw and up into the rocks and timber. An Apache reared up in front of him, hate on the face. Sam shot the brave in the belly and the horses coming up behind mauled the Indian with their hooves.

The ambush having failed, the Apaches settled down to a waiting game. The three were in a fairly good location, but that had been due to luck, not on the skills of any of them. Just above the rocks was a thick stand of spruce and fir.

"We can't let them get up there," Sam said. "I'll take the high place." Then he was gone, moving silently and swiftly up the slope.

While Wellman kept watch, Bodine picketed the horses in a hollow, grabbed two canteens, their spare rifles, a pouch of dynamite, and found himself a good spot from which to fire.

"How many?" Bodine called.

"Don't make no difference," Wellman's reply was caustic. "They'll all be here in an hour. Pony left at a gallop while you was gone."

"I have a little surprise for them," Bodine called in a hoarse whisper. "One I doubt they've ever faced before."

Wellman chuckled. He knew Bodine had been in the dynamite. "This is a good spot for it awright."

Moments later Sam called, "Head's up! Reenforcements have arrived."

"They must have been just over the ridge," Bodine muttered. He turned his head and almost yelled as he came nose to snout with a funny looking varmit.

Wellman laughed just as the varmit took off like a shot, heading for the timber, its long banded tail held high as it scampered away. "Coatimundi. They some relation to the raccoon."

"The expression on your face was priceless!" Sam called down with a laugh. Then he switched to Cheyenne and said, "We are confusing the Apache with all this idle chatter. They don't know what to make of it and some of them have backed away, believing us to be crazy people. So let's keep it up."

"Can you preach, Dick?" Matt called.

"I'll say I can! I can talk the devil right out of any sinner that ever lived."

"Get to it, then. I'm gonna lay out some surprises for our friends."

Dick went to preaching and it was quite a sermon. He ranted and raved and even Sam perked up when the old mountain man began confessing to past sins concerning various ladies.

So far, with the exception of the few shots exchanged by both sides at the outset, the Apaches had not fired at the men.

In Cheyenne, Matt called, "Sam? How close is the nearest bunch to me?"

"About twenty-five feet right directly in front of you and below. I didn't shoot when I saw you laying out the sticks."

"I 'bout run out of things to confess to," Wellman said,

and his Cheyenne was excellent. "Drop about three sticks in on top of 'em, Bodine."

Bodine grinned, picked up four sticks wrapped for throwing, thumbnailed a match into flame, and lit the fuse. He let it burn down dangerously close and then chunked it over the rock he was behind.

The explosives detonated about two feet off the ground and the carnage was extensive. Before the sound waves had stopped reverberating, Matt tossed a bundle to Dick.

The Apaches opened up and Sam returned the fire, working his Winchester as fast as he could and still lay down an accurate fire.

Twice the Apaches tried to get to where the dead and dynamite-mangled bodies of the braves lay, to drag them away. Once, Sam's rifle fire drove them back. The second time they reached the bloody scene only to have Bodine and Wellman throw several sticks of sputtering death in on them.

The fight was out of them for this day. As swiftly as they had opened the initial attack, the Apaches pulled out and the canyon grew silent as the hoofbeats of their ponies faded.

"The bodies of the dead are mangled away," Sam called, not yet ready to leave his high-up position in case the Apaches doubled back. "The same as when they are deliberately mutilated. The souls are doomed to wander forever, never finding a resting place."

"Good," Wellman said, then spat a long stream of brown tobacco juice. "Serves 'em right for ignorin' my sermon!"

"Turkey Creek," Wellman said, and swung down from the saddle, stretching his old bones. "After what we done to them today, we can chance a fire and fix us something to eat here and then ride a couple of miles over to a lake and bed down for the night."

"Smack in the middle of Apache country," Bodine said, pulling his Winchester from the saddle boot.

"That's right," Wellman replied cheerfully. "And you can

bet that right now they're scratchin' their heads and won-derin' what in the hell they done come up agin. Couple more fights like the one we just come through, and Chappo will take his band and head for the rocks, up in the north part of the range. And if they decide to do that, boys, we in for some rough goin'."

"Why?" Sam asked.

"Cain't get through there. Least I don't know no way. It's the gawdawfulest mess a human bein' ever laid his eyes on. Looks like God just picked up all the huge rocks He could find and throwed 'em down all in a jumble. The 'Paches know the way in and out, but I don't. And boys, you don't want to get trapped in there."

Bodine handed the man a stick. "Draw us a map and show us the range, Dick."

Wellman outlined a zigzagging square. "We're here," he jabbed the point into the earth. "Just north of where that Spaniard feller, Coronado something-or-another is supposed to have explored couple of hundred years ago. Way up here is Fort Bowie. They's still some soldier boys there. The fort was built back durin' the civil war and the soldier boys is 'posed to be wagin' war agin the Chiricahua 'Paches. But the Army don't come in here much, so don't get your hopes up about that. They got long years of fightin' ahead of 'em 'fore Geronimo is through. Now somewheres up here," he jabbed the stick toward the top of the crude map, "they's a valley. It's 'posed to be about fifty acres in all. Got good grass and water. But gettin' to it is the problem. The way I heared it, they's one way in and one way out: a canyon, about four miles long. Just wide enough for a horse to manage it. Far as I know, there ain't no white man ever found the en-trance. Or if they did, and they blundered in there, they never come out."

"Then we've got to find it," Matt said simply.

Dick fixed him with a jaundiced gaze. "I figured you'd

say something like that." He poured a cup of fresh-brewed coffee and leaned back against a log. "Boys, the Apaches have two virtues. And as near as I can figure, two is all they got. They live for two reasons: to steal without getting caught, and to kill without being killed. And they're the best in the world in doin' both. And I ain't bad-mouthin' 'em for it. That's just the way they's raised. Once taken by Apaches, they's been precious few men ever got away from 'em. I'm an old man, and I don't personal know but of three men who ever done it. And you met one of 'em back at the fort: Bill Lewis. I've rode into and out of the camps of Crow, Cheyenne, Ute, Comanche, Kiowa, Blackfoot, Sioux, Arapaho, Creek, and ten other tribes. I been tooken unfriendly-like five times, and talked my way out of it. You don't talk your way out of the hands of these Apaches down here. I want you boys to keep that thought in your minds at all times. Now let's eat."

They rode about three miles from the lake, toward the northeast, and bedded down in a cold camp. And the nights were chilly. Come the dawning, they chanced a small fire under a low overhang and fixed coffee, extinguishing the fire as soon as the coffee had boiled. They drank coffee and chewed on stale bread and jerky. Then they mounted up and headed north, toward the Wilderness area. Sam and Bodine saw rock formations unlike anything they had ever before witnessed: strange, almost eerie upthrustings, stately and silent.

"And deadly," Wellman said, knowing what they were thinking, for he had thought the same thing years back. "Blind canyons ever' way you turn. Apaches trap you up in one of them, hang it up."

"Awful lot of country for so few Apache," Sam pointed out.

"Yeah. That's why we still got our hair. They don't know where we are. Yet," he added.

At mid-morning, Wellman called a brief halt and said to Sam, "You think you could take some field glasses and climb up that rock yonder?" He pointed.

Sam rode around the nearly sheer upthrusting, looking for hand-holds. When he returned he said, "Yes."

Wellman and Bodine dismounted and squatted down while Sam pulled off his boots and slipped on moccasins. Matt pulled out the makings and rolled a smoke, as did Wellman. It was dead calm on the twisting canyon floor, and the smoke would linger close with no wind to carry it to un-friendly noses.

Sam stayed on top of the peak for over half an hour, meticulously scanning the terrain in all directions. He carefully climbed down and said, "Nothing to the south of us. Some very faint fingers of smoke to the north and signs of dust to the east."

"How far north?" Bodine asked.

"I'd say five miles north and east."

"Talking smoke?"

"No."

"We got luck ridin' with us," Wellman said. "They don't know where we is. But we know 'proximately where they is. In the Wilderness. They're not going to run for the rocks for three of us. They've gathered and are talkin' about this; tryin' to figure out if their medicine is bad."

"They might not understand dynamite," Sam said. "I remember my grandfather telling me about the first time he heard and felt artillery. He said it was awful. The Indians ran in panic."

"Yeah, that's right," Wellman said. "The Apaches have shore enough seen what mountain cannon can do," he told them. "Back some years ago, while the civil war was goin' on in the east, the Army out here used twelve pounders agin Cochise over in Apache Pass. I heard about it. Whipped old Cochise to a farethee-well that day, and put the fear into him.

Since then the Apache has always been afraid of what they call the thundering guns. They might think that's what we've got. How many cookfires did you see, Sam?"

"Maybe half a dozen all told. I looked several times to be sure my eyes weren't playing tricks on me. They were cook fires."

Wellman smiled. "They've gathered. The dust you seen was others comin' to the gatherin' for a pow-wow.

"We just might get lucky," Matt said. "If you want to chance it."

"What do you have on your mind, brother?" Sam asked.

Matt laid it out.

Wellman and Sam looked at each other and both shrugged. "It's so crazy it just might work," Sam said.

"Well then," Wellman said. "Let's fix us a hot meal and get goin.' "

"Some hot food would taste good," Sam said.

" 'Specially when you take into consideration it might be our last meal," Wellman said with a grin. Then his grin faded. "Something about that area with that balancin' rock you spoke of keeps naggin' at my mind. Well, mayhaps it'll come to me. But I thought that was east of here." Then he would say no more about it.

But both Sam and Bodine could see the old man was worried about something, and it wasn't the bacon and the beans cooking.

Chapter 16

They left the packhorses behind, stripped of their burdens and well hidden and left their own horses about a half a mile from where Sam had spotted the heaviest smoke. He had marked the spot in his mind by a huge balancing rock that was just to the south of the smoke. Twice on the way there, Sam climbed atop high rocks to make certain they were on the mark. Each time, they were dead on.

They watered their horses and left them on picket pins in a small area with enough good graze to keep them content for the time the men would be gone, and they didn't figure on being gone for more than three hours. It was silently understood that if they weren't back by then, they would never return.

Dick Wellman did a lot of quiet grousing about the others carrying by far the heaviest loads, but Matt and Sam stood firm. Dick was still quite spry for his age, but they needed his guns and experience more than they needed his strength in carrying dynamite.

They all knew that if their horses were found, it would, in all likelihood, mean the end for them, for the Apache would sound the alarm and every trail and pass would be blocked.

They walked on into the coolness of the wilderness area. This was lush forest country, with running streams, and a few small lakes dotting the wilderness. They walked on in silence, all of them keeping very alert.

Wellman suddenly stopped them. "No good, boys," he whispered. "I know where they's meetin', now, and there ain't no way we can do what we got in mind." He squatted down and Bodine and Sam squatted down with him.

Wellman said, "They's a small valley just over that rise yonder. Slopes down real gentle like. No way we could get close enough to do any damage with dynamite." He pointed through the riotous colors of fall. "Crick runs dead center of the valley. It should have come to me sooner, but it's been years since I been in here."

"Are you sure?" Bodine asked.

"Positive. That balancin' rock finally brung it back to my mind."

"And you suggest we do what?" Sam asked.

"There ain't no choice in the matter. Sooner or later we're gonna have to fight the 'Paches in them crazy rocks north of here. This ain't no place for conversation. Let's get back to our horses, and bypass this gatherin'. Then we'll talk about it. We're close to death here, boys."

"I like it," Sam said.

They had swung into the saddles and headed back to their pack animals, who seemed very glad to see them. Then Wellman had done something that no Apache would ever believe they would have done: he backtracked to the lake. Both Bodine and Sam now knew that if the Apaches didn't think them crazy men before, they would now, and it would worry them.

"I like it, too," Bodine agreed. "How long will this gathering go on, I wonder?"

"Several days," Wellman told them. "Could be as long as

a week. And they'll argue most of that time. You see, no one chief rules the 'Pache. Each small band got their own leader, and they always feudin' and a fussin' amongst theyselves."

"So we might have time to search for that hidden entrance into the valley where Chappo runs and hides?" Sam asked.

"Yeah," his brother said. "If we could find it, we could plant charges along the sides of that narrow entranceway and turn it into a slaughter house for Chappo and his bunch."

Dick grinned. "I knowed they was something I liked about you, Bodine. I like the way you think!"

They rode out at dawn, heading northwest toward the point where the timber touched the desert. There, they would cut straight north and stay in the timber all the way up to the western edge of the crazy rocks, as Wellman called them.

"We'll only be about eight or ten miles from Fort Bowie when we cut east into the rocks," Wellman said. "But it's a rough ten miles."

"It's hard for me to believe that the Apache could come and go at will just ten miles from an army post," Sam said, shaking his head.

"Wait 'til you see the crazy rocks."

They stayed in the timber and saw no Apaches or any sign of them during the ride north to the crazy rocks.

"I can't believe that they're gathering just to discuss the three of us," Bodine said, over coffee on the morning they were to enter the wild maze of rocks that was Chappo's sanctuary.

"The word I got from Bill Lewis is that Geronimo is tryin' to bring the 'Paches under one leadership," Wellman said. "His. But Chappo is the main hold-out. Chappo ain't gonna follow no other man. He's a devil with but one thought in his head: to either drive the white settlers out of his land, or to kill them. And he'd rather kill them all."

"But despite that, Chappo's at the gathering?" Sam questioned.

"Oh, sure. And so is Geronimo and probably Chato and Nana and half a dozen other chiefs. It will all come to naught, though. They'll fuss and squabble the whole time they're gathered, then all ride off in different directions with their noses out of joint." Wellman tossed the dregs of his coffee into the fire. "Let's ride."

Just after dawn, they topped a small rise and Bodine said, "My God!" as he looked down at the maze of rocks.

Sam was speechless at the wild sight that lay like an impenetrable labyrinth before his eyes.

"As far as miles go," Wellman said, "it don't amount to much. But don't no one yet know just how many miles it does cover. I rode around it three times and tried to get in there more times than I could count. Never could find nothing but blind canyons."

"Did you ever leave the saddle and climb up to a high spot and try to eyeball a way in?" Bodine asked.

"Nope. But I imagine the soldier boys has tried that more'un once. They ain't found the way in yet."

"I wonder if there are any Apaches in there right now?" Sam asked.

"Doubtful," Wellman said, biting off a chew from a dark plug. "This is the last hidey-hole for Chappo and his bunch. Bill Lewis told me that they only use it in emergencies, so they wouldn't want no tracks or smoke to give it away."

"It looks spooky down there," Bodine summed up both his and Sam's inner feelings.

"It is, Matt," Wellman spoke the words softly. "They's some that say ghost riders can still be heard riding in and out of the blind canyons, wailing their fears at being damned for all eternity. So it's spooky, all right. Believe me, it is."

"Have you ever heard any of those ghost riders?" Sam cut his eyes to the man.

Wellman chewed his chew for a moment. Just before he knee-reined his horse into movement, taking them down into the ghostly crazy rocks, he said, very softly, "Yeah, I have, boys."

After only minutes into the wild and weird rock formations, both Bodine and Sam could well believe there might be ghost riders forever lost and wailing in this place of blind trails and lizards, rattlesnakes, scrub bushes, and heat.

They cached their supplies, carefully hiding them with all of them picking out a certain landmark that would enable them to quickly locate the supplies if they had to make a run for it. They found a suitable box canyon—about five hundred yards from their cache of supplies—to picket the packhorses and built a front of scrubs. The horses could get out if none of them returned.

Matt and Sam rode some yards away from the makeshift corral and waited while Wellman carefully concealed their tracks by slowly brushing them out and then gently spreading sand and dirt to cover the brush marks. It would not fool a good tracker, but would go unnoticed to anyone not keeping an eye on the ground at all times.

Rejoining them by hopping from rock to rock, so as not to leave tell-tale tracks around their chosen home base, Wellman swung into the saddle and said, "Let's go take a ride, boys."

They called a halt about an hour before dark. They had ridden completely around the foreboding stretch of land and all agreed it was no more than about fifteen or sixteen square miles. The next day they would begin entering and inspecting the many canyon openings they had marked in their minds.

They fed and watered all the animals, gently reassuring the pack animals that they were not alone and rolled into their blankets after a cold supper. They were up at dawn, moving stiffly, working the cold kinks out of their joints and muscles and silently griping.

At first light, Bodine slipped into moccasins and climbed up a huge upthrusting, lying on his belly atop the peak and scanning the immediate area through field glasses. He could easily see many of the blind canyons they had intended to inspect and made mental notes of them, checking them off the list.

He could see no way into the maze and could not see any secure valley anywhere within. "It's got to be much lower and broken up by rocks that conceal the graze and the water," he muttered.

Back on the canyon floor, he told the others of his suspicions.

"Bill Lewis gleaned that much thirty years ago," Wellman said. "But he still couldn't find no way in."

"Well find it," Bodine said, swinging into the saddle.

"It would be our luck to find the opening and then get caught in there," Sam said, and he didn't exactly brighten anyone's spirits with that thought.

"That's the Indian coming out in him," Bodine said with a grin.

"That's the pragmatist coming out in me," his blood brother countered.

"Whatever that means," Wellman said, taking the point.

At noon they stopped for a break of hardtack and water under the shade of an overhang. Sam sat down and wiggled his butt in the sand, trying to get comfortable.

"What's the matter with you?" Wellman asked. "You sit down in a bed of ant people?"

"Ant people?" Bodine looked at him.

"Yeah. Red ants. Some call them harvester ants. The Hopi and Navaho consider them sacred. They say the red ants have such thin waists 'cause during the great flood that destroyed the world, the ant people shared their food with Those That Came Before."

Sam looked pained for a moment. Then he shrugged. "Makes about as much sense as some of the things my . . . other tribes believe in."

Neither Wellman nor Matt changed expression at the slip of the tongue.

"I assure you, it isn't ants." Sam grinned. "I would be moving much faster than I did. It's some sort of depression in the earth."

"You mean a hole in the ground?" Wellman asked.

"Sort of." Sam began gently brushing away the sand with his hands.

The others scooted over to him. "It's a hoofprint!" Bodine said.

"Made when the ground was muddy and then the sun baked it into the earth," Sam added.

Wellman stood up, stepped back, and looked at the closed faces of the rocks behind Sam. Scrub brush grew at impossible angles, clinging to the cracks in the rocks which nature had split at some long ago time, and the wind had hurled earth and sand and seed into the crack.

"Here's other hoofprints," Sam said, crawling around on the ground, excitement in his voice. "And they've been covered over with sand."

"Yeah, here's some others over here," Bodine said. "A lot of them."

"But what does it mean?" Wellman stepped back, took off his hat, and scratched his head, all the while studying the face of the huge rocks.

"I don't know," Bodine said, walking over to the man. "But I damn sure intend to find out."

He stepped into the shadows of the rocks and fell into darkness, unable to stifle his yell as he tumbled into the unknown.

Chapter 17

Bodine literally fell into the opening of the murky and narrow canyon.

"Brother!"

Bodine could just hear Sam calling for him. "I'm all right," he yelled. He looked up the dark, twisting trail, surrounded by walls of fifty to sixty feet of stone. "I've found the passageway!"

"You want the horses in?" Wellman yelled.

"No. It's too late in the day. We'll get the rest of the gear and come back tomorrow. Look, I'm going to follow this trail for a while. Hand me my rifle from the boot."

Wellman and Sam stepped into the opening and both of them whistled in awe.

Bodine had fallen about three feet down from outside ground level. He first had hit the solid wall of a huge rock, then, stepping to his right, he had found a large opening and had stepped into it, his boots hitting nothing but thin air. He had tumbled, rolled, and came to his boots.

"I'll stay up here and keep an eye out," Wellman called.

"OK, Dick," Bodine said. "Sam, stay with him. Dick?"

Wellman looked at him through the dimness.

"Would you do the same tomorrow morning? We need someone out here."

Wellman hesitated. "Yeah. But I got to see this place one time; then I'll come back and watch your backtrail."

"Deal." Bodine took the rifle from Sam's hands and then knelt down and took off his spurs, handing them to his brother. "I don't know when I'll be back. I'm gonna find the end of this trail. If I get into trouble, you'll hear the shots. See you, boys."

Bodine started walking up the dark, almost tunnel-like trail. For some reason he doubted that the trail was four or five miles. He didn't know why he doubted that, but the feeling was on him. It was cool in the narrow trail, but beads of sweat popped out on his forehead at just the thought of being trapped in here by Apaches. He'd take some with him on his way into that long night, but he'd eventually fall.

He pushed that out of his mind and walked on, keeping a wary eye out for rattlesnakes. And for the deadly coral snake; this would be just right for them. He tried to remember what a desert man had told him once about the colorful bands on the coral snake. Was it red on black, get back, or red and yellow kill a fellow? He couldn't remember.

Damn place was spooky.

He stopped and looked back. He could not see the opening. Naturally! he berated himself. You've twisted and turned a dozen times.

He walked on.

Once he heard a moaning sound and stopped. He finally concluded it was only the wind cutting through the high overhead rocks. He hoped it was the wind. All he'd need now would be to see one of those fabled ghost riders. He put that thought out of his mind, too, and silently fussed at himself for acting like a silly little child.

It almost worked.

He guessed he had walked about a mile; he had been using a trick that woodsmen had been using since the Revolutionary War: he had been counting each time his left foot hit the ground. Each step was approximately thirty inches. A hundred steps was two hundred and fifty feet; he just kept adding and adding. Some woodsmen used a rawhide thong with beads on it to keep track: each time a hundred yards was reached, they'd pull a bead down.

He saw light up ahead, and slowed his pace, walking silently, being very careful where he put his boots down on the worn trail.

He rounded a long curve and stepped out into a valley. He could hear the sounds of water running over rocks. And the place was deserted. He sensed that. He slipped from rock to rock, staying low, presenting less of a target if he was wrong in his guessing.

It took him about an hour to circle the less than forty acre valley, finding both good graze and water. And he knew this after gazing up at the craggy rock walls that surrounded the valley: a person might be able to climb out, but it would be one hell of a climb.

Still? . . .

He walked around the inner walls, looking. There! There was where the Apache climbed up to post lookouts. Bodine slung his rifle by the strap and studied the hand holds.

"What the hell?" he muttered. "Let's see if there is another way out."

He climbed up, taking his time and being very careful where he placed his hands and feet, and thinking: Please, Mister Rattlesnake, don't be curled up in one of these hand-holds catching the sun.

The sun!

He turned his head and silently cussed. It was growing late in the afternoon.

He was halfway up. He hesitated and decided to go on.

When he breached the top, Bodine lay on his belly for a moment, catching his breath. He guessed the clifftop was several hundred feet long, running east to west from the outside canyon inward, and about seventy-five feet high. Lifting his head, he gazed at a panoramic view of the crazy rocks and beyond.

Then he heard voices.

Voices?

Bodine fought to contain his chuckle as the answer came to him. The trail through the rocks twisted and turned, giving one the impression that it was a mile deep. It wasn't; he was hearing the voices of Sam and Wellman. The twists and turns were deceiving, leaving one thinking of a much greater distance.

Bodine grinned and then moaned.

"Did you hear that?" Sam's voice drifted to him.

"I've heared it before. I told you about them ghost riders."

"It was the wind."

"Damn if that's so!" Wellman said. "I wish Bodine would get on out here."

"Place must be spooky in there."

"Oooohhhhh!" Bodine moaned.

Silence from below him.

Bodine had to put his face against the stone to keep from busting out laughing. The tension of the past days ebbed from him in invisible waves as he imagined the expressions on the faces of his friends.

Then he felt guilty about what he was putting them through . . . but not too guilty.

"What's the matter, brother?" he called. "Did I scare you?"

"Bodine! You coyote dropping! Where are you?"

"Just above you. Tie a rock on the end of a rope and toss it up to me. That'll be easier than me going back and wandering through that passageway."

"Ought to leave him up there," Wellman said. "Serve him right."

"I think we'll do just that," Sam said. "Make him spend the night up there for making us worry about him."

"So you admit you were scared?"

"Don't be ridiculous. We were concerned about you, that's all."

"Wooooo!" Bodine moaned.

Sam threw the rock-weighted end of the rope so hard that if it hit Matt on the head it would have knocked him cold.

Bodine secured his end of the rope and scampered down to the canyon floor. There, he pulled the rope tight against the face of the canyon wall and secured the ground end around a thick bush. If the Apaches returned, the rope would not be noticed at night. He hoped.

Working quickly, they covered their tracks and got out of there, Bodine explaining what he'd found as they quickly worked.

"Then we can use the rope to both get in and out," Sam said.

"Yeah. It'll be a lot quicker that way. And from the top of that young mountain, Dick can have one heck of a lookout position. You can see for miles up there."

"You got a plan for placin' the dynamite?" Wellman asked.

Bodine grinned wickedly. "I sure do."

The next morning, Wellman told them both bluntly that he didn't need no gawddamn help in climbing up no rope, so just stand aside and keep your helpful comments to your-selves, boys.

The old mountain man went up the rope like a monkey, and he was the first one up.

He tossed the rope back down. "Send up the supplies, boys, an' be quick about it."

Seventy years old he might be, but Wellman was still all gristle and wang-leather tough, and as he had shown, would be hard to handle in any kind of scrap.

Wellman stood on the lip of the peak and stared at the valley below. "I'd a not believed it," he finally said. "I wish I had me one of them pitcher-boxes so's I could show the world this sight." Then he took the field glasses and slowly and carefully scanned the area in all directions.

"There's the damn fort!" he said disgustedly. "It ain't real plain, but yonder it is." He concentrated on the three other directions and finally laid the glasses aside. "We got time to do our business in the valley. There ain't no 'Paches within a three hour ride of here. You boys get crackin'. I'll belly-down up here and keep an eye peeled for savages."

They lowered the bulky supplies and Bodine and Sam hurried down.

"Brother," Sam said, "I don't like the way you're smiling. What have you worked out in that devious mind of yours?"

"First of all, we find a way to climb up on the lip of this place. One that the Apaches don't use."

"And? . . ."

Bodine looked at him for a long moment, grinning all the time.

"You're not serious!" Sam picked up the mental waves from his blood brother.

"Oh, yeah!"

"You're crazy, you know that? You are positively a raving lunatic!"

"But you love it, right?"

"The plan, if I read it right, does have some elements of intrigue . . . not to mention danger if anything goes haywire."

"You want to do it?"

"What are we waiting for?"

The blood-brothers worked quickly, placing the dynamite, which was the same color as the rocks, in various locations. Bodine had called out to Wellman what he was doing and the man grinned his approval, adding, "I just hope you can find a way up to the lip."

"Use your glasses, Dick," Sam suggested. "Find us some possibilities if you can."

Dick started searching the walls of the valley, marking possibles in his mind.

Bodine and Sam both agreed they would not permanently close the entrance to the valley. When the moment came, Wellman would be in position across from the canyon floor and high-up above the entrance with two fully-loaded rifles, his Colts, and a sack of dynamite for throwing.

Bodine and Sam would be, if they could find another way out, on the lip of the valley wall when Chappo and his warriors returned.

Then the fun would start.

They had done all they could do on the valley floor, and went over the area carefully, smoothing out any tracks they had made. And they had found another way out. It had been a hard climb, but the two young men made it, and it gave them a fantastic view of the valley below them and a great vantage point for shooting.

Dick had climbed down the rope to the canyon floor, and Sam had coiled the rope and climbed down using the Apache hand-holes.

They had left no trace of disturbance. At least they all hoped that.

They took a chance and pulled the horses in close to them, Wellman's horses behind the ridge where he had made himself a home, and the horses of Matt and Sam behind them in a cul-de-sac at the end of a crinkumcrankum.

Then, all they had to do was wait.

And wait they did.

Days passed, and they were running out of food for themselves and for the animals. With despair in his voice, Bodine said, "If they don't show up by tomorrow, one of us is going to have to ride to the fort for supplies."

Despair took wings as Wellman's faint shout came to them: "Dust comin', boys!"

"Good luck, Dick!" both young men shouted, then settled down as still as a waiting snake.

As Chappo and his warriors rode single-file into the valley, Sam whispered, his voice carrying no more than a foot from his lips, "We're seeing history."

"Just as we saw in June," Bodine reminded his brother. "In the Rosebuds."

"But this time we can talk about it."

"That is truth."

It was not all of Chappo's band; the valley could not sustain several hundred warriors and their animals. But it was Chappo and about fifty of his braves. And there were fresh scalps tied onto the manes of their ponies and on their rifles.

"They've been busy," Matt said grimly.

"Very," was his brother's reply. "Some of those scalps belong to children."

The Apaches swung down from their horses and began settling in.

Bodine and Sam looked at each other and smiled, a grim curving of the lips. It was about to become very unpleasant for Chappo and his braves. And Sam had stated coldly that if any renegades deserved it, Chappo and his bunch did—richly so.

They had brought a mule in with them, no doubt stolen during a raid, and a brave killed the poor animal with an axe. Apaches preferred mule meat above horse. Other braves began gathering up very dry wood for a quick, hot, and virtually smokeless fire.

Both Bodine and Sam quietly eared back the hammers on their Winchesters.

Bodine had carefully dug into the cold ashes of old cook-fires and planted a dozen sticks of dynamite just under the ashes of each fire-pit, the fuses up, and then re-spread the ashes. For many of the Apaches, this was going to be a very unusual last meal.

The dry wood was dropped into the fire-pits as the mule was being butchered.

"Just another couple of minutes," Sam muttered.

It was cool in the valley, and many of the Apaches had gathered around the fire-pits, urging the fire-tenders to hurry up and build the fires so they could warm themselves and stuff their bellies full of mule meat.

The fire-builders had knelt down around the pits and were igniting the dry grass and twigs under the piled on wood. Already the Apaches were moving closer to the just-lit fires, hands extended over the pit. Others were coming forward with bloody chunks of mule meat impaled on sticks.

The first pit blew, the dozen sticks of dynamite exploding and knocking Chappo's braves in all directions, many with shattered arms and legs and torn-open chests and rock-mangled heads.

Before the others could react, all the fire-pits blew, the sounds echoing around the closed-in valley and deafening all who were close by.

Matt and Sam opened up, the slugs from their Winchesters knocking the already confused Apaches to the ground as they ran toward weapons. One was climbing up the hand-holds toward the look-out spot. Matt and Sam let him climb. When he was halfway up, his hands tried to get a purchase in the two holes Sam had filled with bacon grease. He fell screaming to the rocks below him and landed on his head, smearing the rocks with blood.

Dynamite had been placed in the rocks above the narrow

valley. Matt and Sam began firing at the primed and capped sticks, exploding them and showering the Apaches below with killing and maiming rocks hurled forth under the charges.

Sam and Bodine spotted Chappo as he ran from his wickiup toward where the horses were corralled inside a crude barricade. They fired as one and both shots were true, taking the guerrilla leader in the belly and turning him around. He went down on one knee and Bodine and Two Wolves fired again, the slugs striking the man in the head and chest.

Chappo's savage and evil career was over.

Chapter 18

The remainder of the band had nowhere to go and nothing to do except die; and they did that.

Several made the twisting entranceway only to be shot down by the rifle of Dick Wellman as they ran out onto the canyon floor. Several more tried to climb up to Matt and Sam. They were killed by thrown sticks of dynamite, their bodies mangled from the blasts.

There was no surrender in those few remaining. They fought to the last man, and the last man died. From their vantage point, there was no place in the little valley for the Apache to hide from the guns of the brothers bonded in blood. When the last of Chappo's band lay sprawled on the ground, Bodine and Sam took careful aim and fired a coup-de-grace into each seemingly lifeless body. A half a dozen of them were not dead before the final bullet struck them. When those sprawled death-still on the ground and among the rocks realized what was happening, they jumped up and tried to run.

They did not make it far.

The buzzards were gathering before the gunsmoke had

drifted away from the valley of the dead, the carrion-eaters gracefully floating in a circle high above, as silent and as knowing as death.

"Dick?" Sam yelled.

"Yo!" came the shout.

"Bring the horses up to the entrance. We'll lead a horse out and lower down Chappo's body over the edge. We'll take him to the fort and bring the Army back."

"I'll be ready when you are."

A patrol rode out to meet the men about a mile from Fort Bowie.

"Lose a man?" the sergeant asked.

"Chappo," Bodine told him.

The sergeant almost swallowed his chew. He jumped off his horse and lifted the blanket covering the Apache war chief. "Holy Christ!" he yelled. "It's really *him!*"

A rider from the patrol was sent galloping back to the fort and everybody there turned out to see the men ride in.

After the colonel had gazed at the dead face of Chappo, he personally escorted Bodine, Sam, and Wellman to his office. There, he seated them with a wide smile and poured them tumblers of whiskey, filled up nicely.

He ordered a man in to take down their story and told them to proceed.

The colonel was all smiles when they finished. "Sergeant," he said. "I will personally take Companies A and B out at first light in the morning. Have those orders cut and recorded. And have the official photographer ready to go. I want this recorded for posterity."

"Yes, sir."

"Would you gentlemen consent to lead us back in?" he inquired.

"Be glad to," Wellman told him. "But don't take no green

soldier boys, 'cause the smell's gonna be enough to gag a maggot. And that reminds me, Colonel: you got anything to eat around this place? We run out of grub waitin' for them heathens to show up." He smiled as he held out his glass for another drink.

They could all see the buzzards long before they reached the valley. And they began to smell the dead not long after that.

Guards were posted all around and above the entrance to the valley and Bodine led the colonel and several of his men and the Army photographer through the winding passageway.

"Incredible," the colonel muttered, stepping out into the valley.

He and the others wrapped bandanas around their faces to give some relief from the smell of the dead.

Photos were taken with the colonel in various poses beside the stiffened dead; the colonel with Bodine, Sam, and Wellman; the colonel standing beside the great holes in the earth caused by the dynamite planted in the firepits; and the colonel holding a rifle with several dried scalps dangling from it.

"Why is he doing all this?" Sam asked. "The fool had nothing to do with this slaughter."

"He's buckin' for general," Wellman said. "And this will probably do it for him."

The men, after soaking in tubs of hot soapy water, had resupplied at Fort Bowie and changed into clean, freshly laundered clothing.

In the valley, they looked at one another, passing silent messages, then walked over to a grizzled sergeant major.

"We're gone, Sarge," Sam told him.

"Wish I could go with you," he whispered. "One other good thing just might have come out of all this, though."

"What's that?" Bodine asked.

"That fool colonel might get promoted and transferred outta here!"

The men were still chuckling as they rode away from the crazy rocks.

They began their search for the outlaws Lake and Porter. Wellman had vowed to kill both of them for killing his kin and taking his Jenny. Bodine and Sam agreed to tag along.

They rode northwest out of the Chiricahuas, heading first for the town of Dos Cabezas, Spanish for Two Heads, a wide-open and rip-roaring mining town. The news that they had trapped and killed Chappo and his murderous band of renegades had preceded their arrival, and they could pay for nothing in the town. They were put up in the hotel and served the finest food that could be prepared for them. But no one could tell them anything about Lake or Porter.

From Dos Cabezas they followed the stage road west to Wilcox and received the same treatment there they had in Dos Cabezas. And got the same lack of information about the men they were pursuing.

"Might have gone to Tucson," Wellman said, lingering over a glass of beer. "You boys game?"

"I don't believe we have anything terribly pressing on our social calendar," Sam said with a smile.

"Not unless President Grant calls us to come to Washington so he can pin medals on us for getting rid of Chappo," Bodine added.

"That colonel back yonder at Bowie will be gettin' them medals, boys."

"He can have them," Sam summed up the feelings for all of them.

* * *

They were just about halfway between Wilcox and Benson when the Apaches hit them. They'd been following the stage-coach road that dipped south for a time before gently beginning its northwest slope toward Tucson.

It was a pleasant morning and the men were riding abreast when the Apaches seemingly came out of nowhere and hit them hard. One Apache was too eager and snapped off a shot that whizzed under Sam's chin. The men put the spurs to their horses and made it into the rocks just as the main bunch of warriors began firing.

Wellman looked around their position in the rocks and said, "I been in better situations. But it beats bein' out yonder in the open, I reckon."

They had the water in their canteens and some food. No graze for the horses; but each man did carry a bait of corn for the animals.

"According to the schedule I read back in town, there'll be a stage along this afternoon," Sam said. "Give or take a day or two," he finished it, knowing that when the Apaches were known to be rampaging, the stages sometimes did not run.

"Which may or may not stop to lend us a hand," Wellman grimly pointed out to them. "And I wouldn't blame them if they just rolled on by. If we're still alive by then," he added.

The rocks in which they had forted up were circular, and with the horses, crowded. Wellman took the position facing the road; Sam took the west; Bodine crawled to cover the other angles. The men had taken their spare rifles and Colts from the pack animals, laying the rifles to one side and shoving the pistols behind their belts. The terrain in front of them looked barren and void of life; but they all knew better.

Sam saw something that just didn't quite fit in with their surroundings and lifted his Winchester, sighting the object in, and waiting. The stick-like object moved—no more than a tremble—and Sam fired. An Apache jumped up, his left arm dangling useless, broken at the elbow by the .44 slug, and Wellman drilled him in the brisket, doubling him over and dropping him to the sand.

After that, nothing seemed to move and no shots were fired for better than half an hour, the Apaches playing their best card: the waiting game.

But the men in the rocks knew the warriors were stealthily moving toward them, perhaps no more than an inch or two at a time, but coming at them all the while.

None of them had any idea how many Apaches they were facing. It could be anywhere from half a dozen to more than thirty. A good bet was somewhere in-between, since Apaches were not known to travel in bands of more than thirty. Chappo had been the exception. But Chappo's head had been cut off and mounted up on a tall pole and placed in front of the fort.

All of the men inside the rocks had moved, one at a time, and gathered up more smaller rocks, to pile in front of them for more protection.

When the Apaches made their move, they came all at once, and they had been very close to the rocks.

Bodine nailed one in the chest, Wellman got lead in another, and Sam shot one right between the eyes before the braves reached the jumble of rocks and breached the natural fort.

Bodine jammed the muzzle of his Winchester into a warrior's mouth and pulled the trigger, blowing away the back of the brave's head.

Wellman clubbed one to his knees and then shot him, the slug severing the man's spine.

With blood streaming down his face from a bullet graze on his forehead, Sam's rifle jammed and he used his long-bladed knife, burying it to the hilt in an Apache's chest.

Bodine was knocked down by a brave who hurled himself over the rocks and landed on him. Bodine kicked the brave between the legs, bringing a wild cry of pain and then pulled a Colt from behind his belt and shot him in the head, ending the yowling.

Wellman had taken a slug in the upper part of his left arm and was using his right hand filled with an empty Colt to batter in the face of a brave. Sam stepped forward and shot the Apache twice in the belly.

The remaining Apaches, having lost far too many warriors, called it quits and vanished into the desert across the road. They galloped away, hugging the necks of their horses to offer a smaller target.

Bodine brought down a horse with a single rifle shot and plugged the Apache when he stood up after rolling on the ground. The pony struggled to its feet and Wellman put the animal out of its misery. It was a better end than the Apache would have given it, since they usually rode a horse to death and then ate it.

That was yet another reason why the Apache was so hated by the settlers.

Sam lifted his pistol to finish one brave who lay on the ground, glaring hate at them through dark eyes, his hands clutching his bullet-shattered belly.

The Apache cursed Sam in English and Sam returned the uncomplimentary remarks in Cheyenne.

The Apache spat at Sam and Sam shot him between the eyes.

"Thoroughly disagreeable bunch of people," Sam said, reloading.

Wellman was plugging the hole in his arm with wet chewing tobacco and paused and laughed at Sam's statement while Bodine tied a kerchief over the wound. "Let's ride," the old mountain man said, "afore them savages find some friends and decide to come back."

"Can we make Benson by dark?" Bodine asked, spilling out empties and reloading.

"I damn sure intend to try," Wellman said.

They mounted up and rode away, leaving the bodies of the Apaches where they lay on the sand and among the rocks. The Apaches who escaped would probably return to gather up their dead if at all possible.

Benson was a little spot on the map, but it had several stores, a saloon, a cafe, and a barber shop with tubs to bathe in out back.

The men stabled their horses and walked over to the cafe. It had a real wooden floor and curtains on the windows and red and white checkered tablecloths on the table.

"Class joint," Wellman said, leaning his rifle against a wall and sitting down.

The men ordered and were eating when the town marshal walked in. He sat down, ordered coffee, and glanced over at the trio, noting the bandage on Sam's face and the bloody shirt sleeve of Wellman.

"You boys run into trouble?" he inquired.

"A mite," Wellman spoke around a mouthful of beef. " 'Paches hit us 'bout twelve-fifteen miles east of town. Them we kilt we left for the buzzards."

The marshal slowly nodded his head, shifting his gaze to Sam. "You a breed?"

"Yeah." Sam said it without looking at the man, and something in the short reply told the marshal it would be in his best interest to let it alone.

He looked at Bodine. "Do I know you?"

"I don't know whether you do or not. I only know that I don't know you." Matt had not looked up; just continued eating his supper.

The marshal almost said something sharp in reply, then thought better of it as the stage rolled in, several hours late. Boots sounded on the boardwalk and the door was pushed open.

The man walked inside, wearing a deputy's badge pinned to his shirt. He looked at the three men eating, checked the bloody bandages on two of them, and sat down at the table with the marshal. "Trouble, Marshal?"

"I don't know, Brun. What'd you doin' this far over?"

"Headin' to Tucson to pick up a prisoner. Signs of a pretty fair scrap twelve-fifteen miles east of town. Driver pointed it out from the box. We stopped and looked around. Injuns toted off their dead, I reckon."

"That's what these men told me. About the fight. And precious little else I asked 'em."

The sheriff's deputy held his tongue while he eyeballed the two guns of Bodine. Twin guns were not the norm; but were not that unusual, either. But there was something about the way this young man wore his that caught the deputy's eyes.

The other patrons in the cafe had fallen silent and stopped eating, listening to the exchange, wondering if there was going to be trouble.

The deputy turned to the marshal.

"You mighty calm about the news."

"What news?"

"You ain't heard about Smoke Jensen headin' down this way?"

"No! You're funnin' me."

"No, I ain't neither. Down here lookin' at cattle, so I was told."

"Man, I shore would like to see that feller just one time."

"I seen him half a dozen times," Wellman said, forking a wedge of apple pie in his mouth. "Me and old Preacher— that's the man who halfway raised the kid—was trappers together back some years ago." He slurped at his coffee and said, "Jensen's a right nice young man. In his thirties by now."

"You . . . know Smoke Jensen?" the deputy said.

"Yeah. Et with him and Sally a time or two. What you all het up about Jensen for?"

" 'Cause he's the most famous gunfighter in the west!" the marshal said.

"Hell, he ain't much more famous than this one!" Wellman said, jerking a thumb toward Matt.

The marshal picked up his coffee cup and looked at Matt. "Who are you?" he demanded.

"Matt Bodine."

The marshal spilled coffee all down the front of his shirt.

Chapter 19

"You told me you never met Smoke Jensen," Matt said to Wellman, after they had left the cafe.

"I lied. If I'd a told the truth you'd a been pesterin' me for weeks on end about him. You'd have never shut up."

"This is true," Sam said solemnly. "Bodine can certainly be a pest and he rattles on and on about the most trivial of matters." He tried, but could not hide his smile.

"What's he like?" Matt asked, giving his blood brother a dirty look and otherwise ignoring him.

"You see?" Sam said. "It's started already. You should never have brought it up."

"We all make mistakes," Wellman admitted.

"Jensen's a quiet sort of fellow. Very much in love with his wife and devoted to his kids. He's a decent man who don't like thugs and punks and outlaws and trash. He wasn't nothing but a kid when he rode into that minin' camp up on the Uncompahgre lookin' for the men who raped and kilt his wife and murdered they baby boy. I don't know how many men he kilt that day. Some say fifteen, others say thirty. But he's a bad man to mess with. Just like you, Bodine. You and

Jensen got a lot in common. He's a little taller and heavier than you. And he might be a tad quicker pullin' iron. Now is that enough to suit you?"

"I'd like to meet him."

Wellman muttered something under his breath.

"What'd you say, Dick?" Bodine asked.

"I said I don't know ifn I want to be in the same town was you two to get together—bein' the peaceful sort of man that I am."

Sam and Bodine were still chuckling as they went to the hotel for night's sleep in a bed.

It was becoming a pattern: no one knew the whereabouts of Lake or Porter. It seemed the outlaws had gone into deep hiding somewhere along Arizona's hoot-owl trail. But nobody knew where.

Or if they did, they weren't talking.

The trio pulled out the following morning, following the stagecoach road toward Tuscon, about fifty miles away. Before leaving Benson, they had inquired as to waterhole and spring locations along the way, and found the information to be right on the mark. They kept the Empire Mountains to the south of them and made the ride without seeing any sign of Apaches.

Tucson was where Wellman felt they might pick up the trail of the outlaws, more than likely in one of the rougher saloons, where a man placed his life in the hands of the Almighty just by pushing open the batwings and stepping inside.

"You want to take Mex town, Sam?" Wellman asked. "I think they'll probably talk to you whilst they wouldn't to me or Matt."

"I'll give it a whirl."

"I'll take the miner's hangout and you get all spiffed up,

Matt, and take the saloon where the fancy-dans gather. We ought to come up with something."

Bodine bathed and got a shave and a haircut and his clothes laundered before heading to the Hall, as the better of the saloons in town was called. It was the gathering place for businessmen and ranchers and mine owners and the like.

Bodine introduced himself as Matt and left it at that. He could talk cattle and horses with the best of them, and did so, every now and then dropping in something like, "I heard some ranchers between here and Phoenix have been having some trouble with an outlaw gang; supposed to be fronted by two men called Lake and Porter."

Finally he hit paydirt.

"It ain't just ranchers," a mining equipment salesman told him. "They're working on gold shipments as well. It's a big gang and they control a lot of country up thataway. They come bustin' out of the Tonto Basin to strike and then run back in that wild country to hide out. Least that's what I been told."

Bodine left shortly after that to hunt up Sam and Wellman. He found both of them in the roughest saloon in town.

Before he could share his information, a rough-dressed, unshaven, and smelly lout popped off at him. "Well, well, would you take a look at the dandy. All duded up in his pretty new suit." Bodine was wearing a black suit he'd just purchased, with a white shirt and string tie. His boots had been blacked while he was bathing.

Bodine ignored the man.

But the bully wasn't going to be put off that easily. "Hey, pretty boy! I'm talkin' to you."

Bodine said to Wellman and Sam, "Word I got is that Lake and Porter are just northeast of Phoenix. They've got a big gang of men; working at rustling and robbing gold miners."

"That's what I heard, too," Sam said.

"Goddamn you, pretty boy!" the bully shouted, banging a fist on a table. "You turn around an' talk to me."

Bodine told the bartender to draw him a beer, and while his beer was being drawn, he turned to take a look at the bigmouth. And the man was huge. Bodine figured him at six-five and probably weighing two-hundred and fifty pounds, or better. But Bodine had fought other men of the same size . . . and won. With both fists and guns.

"What's your problem, pig-face?" Bodine asked.

The crowd hushed and moved away from the path of the big man.

"What'd you call me, fancy-dan?"

"Pig-face," Bodine repeated. "You know. Like in oink-oink?"

The big man blinked. He shook his head and stared at Bodine. Nobody talked to him like that. Ever. Not and got away with it.

"I think I'll tear your arm off and beat you to death with it!" pig-face grunted.

Bodine laughed at him.

That infuriated the man. He picked up a chair and hurled it across the room, the chair splintering against a wall.

"Did you ever see anything so impressive?" Bodine asked.

"Never in my borned days," Wellman said. "Scares me half to death. I ain't never seen such a sight in all my life. And did you ever see anyone so *ugly?* "

"I'm so frightened I might run screaming out into the street," Sam said.

Then the three of them laughed at the man.

"I'm Jack Bennett!" the bully shouted, his face flushing.

"Is that supposed to mean something to me?" Bodine asked.

"It will when I stomp your guts out!"

"You like to hurt people, huh?" Bodine asked, feeling that old familiar coldness begin to spread throughout him. He hated a bully; especially men the size of Bennett who threw their weight around, intimidating others.

"Damn right!" Bennett said.

A woman had been standing on the balcony of the second floor, watching and listening. She ran a string of soiled doves, operating on the second floor. "That's Matt Bodine, Bennett," she called.

The bully had started forward. He stopped as if running into an invisible barrier, his face a study in conflict. He knew that he had made his brags and to back down now might well mean his leaving town in disgrace, the laughter and taunts of the others ringing in his ears.

But Matt Bodine! Nearabouts as famous a gunhand as Smoke Jensen.

And Bennett knew well the ways of the west. He was wearing a gun, and in the west, when a man or boy strapped on a gun, he better be willing, and more important, able to use it.

But against Matt Bodine!

Bennett was better than the average with a gun. But nowhere near Bodine's class.

What to do?

Bodine settled it for him.

Within every good man, and Bodine was a good man, there runs a darker side. Oftentimes the dislike of a certain type of person—the bully Bennetts of the world—can turn as unreasonable as the bully's mind.

Bodine was more like Smoke Jensen than even he knew.

Bodine knew he could tell the man to sit down, buy him a drink, and it would be over, with the bully saving face. But how often had the bully allowed any of his victims that option?

Never, Bodine would bet.

"Hello, Patty," Bodine said, flicking his eyes to the woman for a brief second, then returning them to stare at Bennett.

Bodine had noted that the bully was wearing a gun.

"Matt," Patty said. "Bennett's no hand with a gun, Bodine."

"That's his problem." Matt's eyes bored into the eyes of the bully. "How many men have you given a break, pig-face?"

Bennett chose not to reply.

Suddenly, Matt smiled, albeit a cold, thin smile. He took off his suit coat and folded it, laying it on the bar. He untied the leg straps and unbuckled the gunbelt, placing it beside the coat. "You've used your fists on no telling how many innocent men, pig-face. You've bullied your way all your low-down, miserable life." Bodine was walking toward the bigger man, shoving tables out of the way. "Always being very careful to pick your victims. And always sucking up to men you knew you couldn't take."

Bodine abruptly picked up a chair and hit Bennett smack in the face with it, the blow knocking the big man sprawling, his face bleeding.

Bennett was up with a bound, grabbing for the gun he wore.

A dozen hardcases jerked iron, jacking the hammers back. "No, you don't, Bennett," one said. "Lay your gun on the table and take your beatin'. You started this."

"Beatin'!" Bennett laughed. "Not from this punk." He tossed his pistol to Matt. "I'll even give you an edge, pretty-boy." His face was bloody but his confidence was fast returning.

Matt tossed the six-shooter on a table and said, "Then come on, lard-butt. Show me how tough you are."

Bennett jumped at Matt, both fists swinging. Matt side-stepped and clubbed the big man on the ear with a right fist. He had slipped on black leather riding gloves—that had been hand-made for him. The leather gloves not only enabled him to hit harder, but they also protected his hands.

Bennett recovered quickly and busted Matt on the jaw with a rock hard and flat-knuckled fist that hurt. Matt backed up, shaking his head, and Bennett made the mistake of pursuing him. Bodine faked the man out and drove a straight right fist into the man's face, pulping his lips. He followed that with a punch to the bully's wind, then sidestepped away and kicked the man on the kneecap, bringing a howl of pain.

Bennett backed up and changed tactics, deciding to box Bodine.

That was a mistake, for Bodine's dad was still a good boxer and had taught his sons well.

After Bodine smacked Bennett several good blows, going right through his guard, the bully decided he'd better stick to rough and tumble.

That wasn't too bright on his part either, since Bodine could hold his own in gutter fighting as well as Indian wrestling.

Bodine showed him that by rolling the bigger man over his hip and tossing him to the dirty barroom floor. Bodine kicked the man in the side, bringing a grunt of pain, then backed up, allowing the bully to slowly get to his boots.

"How many men have you humiliated, Bennett?" Bodine asked him. "How many men who had done you no harm have you beaten in your life?"

Bennett's reply was a roar of rage. He picked up a chair and charged Matt, screaming incomprehensible animal sounds.

Matt tripped the big man, sending him crashing into the bar near Sam. Sam looked at him, lifted his glass of beer in a mock salute, and said, "Not having too good a day, I see."

Bennett heaved himself away from the bar just in time to catch a left and a right to the jaw—both sides. He lifted his hands to protect his face and Bodine started working on his mid-section; hard, trip-hammer blows that hurt and tore the wind from the bully.

Those who had shouted out bets on Bennett now sat or stood quietly, all knowing what the smaller man was going to do. Not all of them liked it, but no one tried to interfere.

Bodine was going to destroy the man.

Bennett swung a heavy arm and knocked Bodine back, giving the man time to collect his wits and wind. Bodine stood in the center of the barroom, his shirt ripped open, and all could see the hard-packed muscles of the man, put there by years of wrestling steers and breaking horses and digging post holes and cutting and stacking and manhandling heavy bales of hay.

"Come on, bully-boy," Bodine panted the words. "Come get what you've been dishing out to others for years."

"Why are you doin' this to me?" Bennett shouted the question.

"Because you deserve it, you son of a bitch!" Bodine stepped in and hit the man flush on his red nose, breaking it and sending blood squirting.

Bennett once more fell back against the bar and Sam said, "Some days it just doesn't pay to get out of bed, does it?"

With a wild curse, Bennett lumbered away from the bar and the smart-aleck Injun-lookin' man and faced Bodine in the center of the room.

Bodine lifted his fists, holding them close to his face, the left slightly higher than the right. He was signaling Bennett to box.

"All right," Bennett said. "To box it is then."

The men stood toe to toe on the barroom floor and fought it out, with both of them drawing blood. Bennett toe-hooked Matt's ankle and sent him crashing to the floor. Matt rolled to avoid Bennett's kick and came up on his knees. He drove one fist into the bully's crotch and Bennett doubled over, screaming in dizzying pain. Bodine jumped to his boots and hit the man as hard as he could over one kidney, driving the bully to his knees. Bodine circled and brought a knee up into the man's face, jerking the man's bloody face up with the impact.

"That's enough, Bodine!" a man yelled. "You're goin' to kill him!"

Bodine told the man where he could put his words and continued smashing Bennett's face with hard left and right combinations. One of Bennett's ears was dangling by a thin flap of skin. His nose was smashed flat against his face and his mouth was a bloody smear; teeth littered the dirty floor.

Bodine grabbed the bully's bloody shirt front and literally muscled the big man up on his boots. He turned him around and with one hand on the back of his dirty shirt collar and the other gripping the seat of his baggy pants, Bodine propelled the man through the batwings and tossed him into the dusty street. Bennett landed on his face and lay still.

Bodine looked around him. A small boy with a little dog by his side stood staring up at him.

"He kicked my dog one time, mister," the boy told him. "For no reason other than he just wanted to hurt something. Thud still walks with a limp where Bennett broke his hip."

Bodine patted the boy on the shoulder. "Then that in itself justifies what I did to him."

Chapter 20

Bully Jack Bennett was dragged off the street and taken to a doctor's office for treatment. The doctor found that the man had a broken jaw, half a dozen broken ribs, and all his front teeth—top and bottom—either knocked out or broken off at the gumline. One ear was amputated and his nose reset.

When he was able to travel, Bully Bennett left town, swearing to someday kill Matt Bodine. By that time, Bodine, Sam, and Wellman had bought what supplies they needed, rested up, and were once more on the trail.

"What's that country like north and east of Phoenix?" Matt asked.

"Wild and rugged," Wellman said. Both Matt and Sam had noticed the man had lost weight and was in some degree of pain most of the time. He had bought several bottles of laudanum in Tucson, but used the pain-killing liquid sparingly, and never while Sam or Bodine were watching. Or so he thought. "Be good to see it one more time."

Both Sam and Bodine wondered if the old man would live that long.

"How's your hands, Bodine?" Wellman asked.

"They're all right." Matt's hands had been swollen after the fight in the saloon. He had soaked them several times a day and used liniment to keep the swelling to a minimum. "Dick?"

The old mountain man looked up, the pain in his body now clearly showing in his eyes.

"Get on a stage and go back home, man. Spend some time with Jenny and Laurie. I give you my word we'll track down Lake and Porter."

Wellman shook his head. "I'd never last the trip, boys. I'm kinda like ol' Cochise. You know he called the hour he'd die? That's right. And he was right on the mark with it. I'll be dead in a week, boys. By that time we'll be deep in the Tontos— that's what we used to call it. Bury me high up so's I can look out on the wilderness and hear the wind sounds. You'll do that?"

Both young men nodded in agreement. They were of the frontier and understood the request.

"Then let's ride!" Wellman said.

"Over yonder's the Superstitions," Wellman pointed out. "Somewheres in there they's a Dutchman named Walzer. He's been haulin' gold out of that area for some years now. Millions. You fight shy of that man. He's a cantankerous old coot who's likely to shoot you on sight if he thinks you're after his gold. Lives with an Apache woman. Her people raided his place some time back and took her. Tore her tongue out as punishment. I 'spect we'll find some of Lake and Porter's men hangin' around the Superstitions. If we do, you boys just hang back and let me have my go with them."

"When do you want us to step in, Dick?" Sam asked.

"When I've tooken enough lead to put me down."

They headed for the Superstition Mountains, about a

day's ride away. With Iron Mountain in sight, they came up on a small placer operation.

"You boys been havin' trouble with thieves?" Wellman asked one miner.

"Shore have!" the man said. "And can't get no law out of Phoenix to do nothin'."

"You know who's robbin' you?"

"Hell, yes! They're camped right over yonder in the Superstitions. But knowin' and provin' is two different things."

"They ride horses with the Triple-V brand?" Bodine asked.

"Shore do! Some of 'em, anyways."

The miners gave them directions to the outlaw camp and the men pulled out.

"How come the law doesn't handle Lake and Porter?" Sam asked.

Matt answered that. "Phoenix is only about eight or nine years old. The newspapers I read said that the town is woolly and full of fleas. I guess the law—what there is of it—has their hands full close to home."

Wellman took the point and rode right into the outlaw camp. The men around the campfire looked up in surprise but no one grabbed for a gun. The trio swung down from the saddle and spread out, listening as Wellman came right to the point.

"You boys ride for Lake and Porter?"

"Yeah," a man said. They had all stood up. "If that's any of your business, old man."

"You know who we are?" Wellman asked.

"No, and don't care. Git outta here."

"My name's Wellman." They all tensed at that. "And you're part of the bunch that grabbed my little Jenny. Now fill your hands with guns, scum!"

The camp erupted in gunfire. Wellman put two outlaws on the ground before a bullet turned him around and another slug hit him in the back. On his knees, Wellman's longbarreled Colt spat fire and death until it was empty. Then he grabbed for another Colt behind his belt and took another outlaw out.

Bodine and Sam were standing and firing, with a six-shooter in each hand. It had all happened so fast, as it usually does—the outlaws were caught totally unprepared for the violence.

Bodine's hat had been knocked from his head by a .45 round and he had a burn on the outer part of his right thigh. Sam had taken a graze on his left arm. This bunch of Lake and Porter's hoot-owl riders were on the ground, dead or dying.

And so was Dick Wellman, one of the last breed called mountain man.

"Straighten me out easy, boys," he whispered. " 'Cause I shore hurt."

Bodine made Wellman as comfortable as possible while Sam stirred up the fire and heated up the coffee, knowing that Dick would want a cup, gut-shot or not.

"You boys take my personals," Dick said. "So's no thieves will disturb my restin' place a-grave-robbin'."

"We'll see that Jenny and Laurie get them," Bodine assured him.

"Kind of you." He took the tin cup of coffee and sipped it. "Good. Don't mark my grave. I don't want to be disturbed."

"Do you believe in God, Dick?" Bodine asked.

"Heaven?" Wellman whispered.

"Yes."

"You know what ol' Cochise said when asked that on his death bed?"

"No." Bodine's voice was thick with emotion.

"He said that he believed good friends will meet somewhere."

Dick Wellman closed his eyes and died.

* * *

They wrapped Dick's body in a blanket and buried the old mountain man deep in the Superstitions, on the crest of a high windy peak that overlooked the desert. Bodine said a quiet prayer in English while Sam chanted a death song in Cheyenne. They buried his saddle and his guns with him, then turned his horse loose to run wild and free. They would ship Dick's personal belongings to his ranch when they got to Phoenix.

Matt Bodine and Sam Two Wolves mounted up and rode away from the lonely gravesite. They did not look back.

They rode into Phoenix and put their horses up at a livery just off Jefferson Street. The main drag was a wide, muddy, and rutted street, filled with teamsters driving wagons pulled by mule teams, carrying freight out to the miners. Few of the stores had boardwalks; some didn't even have wooden floors inside, only hard-packed and swept dirt floors. They found a room at the hotel and stowed their gear, then went looking for a hot bath and clean clothes. Then they would sit down to a meal they didn't have to fix.

On the way to a cafe, clean-shaven and with the trail dust and fleas off them, the young men walked up and down both sides of the wide street, checking brands. They saw no Triple-V brands.

They didn't talk much, for the death of Dick Wellman had left a temporary void in their lives. Both had liked and respected the ornery old coot, and they missed him very much.

They ate slowly, enjoying the hot food and the apple pie. Over a cup of coffee, Sam finally broke the silence. "Dick would not have wanted us to feel this way."

"I know. I just didn't think I had become this fond of the old goat."

Sam chuckled. "He was ornery, wasn't he?"

Before Matt could reply to that, his eyes picked up three

men walking across the street, all of them wearing badges. "I think the law is looking for us, brother."

"Let them come on."

They came on, pushing open the cafe door and walking across the room and sitting down at a table. The sheriff waved away the counterman's offer of coffee and looked at Bodine. "You boys just ride in?"

Bodine met his eyes. "Yeah."

"From the Superstitions?"

"Yeah."

"Half a dozen men found dead up near a minin' camp. My deputy said it looked like a hell of a gunfight."

"About time one of your deputies got up there."

"What do you mean by that?" The sheriff's voice took on a hard edge.

"The miners told us they've been robbed for some time and the law wouldn't do anything about it."

"So you boys took the law into your own hands?"

"Nope."

"Well, damnit, somebody shot those men!"

"That's right. Somebody sure did. A man by the name of Dick Wellman."

"The old mountain man?"

"That's right."

The sheriff waited and watched with exasperation on his face as Bodine finished his pie and called for another cup of coffee.

"Well?" the sheriff demanded.

"Well, what?" Sam took it up.

"I don't need no lip from a breed, boy."

Sam stood up, his hand by the butt of his .44. Bodine stood up with him, and the three lawmen noted the twin Colts, tied down low. There was something about this young man—hell, about *both* of them—that triggered a silent scream of warning in the sheriff's brain.

"I don't fight my brother's battles for him, Sheriff. But I do stand beside him. Your remark was uncalled for. Now apologize."

"I'll be damned if I'll apologize to any goddamn Injun!"

"You'll be dead if you don't," Bodine spoke the words softly.

"Do you know who that is, Sheriff?" the counterman called from the kitchen.

"No. And I don't much give a damn!"

"That's Matt Bodine and Sam Two Wolves."

It was like letting the air out of a balloon: the sheriff and his two deputies seemed to deflate. The sheriff of Maricopa County, Arizona Territory, was no coward. He'd faced men across the barrel of a gun and brought in his share of hardcases, both alive and tied across a saddle. But he was no match for Matt Bodine and he knew it. To make matters worse, now he had two of the most famous gunslingers in the west in town. Smoke Jensen and Matt Bodine; and he knew from reports he'd read that Sam Two Wolves wasn't far behind his blood-brother in speed and accuracy.

"If you took any umbrage in my remarks, Sam," the sheriff chose his words carefully, "they won't be repeated again from me."

It wasn't much of an apology, but Sam accepted it. Both young men sat back down.

"Would you tell me what happened up yonder in the Superstitions?" the sheriff asked. "Either of you."

Bodine laid it out for the sheriff, taking it from the beginning.

The sheriff listened and finally nodded his head. "That's fair enough, I reckon. I'll write it up that way. You boys gonna be in town long?"

"We'll be in and out," Bodine told him.

"I won't stand for no trouble. I'm no fancy gunhandler,

boys. But I will arm me and my men with express guns and handle you that way. And that ain't a threat; it's a warnin'."

"I'm no trouble-hunter," Matt told him. "But I won't back away from it if it comes at me."

"That's fair enough. You got anything agin Smoke Jensen?"

"Never met the man in my life and I don't notch my guns."

"Didn't figure you did. You ain't got the reputation of a tinhorn." He cut his eyes to Sam. "Neither one of you."

When Matt or Sam did not reply, the sheriff asked, "You boys goin' to hunt them others who was in cahoots with Chappo?"

"Yes," Sam answered for both of them.

The sheriff sighed and fiddled with the salt shaker on the table. "Keep it out of town."

"We'll do our best."

"I can't ask for no more than that, I reckon. Not and get it granted," he added drily.

Bodine and Sam cut their eyes to a man riding a mean-looking stallion with the outline of a knife on the animal's left rump. The man tied up in front of a bank and slowly looked all around him. He was a big man, with massive shoulders and lean hips. He wore two guns, one of them butt-forward.

"Who is that?" Sam asked.

"That, boys," the sheriff said, "is Smoke Jensen."

Chapter 21

That was the only glimpse Matt and Sam saw of Smoke that day. They retired early and were in the saddle and riding out to look for Lake and Porter at first light. Jensen, they were told, was not much of a drinker and seldom visited the saloons in town, preferring to stay in his hotel room reading whenever he was away from home . . . unless somebody pushed him. So far, none of the hardcases in town had tried to brace the man.

"Where do we start?" Sam asked, as Phoenix faded behind them.

"We'll head north first. All the way up to Camp Verde. Then work our way back down through the Mazatzals. I got a hunch that Lake and Porter left this part of the country after they got wind of the shooting."

"Time we work our way back to the Mazatzals, they'll be snow in the high up."

"One extreme to the other," Matt summed up as much of the territory as he'd seen.

This was still Apache country, so the pair rode alert at all times. They made camp along the northern tip of the McDowell Mountains and the next morning headed out for Bloody Basin. From there on up to Camp Verde, some seventy-five miles as the crow flies, was pure virgin wilderness. There was one trading post on the East Verde River, just east of Turret Peak, so they'd been told in town, and the men intended to stop there for information. If they reached it at all.

The farther north they went, the more mountainous it became, with thick stands of timber. They passed through a transition zone; from cedars, junipers, and piñons, into chaparral brushlands. They did not see one living soul for four days, until riding into Camp Verde.

Neither one of them knew exactly what month it was, so they asked at the cafe over a hot meal.

"November, boys. Thanksgivin' ain't too far around the corner."

"Going to have turkey?" Bodine asked.

"Naw. Beans and beef and taters. Gonna be around?"

"I doubt it. You got any hardcases working this area? Some of them would be riding the brand Triple-V."

"I ain't seen no one ridin' that brand. They'd probably fight shy of Camp Verde; the Army bein' here an' all."

He wandered off when another customer hollered for some more coffee.

"We'll find them wherever there is gold," Sam said.

"And we don't really know that they went north. There's been gold strikes all over the state. Eat up and then let's go talk to the commanding officer at the Camp."

The colonel was not unfriendly, but neither was he bubbling over with excitement at seeing Matt Bodine. But he did give them a few minutes of his time.

"Make it fast, Bodine," he told him.

His overbearing attitude irritated Matt, but he held his temper in check. "We're looking for some outlaws. The group is headed by two men, Lake and Porter."

"I know who you're looking for, Bodine. I received a dispatch from Fort Bowie. And I don't approve of what you're doing."

"You disapprove of us killing Chappo?"

"That was a commendable act, of course. It's this vigilante business that I personally find abhorrent."

"They sold young kids into slavery, Colonel. They armed Chappo and his band in return for young girls. My God, man, I . . ."

"That will be quite enough, Bodine!" the colonel said sharply. "Those allegations were never proven."

"The Mexican government down in Sonora thought they were."

The colonel waved that aside.

"And the Mexican Army was a hell of a lot more cordial to us than you're being," Sam pointed out, reaching for his hat, for he knew with that remark, they were on their way out.

Standing outside the post, Bodine said, "You know what I think, brother?"

"I am afraid to ask. You might want to ride to Texas or some other Godforsaken land."

Bodine laughed at him. "No! I just now figured out why the Army is mad at us."

"Oh? Are you going to enlighten me?"

"We did what they couldn't do."

"And not just rescuing the kids, either."

"That's right. We killed Chappo. Found his hideout and killed him. Not just him, but a lot of his followers. That's why they're behaving like a bunch of spoiled children."

"Just some of the officers, me boys," a sergeant said, walking up to them. The Irish was thick in his speech. "Not the enlisted men, or really, most of the officers."

They introduced themselves and shook hands all around and the sergeant motioned them away from the HQ building.

"The men you're looking for moved west," he told them. "They're plannin' on robbin the miners who come into Ehren-berg for supplies. I got that from a U.S. Marshal."

"Where is Ehrenberg?"

"Right on the California line. The Colorado River is the dividin' point."

"Desert?"

"Like the fringes of hell, boys."

They headed out the next morning, crossing the Verde Valley and aiming for Horsethief Basin. They would cross Turkey Creek, cut south, and head for the mining camps around Snyder's Station, later to be renamed Bumble Bee. The sergeant said pickings for outlaws were real good around that area—big strike in there—and it might behoove them to try there.

They rode into town late one afternoon, dusty from the trail and wanting a bath and something to eat. They had planned to bathe in Turkey Creek, but it was just too damn cold!

As towns went, this one wasn't much, but it did offer a small hostelry and stable, a saloon, and a cafe. And the first thing both men noticed when they swung down from their saddles at the stable, was several horses wearing the Triple-V brand.

They looked at each other and smiled, both of them slipping the hammer thong from their Colts.

And that move did not escape the eyes of the boy who worked at the stable.

"They's bad ones in town," he said. "Over to the saloon. They brag about being part of the biggest outlaw gang in the territory. They got the marshal treed."

"Must not be much of a marshal," Bodine said.

"He ain't. But we ain't used to havin' much trouble in this town, neither. Mostly Old Weaver just handles the drunks and like."

"He's an old man?" Sam asked.

"Yes, sir. Got a bum leg from a minin' accident."

"Where is he?" Bodine asked.

"In his office. They told him if he came out they'd kill him."

"His office got a back door?"

"Yes, sir. Third door down yonderway." He pointed it out.

"Rub the horses down and give them some grain," Bodine told the boy. "And stay off the street."

"You fellows the law?"

"No," Sam told him.

The big-eyed boy stared at the men.

"How many town people are in the bar?"

"None, that I know of. Them hardcases just tooken it over and throwed what few people was in there out the door."

"When did all this happen?" Sam asked, knowing that under normal circumstances, nobody trees a western town, for the men would all be armed, and most would be veterans of the war between the states, or experienced Indian fighters, or ax-cavalry.

" 'Bout noon. They was a big strike over to the flats. Thataway," he pointed it out. "And most of the men pulled out yesterday."

"Have the outlaws bothered any women?" Bodine asked.

"No, sir. Not yet anyways. They ain't but ten or twelve in town noways."

"Stay in the barn," Bodine told him.

Sam and Bodine walked up behind the short street to the back door of the marshal's office. Bodine tapped lightly on the door.

"Go away!" the voice spoke from within.

"We're here to help," Sam told him. "We're coming in."

Sam gently pushed the door open and his eyes narrowed and his lips tightened at the first glimpse of the man. He had been badly beaten.

"Pistol-whipped," Bodine said, stepping inside.

Sam put water on the stove to heat while Bodine looked around the small, two-cell jail. "What happened, Marshal Weaver?"

"Marshal!" the man spat the word. "I ain't much of a marshal, now, am I?"

"You did all you could do against them," Sam said, bathing the man's face with warm water. He had been terribly beaten. "You're lucky they didn't kill you."

Bodine had taken two double-barreled, sawed-off shotguns from the gun rack and had loaded them, stuffing his pockets with shells. He handed a shotgun to Sam along with half a box of shells. "What happened, Marshal?"

"I heard 'em ride in and stable their horses. They was a loud talkin' bunch. Used a lot of bad language. Run all the women off the street that was out shoppin'. I recognized them from reports I got. I knew it was a stupid thing for me to do, but the people in this town pay me to enforce the law, so I tried to do just that. Them hardcases laughed at me and took my shotgun away. I ain't never been much good with a six-shooter so I don't even carry one. Then they just pistol-whipped me. No reason for it; they just done it. Then they throwed some old men out of the saloon and took over."

"How many of them?" Sam asked.

"Must be a dozen or more. I'd say eight of them are bad. The rest are young tinhorn punks. You know the type: hair all slicked back and wearing shiny six-shooters, tied down low."

"We know the type," Sam said. "We've been following this gang of scum for weeks."

"Who are you boys?" Weaver asked, holding a warm, wet rag to one side of his face.

"I'm Sam Two Wolves. That's Matt Bodine."

The marshal smiled grimly. "Heard of both of you. Give them rowdies hell, boys."

"We intend to give them hell, Marshal. We intend to send them there!"

Matt and Sam slipped in through the back door of the saloon, the express guns in their hands, the hammers jacked back. The marshal had loaded his own shells, and they were filled with bits of nails, rusty screws, and ball-bearings. At close range, the sawed-off shotguns would literally tear a man apart.

Bodine kicked open the door and he and Sam went in fast and low.

"Party's over, boys!" Bodine shouted.

"The hell it is!" a hardcase yelled, and grabbed for his gun.

Sam gave him one barrel and spread the man all over the front of the bar.

Every man in the place grabbed iron and Matt and Sam dived for whatever cover they could find as the smoky, beery air was filled with lead and death.

Bodine gave an outlaw a bad case of indigestion by blowing a hole in his belly just as Sam gave another the second barrel of his express gun.

"Goddamn you, Bodine!" a man yelled, just as he jumped through a window and hit the ground outside the barroom, running toward his horse tied to a hitchrail across the street.

Bodine felt the shock of a bullet hitting his leg and the leg buckled under him. As he was going down, he unloaded the second barrel into the face of a young punk. The face vanished as the head was torn from the torso. Bodine grabbed for his Colts as he hit the floor and rolled over on his stomach. Bodine eared back the hammers and let his guns bang.

As the door was kicked open, the barkeep had gone belly-down on the floor behind the bar and stayed there.

"Holy jumpin' Christ!" the barkeep hollered, trying to hug the floor a little closer. He couldn't; his buttons kept getting in the way.

Sam was knocked back against the bar, a bullet wound in his side. He fired his last round into the man who'd shot him and grabbed for the pistol he carried tucked behind his belt.

Bodine rose to his knees, a Colt in each hand, and began doing his part in clearing the barroom of all hostile living things.

Sam had staggered behind the bar, the empty shotgun in one hand, and reloaded all his guns, keeping the locations of the hardcases in his mind. He crawled to the other end, shoving the frightened barkeep out of the way, and stood up, firing at an overturned card table. The charge blew the table apart and killed the two gunnies who had been crouched behind its dubious protection. He jerked out a Colt, thumbing back the hammer, when he realized there was nothing left to shoot at.

He glanced at Bodine's bloody leg. "You hard hit?"

"I don't think so. Went through the fleshy part. Just hurts. You?"

"Caught one in the side. I don't think either of us will be doing much riding for a few days."

A gunslick moaned from his intense pain and Bodine and Matt limped over to where he lay. He'd been gutshot twice.

"You're not going to make it, pardner," Bodine said, kneeling down beside the man. "Why not go out with a clean slate?"

"Why don't you go to hell!" the man gasped out the words.

Bodine shrugged and rose painfully to his boots. A crowd had begun gathering outside the saloon, all of them peeping inside at the bloody carnage visible through the lingering gunsmoke.

By another badly shot-up outlaw, Sam said, "Lake and Porter . . . where are they?"

"Headin' for the California line," the man moaned. "By way of Wickenburg."

Matt had limped over to where he lay. The outlaw looked up at him. "You boys played hell with us. But I can't figure out why. We ain't done nothin' to you."

"We gave our word to an old man."

"Dick Wellman?"

"Yes."

"I knowed Chappo hadn't oughta tooken that little girl. Soon's I heard her grandpaw was Dick Wellman I knowed we was in trouble."

"Chappo's dead," Sam told. He watched the outlaw's eyes widen. "We killed him over in the crazy rocks and the army cut off his head and stuck it up on a pole."

The outlaw had been shot through and through, the slugs puncturing both lungs. Each breath was a painful wheeze and pink froth was gathering on his lips. "Letter in my saddle-bags from my Ma. Address on the envelope. Write her and tell her where I'm planted. But don't tell her I turned bad. I was her youngest and she had high hopes for me."

"We'll do it," Bodine told him. "We'll tell her you died an honorable death."

"Much obliged." The man closed his eyes and took his last ride.

Marshal Weaver pushed his way inside the saloon and whistled at the sight. "Lord have mercy! When you boys git on a rampage, you do it right, don't you?"

"You got a doctor in this town?" Sam asked.

"Got a feller that passes for one. When he's sober. I'll send for him. He's real good with horses and dogs."

Chapter 22

Their wounds were painful, but not serious, with Sam's wound requiring the most attention. The doctor, and he really was a doctor, gave them both a long lecture about people who live by the gun, charged them twenty dollars apiece, gave both of them a bottle of laudanum, and went off to get drunk.

"Don't you think twenty dollars is a bit high?" Sam asked.

"I don't know," his blood brother said, unable to pass up a good chance to stick the needle to Sam. "Unlike you, I've never been sick a day in my life."

Sam, speaking in Cheyenne, called Bodine some perfectly awful names.

The pull of the trail proved to be too strong for the restless young men. After two days of lounging about, they packed their gear, saddled up, and headed out, aiming for Wickenburg.

Wickenburg had been in existence for about fifteen years, and had good law officers. If Lake and Porter had stopped there, both Bodine and Sam had a hunch they wouldn't stay long and would behave themselves while in town.

The change in scenery was abrupt and dramatic. They left

timber and rode into the desert, riding between the hot springs to the south and Thoma Butte to the northwest. The Hiero-glyphic Mountains—misnamed when someone confused pet-roglyphs (Indian rock carvings) with hieroglyphics—were a mess to get through, the mountains filled with boulder-choked canyons, twisting passes, and a pronounced absence of water.

The weather had turned sour, with a cold north wind blowing and even hard bursts of sleet from time to time, so Matt and Sam were glad to see the mining town of Wickenburg emerge in the distance. They had been told back at the Station that Wickenburg got its name from a Prussian prospector, one Henry Wickenburg. Henry, so the story goes, started the gold rush into the area when he threw a rock at a stubborn mule only to have the rock crack open, full of gold. It is not known whether or not Henry hit the mule.

Matt and Sam went first to the marshal's office and laid their cards on the table to the town marshal and his deputy.

But the marshal shook his head after hearing them out. "You're wasting your time here, boys," he told them. "If this Lake and Porter came through here, they didn't stay long and didn't cause no trouble while they was in town. We got a couple of people chained to the tree, but they're locals."

"Chained to the tree?" Sam asked.

The marshal smiled. "We ain't got no jail, as you boys can see plain. But we do have a jail tree. Over yonder," he waved his hand, "on the corner of Tegner and Center streets. Good solid mesquite tree. We just chain them sentenced to do time to the tree. It ain't that bad. Their families can come bring them lunch on Sundays."

"What if it rains?" Bodine asked.

The marshal shrugged. "They get wet."

The marshal had warned them. "You're goin' to have about seventy miles of practically nothin,' boys. Nothin' but desert and Apaches, with no dependable water holes." He found a stub of a pencil and traced their route on a piece of paper.

"Right here, on the southern tip of the Granite Wash Mountains is a little two-bit town that ain't even got a name. But it has water. It's about sixty miles from here. There might be water here," he pointed, "and here. But don't count on it." He smiled. "Good luck."

"If hell is anything like this," Sam groused, looking around the desolation and grimacing, "I am changing my ways immediately."

"Going to become a man of the cloth, Sam?" Bodine asked with a smile.

"Let's don't take it that far. And speaking of far? . . ."

"We should be seeing that little town pretty soon."

At that, they reined up and dismounted, checking their guns, wiping them free of dust and loading them up full. There was a good chance some of the outlaw gang would be in the town. Both were reasonably sure the one man who had escaped the carnage back at the Station had rejoined his buddies-in-crime. If so, they would be alert and waiting on the brothers.

They rode on a few more miles in silence, only the clop of their horses' hooves and the dust to keep them company on the lonely trail.

They were in a land of saguaro and creosote bush, populated by coyotes, deer, bobcats, and Gambel's quail, along with rattlesnakes, kangaroo rats, and foxes. It was a strange place for the young men, seeing it for the first time. Hot during the day and cold at nights; but they had learned to enjoy the fragrance of a mesquite fire. Back at Wickenburg, the marshal had told them of summer in the desert country, when the flowers and plants bloom at night under the moon, and close up against the heat during the day.

South of them, according to the marshal, in the Kofa Mountains, were groves of palm trees. Sam and Bodine had looked at one another and offered no comment. Neither of them knew what a palm tree was.

Sam spotted the thin fingers of smoke, seeming to rise from the vastness without root. "That'll be it."

Their wounds had very nearly healed, the pure clean air of the country helping the healing along as much as the medicine. Neither of them were quite up to any fistfights; but they could handle a gun.

They reined up about five hundred yards from the no-name town and looked it over. Like the marshal had said, it wasn't much. From the crest of the rise, the men could see seven buildings—not counting the outhouses.

"The corral's full," Bodine pointed out.

A few of the horses wearing the Triple-V brand, both noted as they swung down from the saddle, handing the reins to a man with one gimp leg and a tobacco-stained beard.

"Treat them right," Bodine said. "They've had some hard traveling."

"Your name Bodine?"

"That's right."

"Figured it was. Bunch of hardcases over to the saloon waitin' on you."

"A set-up?" Bodine questioned.

The man spat in the dust. "Nope. They said for me to tell you that they want to talk. They've had enough of bein' chased all over the country."

"You believe that?" Bodine asked.

"Yep. You will, too, when you walk in the bar. Their guns is a-hangin' on pegs on the wall."

Bodine pushed open the batwings and stepped inside the bar, Sam right behind him. Not being very trusting types, neither had taken off their Colts. Guns on pegs notwithstanding, any or all of the men could be wearing a hideout gun.

Spurs jingling softly, they walked across the sawdust floor and to the bar.

The barkeep looked very nervous, and there was a quiver in his voice as he asked, "What'll it be, boys?"

They ordered and turned to face the crowd of hardcases, all looking at them.

As before, none of the known gunslingers was in the crowd, and neither was Porter. Bodine didn't know Lake, but he doubted the man was anywhere around.

"It's over, Bodine," a bearded man finally spoke. "Lake and Porter is out of the girl-tradin' business. So there ain't no more need for you to be follerin' us all over the damn country."

"It's a free country," Bodine said, after taking a sip of beer. "We'll ride wherever we please."

"Why?" another asked. "You ain't the law. You got no stake in nothin' we do. Why put your life on the line for nothin'?"

"It's like we told one of your buddies back up the line," Sam said. "While he was dying on a barroom floor. We made a promise to a friend."

"Dick Wellman?"

"Why do I get the feeling we've had this conversation before?" Bodine smiled at Sam. "Yeah. Dick Wellman."

"This is a fair warnin' to you, Bodine," the bearded man picked it up again. "We're ridin' out of here shortly. You follow us, and it's open season on your butts. Now let me tell you how it is: there ain't no dodgers out on any of us. Leastways not west of the Muddy. And that's what matters. So there ain't no reward money on us. In the eyes of the law—what law they is—you shoot us now, unarmed, and it's murder charges agin you."

"Get to the point," Bodine told him.

"You and that damn breed is hay-rassin' us by follerin' us all over the country, and a-pickin' fights with us. Now enough is enough. We're gonna get you off our back-trails one way or the other, and I think you get my drift."

"That all you got to say?"

"That's it, Bodine."

"Fine. Now you hear me. We're going to follow you until one of two things happen: you either get enough lead in us to put us in the ground, or you're all dead. Now that's all I got to say."

Two gunslicks stood up and walked to the pegs along the wall. "We're through, Bodine. I think you and that damn Injun is just crazy enough to keep on comin'. So we're headin' the other way."

They picked up their gunbelts but did not strap them on. They hung them over their shoulders and walked out of the saloon, heading toward the stable.

The bearded spokesman shook his head and stood up. "We're pullin' out now, Bodine. You been warned."

"And so have you," Bodine reminded them all. "Next time we meet, have your hands full of guns."

One by one the outlaws filed past the pegs, looped their gunbelts over their shoulders and walked out. None of them looked back.

When the last one was gone, the barkeep let out a long sigh. "Boys, I just aged ten years in the last five minutes. I would have bet my last dollar this place was gonna bust wide open."

"You got anything to eat here?" Bodine asked.

"Beef and boiled potatoes. Mex woman in the back's a right good cook."

They ordered another beer and some food and sat down at a table, letting the tension of riding across Apache country and then facing a room filled with gunslicks slowly ebb from them.

"Decision time, brother," Bodine said, rolling a cigarette.

"A promise is a promise, brother. I have never gone back on my word and neither have you."

"We'll be riding looking for one ambush after another," he reminded Sam.

"Yes."

The sounds of the hardcases leaving town came to them as the knot of riders walked their horses up the wide street. They were riding west, taking the stagecoach road toward Ehrenberg.

"It's confusing to them," Sam said, as the last of the hardcases rode west, out of town. "They are men totally without honor, so they cannot possibly comprehend what we are doing."

"And what are we doing?" Bodine softly posed the question, his eyes on his brother's face.

"Running away from a sight that has been branded into our brains."

"Are you saying it will be with us always?"

"It will fade as the years pass. Much more easily for you than for me, I'm afraid."

Bodine knew what he meant. For in the Rosebuds, Sam had not only seen his father die in the Custer fight, but with it, a way of life that both knew would never return. "When you're ready to go back to our homelands, brother, let me know."

"It will be a long time coming."

The bringing of the food put an end to conversation for a time, for in the West, eating was serious business. When the sharper edges of their appetite had been blunted, and they were working on their second pot of coffee, Matt broke the silence.

"I think we had best not follow the stage road to Ehrenberg. Let's cut north, between the Plomosa Mountains and the Granite Wash and come in that way."

Sam chewed reflectively for a moment. "You know anything about that country?"

"Just about as much as I know about women."

Sam shook his head, a mournful expression on his face. "If that's the case, we're lost before we start!"

Chapter 23

Possible sources of water had been pointed out to them by the barkeep just before they pulled out the following morning. And they were warned that there were still hostiles in the land they would be riding through. Not all the Indians had chosen to be herded onto the reservation next to the Colorado River.

The men ate a quiet and leisurely breakfast before leaving. If any of Lake and Porter's men were lying in ambush somewhere along the stagecoach road, Bodine and Sam wanted them to remain as uncomfortable as possible for as long as possible.

They left the no-name town and headed north.

At Cunningham Wash they cut west, riding through the dry emptiness of the Plomosa Mountains, Cactus Plain to the north. They rode with Winchesters across the saddle horn, always alert for trouble, from the Indians or outlaws. They saw no living beings, friendly or otherwise, as they came down the west side of the Dome Rock Mountains and picked up the stagecoach road about fifteen miles outside of Ehrenberg, following that on into town.

"Yeah, they was here," the marshal told the trail-weary men. "But they didn't cause no trouble. They was right nice and po-lite. Real gentlemen, all of 'em."

"Which way'd they go?"

"South, toward Yuma." The marshal fixed the pair with a hard eye. "You'd be the gunfighter, Bodine. And you'd be Sam Two Wolves, right?"

"That's right."

"They said you'd be along. Yuma's a tough town, boys; they ain't put up with no crap down there."

"We don't intend to start any."

"That's good. Right proud to hear that." His expression changed from hard to curious. "I overheard something from one of them hardcases. Didn't mean nothin' to me. Still don't. Does the *Virgin Princess* mean anything to you boys."

"Yes," Sam replied. "It's a slave ship."

"Is that right? Well, this hardcase was whispering something about meeting up with it and somebody named Morgan."

They chatted for a few more minutes, then thanked the marshal and headed for a nearby saloon. They didn't have to look far; two or three steps in any direction would have taken them through batwings.

Over a beer and food in the coolness of the adobe structure, the men talked in low tones.

"You pegged it right when you said they had no honor," Bodine said. "All that talk back at that no-name town was just that: talk. They knew all along they were back in the slaving business. You heard what the marshal said about there being only a dozen of them but they bought supplies enough for a hundred men and wagons and mules."

"Yes. And as they use up the supplies, they'll fill that space with stolen children . . . girls. But they're not going to find many girls in this area, brother."

"No. I think that 'going to Yuma' business was a lot of crap."

Sam held up a hand. "Maybe not. Maybe they do plan on going to Yuma, pretending to be hauling freight, and then cutting across into California, staying close to the Mexican border, raiding small farms and ranches as they go. How far across to the ocean is it?"

Matt shrugged. "Your guess is as good as mine, brother."

They asked the barkeep.

"Oh, 'bout a hundred an' fifty miles, I reckon. I ain't never been there personal."

"Do we check out Yuma?"

"We'll leave in the morning."

As they pulled out before dawn, both were thinking that if Yuma was any worse than Ehrenberg it was a hell-hole. They were leaving behind them a town where all water had to be hauled from the muddy Colorado; where four to five inches of dust lay in the streets, and where flies and other insects swarmed everywhere, biting and stinging and covering food almost as soon as it hit the table. Not only was it a nuisance, it was a health hazard.

They followed the river south and at a tiny four building town about twenty-five miles south of Ehrenberg, they found their suspicions to be reality.

"I sure did see them wagons," the barkeep said, wiping off the bar with a dirty rag. "It was an odd sight, too."

"Why?" Sam asked.

"All them sleepin' kids. Well, I say all of them. 'Bout half a dozen of them in one wagon. I 'spect the other wagons had kids in them, too."

"Sleeping? All of them?"

"Ever' last one of them. All girls, too. I don't think I was 'posed to see 'em, neither. Made one of them hard-lookin' hombres mad. Then he kinda forced a grin and said they was totin' them kids to an orphanage as soon as they dumped the supplies in Yuma. I didn't think no more about it 'til you fellers asked."

"Did they buy anything in town?"

"Let me think. Yeah. Yeah, they did. They bought all the laudanum Riley had over to the general store."

"Bastards!" Bodine spat the word. "They're keeping those girls drugged during the day and probably covered with a tarp so they can't be seen."

"But where did they get them?"

"They probably had them all along; all the time were making that noble speech to us. Probably been stealing them as they rode west."

"Well, there are the wheel marks. We were right in thinking we were following the right tracks."

"And now? . . ."

"We know the girls are all right. Unhappy and scared, but unhurt. We go busting up in there, and some of them are sure to get hurt in the gunfire. Let's wait and see what they do next."

They followed the tracks south, staying well back, as the wagon train followed the meandering route of the Colorado. Both felt the wagons would not enter Yuma, and several days later, their theory proved to be correct. About ten miles north of the town, the wagons pulled over and the men made camp. The two had to lay back for cover, but using field glasses, they could see through the distance as the outlaw size was strengthened by the arrival of a dozen riders, coming up from the south.

And they brought with them another group of girls. Even from their distant vantage point, both men could see that the girls appeared drugged by the way they moved.

"Now what?" Sam asked in a whisper, even though they were hundreds of yards away and a shout could not be heard from their location.

"Circle around and find the law in Yuma?" Bodine returned the softly-spoken words, then added, "Why are we whispering?"

"You can bet they've got papers of some sort," Sam said. "After what we did to them on the border, they'll be doubly cautious."

"And they'll probably have men in town watching the sheriff's office."

"Right. So that leaves? . . ."

"Us," Bodine finished it.

The wagons remained in place for another day. On the second day they were joined by other wagons and more out-riders, bringing the force to about fifty men and twenty wagons.

"Figure three or four girls to a wagon," Bodine said, "and that comes out to between sixty and eighty girls."

Sam pointed to the south. Four riders were approaching the encampment. Lifting the field glasses, he picked out the badges pinned to the shirts of the riders. "Lawmen," he said, handing the glasses to Bodine.

"Now we'll see how well they've prepared," Bodine muttered.

He watched as papers were presented to the lawmen, the papers inspected, the tarps pulled back, and the girls looked at.

"Probably telling the deputies that it's easier on the girls to keep them sleepy," Sam said. "Orphans aren't given much of a break in your society."

Bodine could not argue the point. His blood-brother was right.

Apparently satisfied that everything was on the up and up, the lawmen shook hands and rode away, back toward the south.

"Did you see any money change hands?" Sam asked.

"No. I don't think they're trying to buy anyone off. Those papers they've got are doing the trick. They finally got smart and had some documents forged. Brother, I've got a feeling that we're looking at one tree in a big forest—if you know what I mean."

"Yes. I've been thinking about that. Say they're getting a thousand dollars a head for the girls. And say there are seventy-five girls down there. That's seventy-five thousand dollars split among fifty or sixty men. It wouldn't be worth their while. So I would have to conclude there are more girls either on the way, or being held prisoner close to the sea."

"I pick the latter."

"Yes. That would be the logical choice." He smiled; it was too good to pass up. "You're improving, Bodine. No telling what other great strides you'll make over the years."

Bodine switched to Cheyenne and told his brother how closely he resembled a toad.

Bodine headed south that day, riding for the Mexican border, leaving Sam to watch and to follow if the wagon train pulled out. He'd catch up with him if that was the case.

He did not stop in Yuma, instead riding for the border as hard as he dared push his horse. It was a hard ride for both rider and horse. At the border, he found a cantina and relaxed over strong Mexican beer, making friends with several of the men in the bar. After a time, he asked if any of them was acquainted with a Major Luis de Carrillo?

Their faces brightened. They all knew the major, and all stated that he was a very honorable man. Why did Bodine ask?

Matt told them about Porter and Lake and how he and Sam and Wellman and Laurie had rescued the children from the old fort.

They applauded the deed and their bravery and lifted their glasses in a toast. Then Matt told them about the wagon train north of the border.

They were horrified, for most Mexicans revere their children.

"How can we help?" they asked.

"Do you think you could find Major Carrillo?"

They could. The major and his men were in this part of Sonora now, helping to rid the country of outlaws and pistoleros. The major was no more than a day's ride away.

Matt requested pen and paper and wrote out what was taking place and where he felt the wagon train was heading. He requested that the major and his men pace the wagon train on the Mexican side of the border, while he, Bodine, would ride back to where he had last seen the wagons and rejoin Sam.

A slim vaquero folded the paper and put it in a pouch. "I will find the major, Matt Bodine. God go with you and your brother on your journey to save those poor children."

Matt traded horses in the town, getting a fine heavily muscled steeldust gelding that was built for traveling the rough country and was chomping at the bit, ready to go. Diablo was the animal's name, and he liked Bodine, the smiling vaquero said.

"How can you tell?" Matt asked.

"Because you would have not have been able to get close to him if he didn't. He is better than a dog at keeping watch while you rest. He will kill any person who approaches you. *Vaya con dios*, Matt Bodine."

* * *

Sam had left Indian sign for Bodine, showing him when the wagons had pulled out and in what direction. They had crossed the river and headed into California. They had been gone for three days.

Bodine figured he could overtake them in a day and a half, for the wagons would be traveling at a much slower pace than a mounted rider.

He rode through a land virtually without water, following the tracks of the wagons and the hoofprints of Sam's horses, which he knew well. The first couple of days out were the roughest, traveling on the southern edge of the Imperial Desert, and cutting south toward the Mexican border.

At the southernmost tip of East Mesa, Bodine caught up with Sam just at dusk.

"Any changes?" Bodine asked.

"None. But they know where the border is and they're staying very close to it. You find Major Carrillo?"

"I sent him word. He shouldn't be far behind us. I asked him to stay on his side of the border and when the time comes, we'll push the wagon train into his territory."

Sam arched one eyebrow. "There are two of us and about sixty of them. How do you propose to do that?"

Bodine grinned. "I don't have the vaguest idea, brother."

Chapter 24

Since following the wagons was a slow and tedious task, Sam had been stopping often along the way, making conversation with anyone who would talk to him and had something of value to share.

"There are water holes other than those known by Porter and Lake," he told Bodine. "And there are little towns all along the route. Towns that the slavers will not enter for fear of being exposed." He smiled. "But we can."

"Indians?"

"Many tribes but not many Indians. Cuyapaipe, Manzanita, La Postas, Viejas, Campo, Los Coyotes . . . half a dozen other tribes. They present little danger now."

"Back at the cantina, they told me about a town right on the border. Nobody really knows which side of the border it's on. Major Carrillo is supposed to meet us there if at all possible."

"Does it have a name?"

Bodine shrugged and drank the last of his coffee. "I don't think so. It's just a town. We ought to come up on it tomorrow."

* * *

Bodine spotted the major and a few of his men, sitting on benches in front of a cantina. They were all dressed in civilian clothes.

After a nod from the major, Bodine and Sam tied up at the hitchrail and followed the man into the coolness of the cantina. Carrillo's men remained outside, to keep watch.

Over beans and tortillas and beer, the men relaxed and talked.

"I have put people in place on your side of the border," Carrillo said. "All the way to the Gulf of Santa Catalina. I suspect the plans are that Captain Morgan will lay off-shore and the girls will be taken to the ship by longboat."

"How many men do you have, Luis?" Bodine asked.

"Sixty. They are all seasoned fighters."

"Can we expect any help from the Army on our side of the line?"

"That I cannot say for sure. But I must warn you that my first thoughts would be no. Emphatically so. I have had people busy with the *telegrafo*—on both sides of the border— and the news they received is that the papers of Porter and Lake are proper, legal, and in order. It seems that Lake has a judge under his thumb, so to speak, and the judge drew up these papers. And there is this to consider: at the present time, relations between our countries is somewhat strained. I would think that if anything is to be done, we alone will have to do it."

"I hate politicians," Sam said bluntly.

Luis laughed softly. "They are the same worldwide, I think. They are . . . what do the *Norteamericanos* call it? Yes. A necessary evil."

They all agreed on that, Bodine saying, "And of course you and your men are not allowed to cross the border, right, Major?"

"Oh, heavens no!" Luis said with a quiet laugh. "We would never do that. Anymore than your soldiers cross our borders searching for Apaches and Comancheros."

The three of them laughed at that, all knowing the cavalry and various lawmen crossed into Mexico routinely and with arrogance.

"Well, then," Matt said, "we'll just have to make sure the wagons somehow get into Mexico."

"The two of you?" Luis replied, arching one eyebrow. "I would be most interested in hearing your plan."

"He doesn't have one," Sam said. "And neither do I. We'll just charge headlong into the fray and do our best to tilt the windmill south . . . so to speak."

The major studied Sam for a quiet moment. "You speak as quite an educated man, Sam. Yet, like Bodine, you have the reputation of a gunfighter. I find that most interesting. And yes, I have made discreet inquiries into the backgrounds of both of you."

"My mother's deathbed wish was that I would be educated at a university back east. I stood it for as long as I could before returning home to my father and the Cheyennes."

Luis shifted his eyes to Bodine. "And you have extensive land holdings in Wyoming—both of you. You are both moderately wealthy men. And yet you drift, living by the gun and staying on the thin line of danger. We must sit and talk at length someday; discussing things of a philosophical nature. I think the talks would be most enlightening."

"For whom?" Sam questioned.

Luis laughed. "Good question."

Major Carrillo stayed south of the border, while Matt and Sam returned to the American side, tracking the westward progress of the slave wagons. Carrillo and his men paced the wagons, never staying more than five miles away from the border.

Luis had given Bodine a map of southern California and Matt had studied it carefully.

"The stagecoach road veers north at Tecate," he said. "I can't believe they'll take that route. I'm going to take a chance, Sam, and go on ahead. I think they have a route already checked out, running right along the border. About halfway between Tecate and Tijuana, I'm going to throw up a detour and see if I can force the wagons across the border; or close enough so that it won't matter to Luis and his men. I don't know how I'm going to do it; I'll just have to play it by ear."

"You be careful, brother."

"That's my middle name," Bodine said with a laugh as Sam rolled his eyes heavenward.

Bodine cut south, crossing the border and linking up with Major Carrillo. He told Luis of his plan.

"It might work," the major agreed. "I will send two of my men with you. Benito has traveled extensively in this part of the country and thinks he knows what route the scum are taking. Vasco is a crack shot. They are both good men to have at one's side. Go with God, my friends, and remember that the lives of many innocent children are in our hands."

Around the small fire that night, just north of the border, Benito drew a map in the sand. "They will have to water here," he said, pointing at a spot. "For there is nothing between there and Tijuana. At least not enough to sustain as many people and animals as they have. They will have to fill many barrels of water at that spot, and doing that will certainly cut down the travel time of each day. I am absolutely certain they are taking this old road that runs along the border. It is passable for wagons, but just barely. A wash cuts through here," he said, pointing, "and it is there I believe we can make them cut south into Mexico. We will have to work very hard and very quickly to block this route, and then cleverly disguise what we have done to make it appear it was nature's work and not the work of men."

"Will doing this put them into Mexico?" Bodine asked.

Benito flashed a dazzling smile, but his eyes were killing cold. "Close enough," he said. "We won't quibble over a few miles."

Major Carrillo and his men spread out and made camp within gunshot sound of the wash while Bodine and the two Mexican soldiers worked feverishly to throw up a natural-looking blockade of the narrow, twisting old road.

Carrillo had sent one of his men riding to intercept Sam and bring him to the ambush site. Sam rode into the major's main camp, quickly ate a hot meal, then rode north to join his bloodbrother.

The slave wagons stopped and made camp less than five miles from the ambush site.

"Two men rode into camp last night," Sam told Bodine. "They didn't stay long. One of them was Porter."

"And it would be a safe bet that the other was Lake," Bodine replied.

"Yes. When they left, they headed toward the stagecoach road that runs between Tecate and San Diego."

Bodine swore softly. He had hoped the elusive pair of outlaw-slavers would stay with the wagons and be caught up in the killing fire of the ambush.

"It'll never end until we put those two out of business," he told Sam.

"This is truth."

"Is this going to be our destiny?" Bodine asked. "Chasing after those two scum?"

"It would appear to be. Either those two are exceptionally clever or they are the world's greatest cowards," Sam remarked.

Vasco looked across the coals of the dying fire. "There is nothing so dangerous as a coward one has pushed into a corner," he told them. "As a boy, I fought another boy in my village. I whipped him and he ran. I made the big mistake of chasing after him and an even worst mistake of catching him. That was one of the worst beatings I ever received. The boy changed before my eyes, fighting with the ferocity of a mountain lion. I learned a valuable lesson that day."

"Lake is no coward," Benito said, pouring them all the last of the coffee. "I do not know this other person, but I have heard of Lake. He is a . . . how do you say it? A *mercenario*. A soldier for hire. He has been a member of many armies and is a skilled warrior. This is what I have heard from several people. His code is that of, he who fights and runs away, lives to fight another day. I think this Lake person is a very dangerous man. Not one to be taken lightly."

"Like the Apache," Vasco said. "And no one with any sense would call the Apache cowards."

"Is there anything else you know about him?" Bodine asked. "Either of you?"

Both Mexican soldiers shrugged. Vasco said, "I have heard that Lake is not his real name. I have also heard that he fought as a *mercenario* in the French army. I have heard that he is a very educated man. And that he was a gunfighter in Texas before going overseas. How much of what I have heard is truth I do not know and cannot say."

Benito shook his head in agreement. "That is what I have heard, too. And that he is a very elusive man, who can change his appearance by disguise. But any man who steals children to sell into prostitution is filth. Beyond any religious redemption. Shooting this snake would be much too easy a way out for him. He should be publicly flogged and then hanged, to dangle at the end of a rope—very slowly. And then left there to rot."

All agreed that would indeed be a very suitable punishment for the outlaw Lake, and for the men who rode with him and for him.

"So if this Lake is not with the wagons come tomorrow," Vasco asked, as he hand-rolled a cigarette, "you will continue your pursuit of him?"

"Yes," the bloodbrothers replied quickly, and as one voice. Sam added, "If the law won't touch him, who does that leave?"

"I think this Lake person might have some connections in very high places," Benito said. "He would have to have some sort of protection in order to travel across two states with wagons filled with stolen children."

"He will not be with the wagons tomorrow," Vasco stated flatly. "Nor will his *compadre* in crime. They are too smart to be trapped like this. But be careful of chasing them into San Diego," he warned. "San Diego is no place for open gunfights. They do not tolerate it there. It is a very old and settled town; more than a hundred years old. Actually settled more than two hundred and fifty years ago by a man named Cabrillo. They have laws that are strictly enforced. That is probably why Lake has made the town his base."

"He'll have to leave his hidey-hole sooner or later," Bodine said.

Benito grinned. "But be aware that men such as Lake are like the rabbit, my friend. He will surely have more than one hole from which to run."

"And there is always the sea," Vasco added. "And the docks of San Diego are not a friendly place. I know; I have been there. It is a dangerous place where many men have been knocked on the head and kidnapped, taken to sea as no more than slaves. More often than not, they are never heard of again."

"Have either of you ever seen the ocean?"

Bodine and Sam shook their heads.

"You should. It will take your breath from you. Truly one of God's greatest creations."

"But dangerous," Benito said. "Filled with huge fish that can swallow a man whole, and creatures with many arms that can crush a man."

"Octopuses," Bodine said.

"Octopi!" Sam corrected.

"There's more than one of them, ain't they?" Bodine said.

Sam sighed.

"Octopuses," Bodine insisted.

Sam rolled up in his blankets and went to sleep.

Chapter 25

Major Carrillo and his force moved into position several hours before daylight. As quietly as possible he positioned his men on both sides of the ravine the wagons would be forced to use once they hit the blocked road.

Then they waited in the cold hours before dawn.

Once the children were in safe hands, Major Carrillo and his men would transport the girls back to Tecate and turn them over to the Catholic sisters at a local convent and school. The Mexican and American governments would then work out the politics of returning the kids to their families.

"God help the kids waiting for those bumble-bee brained politicians on both sides of the border to act," Sam said disgustedly.

Carrillo had laughed softly. "If we all dislike and distrust politicians so much—as we all seem to—why then, do we have them?"

"I don't like rattlesnakes either," Vasco said with a grin. "But we have them, no?"

"Are you equating a politician with a rattlesnake, Vasco?" Carrillo asked.

"Don't they both possess some of the same qualities?"

No one among them could argue that.

Bodine and Sam and Luis had agreed that they would not give the slavers a chance to surrender. Giving them even a split second's chance might endanger some of the girls. So the first volley was going to have to empty wagon seats and saddles. After that, if any wanted to surrender, they would be taken into Mexico for trial.

"Are we in Mexico?" Sam asked.

"For all intents and purposes, yes," Carrillo said, chewing on the stub of a thin cigar.

"And if they're found guilty?"

"They will be put to work in labor camps. There is only one way they will return to the United States." He spat on the ground. "In a box!"

At first light, the men heard the wagons coming. They heard the scout call for a halt and for the wagon master to come forward.

The soldiers hugged the ground as the scout left the old road and followed the ravine for a time. He rode through the wash and then back again, stopping right in front of Sam. "All right!" he shouted. "We can get through here. Bring those wagons around. I want to get to San Diego and find me a hot tub and a hotter woman."

What he got was a bullet through the head as the wagons came into position and the men on the ridges opened up with a deadly hail of rifle fire.

Half of the slavers were knocked out of saddles and off wagon boxes during the first volley. Ten of Luis's men were hidden near the mouth of the wash and at the opening. They swung around and sealed the slavers in, all of the men being very careful to keep the lead out of the wagon beds.

It was a roaring, shattering, and bloody ninety seconds. The only casualty among Carrillo's men was when a cartridge misfired and a soldier got a cut on the side of his face.

It was a slaughter among the slavers.

Twelve survived the ambush and three of those were so badly wounded they did not have long to live. Nine badly shaken and frightened slavers surrendered.

Bodine and Sam walked down to the rocky wash floor and stared at the sullen outlaws with their hands in the air. Carrillo and a few of his men were seeing to the needs of the children.

"Bodine!" a slaver said, disgust in his voice.

"In person," Bodine said with a smile, punching out empties and reloading his Colts. "I told you boys back at the barroom to give it up."

"What happens now?" one asked.

"You'll be taken to Mexico for trial," Sam told him, enjoying the look on the men's faces at his words. Mexican justice was harsh.

"But this ain't Mexico!" an outlaw screamed.

"Really?" Sam asked. "I think you're lost is all."

The man cussed him.

"Lake and Porter?" Bodine said. "Where are they?"

The slaver made a very obscene suggestion.

Bodine shrugged and walked away, joining Major Carrillo by a wagon. "The girls?"

"They have not been molested . . . as far as I can tell. Don't worry, Matt; the sisters will take good care of them and they'll be reunited with their families just as quickly as possible. I will break this scum and find where the other girls are being held. I promise you that." He looked at the slavers. "I do not think they will hold up well to pain."

"We'll ride now, Major," Bodine told him. "These men probably know where the girls are being held. But I doubt if they know the whereabouts of Lake and Porter."

"Nor do I," Carrillo agreed. "Lake is a very cautious man. However, if I do learn something from these . . ." He cut his eyes to the outlaws. ". . . scum, where can you be reached?"

"I honestly don't know. We'll try San Diego first. And hang around there for a few days. But I think once the news of this reaches Lake and Porter, they'll leave California and head for another spot."

"That is my thought, as well." The major smiled and stuck out his hand just as Sam walked up. He shook hands all the way around and said, *"Vaya con dios, amigos*—and good hunting."

They rode into San Diego, two trail-weary and dusty men. In the few days since the wagon train was ambushed and the girls rescued, the news had spread like raging wildfire all over the nation, the story being headlined in every newspaper, and the telegraph wires were fairly humming with the rescue.

It was still on the front page of the San Diego paper when the men walked into the hotel lobby. With Matt Bodine and Sam Two Wolves mentioned several times. And the law was hunting Lake and Porter.

The desk clerk got so rattled when he saw who his guests were he started stuttering, turned over the ink well, and dropped the room keys several times.

They left suits to be cleaned and ironed and went to their rooms to wash up; water was being heated for the tubs at the end of the hall. They set their boots out to be blacked.

When the young men emerged, all decked out in suits and white shirts and string ties, the sheriff met them in the lobby. He was not wearing a very friendly expression on his tanned face.

"We'll talk, boys," he said, pointing to the hotel restaurant.

The sheriff allowed the men to order food and coffee before he began. When he began, he made his position clear and straight to the point.

"Some people are callin' you boys heroes, and maybe you are, but to my mind you're both trouble-hunters. I'll not have it in this town. Lake and Porter were here. They pulled out when the news of the ambush hit the streets. And you two are going to pull out in the morning.

Bodine got his back up at that. He met the sheriff's hard eyes and said, "And if we don't? . . ."

"I can put together a hundred men in the time it takes you to pull on your boots. Look out that there window, boys." He cut his eyes.

Matt and Sam could see at least five deputies spread out, on their side of the street and on the boardwalk across the street. They were all carrying rifles.

Matt and Sam got the point, Sam asking, "What have we done to warrant this, Sheriff?"

"Nothing," the sheriff was honest in his reply. "But I'd do the same thing if I was lookin' at Bat Masterson, the Earp boys, or any other gunslinger."

"We've never hired our guns, Sheriff," Bodine said.

"I believe that, too. But you got the reputation. Now listen to me, boys: I got half a dozen young would-be gunslicks in this town just a latherin' at the mouth for a try at either one of you. I'll not have no shootin' on these streets. This is a respectable town and gettin' more so ever' day. I intend to keep it that way."

"Are we confined to this hotel?" Sam asked.

The sheriff sighed. "No," he finally said. "I ain't got the right to do that. And I ain't got the right to tell you boys you can't wear your iron when you leave here for a drink or whatever. That'd be hangin' a death sentence on the both of you. I just want you gone from here come first light. And I truly wish to hell you'd never have showed up." He shoved back his chair and walked out of the hotel dining room.

"I have taken a very sudden dislike for this town," Sam said.

"As have I, brother. We'll pull out before dawn and ride north, up the coast. I intend to see the ocean and no one is going to stop me from doing that."

They ate slowly, enjoying the food and the coffee— although the coffee was a tad on the weak side. They bought cigars and stepped outside to smoke them in the coolness of fading afternoon.

The sheriff and two deputies sat across the street, watching them.

"Isn't it wonderful to be the center of so much attention?" Sam said, a hard edge of sarcasm to the words.

"I could do without it," Matt replied, leaning up against an awning post.

They smoked in silence for a few moments, both of them aware that a crowd was gathering across the street and the sheriff had gotten out of his chair, a very worried look on his face.

"Something's up," Sam said. "And I don't think it's the mayor to present us with a civic award."

"Here it comes," Bodine said, cutting his eyes up the wide street.

Three young men, in their early twenties, and all wearing two guns tied down low were swaggering down the street.

"Damnit!" Sam whispered.

"You boys get on back home!" the sheriff hollered to the young men.

"You just stand aside, Sheriff," one of the young men returned the shout. "This ain't none of your affair."

"By God, I can make it my affair!"

"Then you're likely to get caught up in the crossfire," he was warned. "We're callin' out Bodine and that half-breed."

"Don't be fools, boys!" the sheriff yelled, an urgent note in his voice. "We'll be buryin' you all come tomorrow."

They sneered at that and came swaggering on, their hands close to the butts of their guns.

"Idiots," Sam muttered, slipping the hammer thong from his Colt. Bodine had already done so.

"Step out in the street, gunfighters!" the third young man found his voice.

"We've got no grievance with any of you," Bodine called. "There is no need for this."

The sheriff was watching the pair closely. His face was unreadable.

"What's the matter, gunfighter?" a young man yelled. "You afraid of us?"

"You know better than that," Bodine's voice was calm. "But this doesn't make any sense. We've done you no harm."

"I'm the Santa Ana Kid!" he called.

"Good Lord," Sam whispered. "A would-be tough trying to make a reputation."

"Glad to meet you," Bodine said. "How about a drink?"

The trio stopped in the street. "No time for that," the Kid called. "We'll have all the drinks in the world for free after we kill you."

Bodine looked at the sheriff. The sheriff shrugged his shoulders.

"You won't kill either of us, boy," Bodine told the young man. "Now go on home before hard words are said that you can't back away from."

"I ain't never lost a gunfight in my life!" the Kid screamed the words.

The crowd was silent, watching.

"Have you ever had one?" Sam asked, his voice low but carrying to the trio.

"You damn right! I've had plenty of fights. I got four notches on my guns."

Nobody but a tinhorn cuts kill-notches in their gun grips.

"Yeah!" another would-be tough yelled. "How many notches have you got, Bodine?"

"Boy," the sheriff called, "if Bodine notched his guns, he wouldn't have any grips left on them."

"Shut up! You stay out of this. I got a right to call out a gunfighter."

Only a half-truth. The laws were changing in the West, but very slowly. The sheriff knew that if he tried to intervene, wild shots would be fired, and someone in the crowd was sure to get hit, for the crowd had swelled to several hundred, lining both sides of the wide street. The sheriff was caught between that rock and a hard place. He exhaled slowly and made up his mind. He would let the men settle it . . . he already knew what the outcome would be. He silently cursed the moment that Matt Bodine and Sam Two Wolves rode into town, all the while knowing that this was not their fault. They had provoked nothing; had caused no trouble.

"I think they're both yellow!" one young man sneered the words.

"Yeah, Red," the Kid said. "It sure seems that way to me, too. Ain't that the way you see it, Sandy?"

"Yellow dogs," the third young man agreed.

The Santa Ana Kid, Red, and Sandy spread out in the street.

"What's your problem, you greasy damn half breed?" the Kid yelled at Sam. "You're like all Injuns: not only do you stink, you're yellow."

Sam's dark eyes were flint hard, his face expressionless.

Then the Kid stepped into his coffin. "Come on, Bodine, Sam Yellow-Coyote, you sons of bitches!"

Red and Sandy laughed at that.

The sheriff did not laugh. He knew it was over. No man could be expected to take that slur.

Bodine and Sam brushed back their suit coats and stepped off the boardwalk.

Chapter 26

There had been the faint sound of murmurings and whisperings coming from the crowd. Now there was only a deadly silence as they watched the men step down from the boardwalk and slowly walk to the center of the street, turning to face the three young would-be gunhandlers.

"There is still time for you all to walk away," Sam told the trio. "Retract that slur against our mothers and we'll call it even."

The sheriff nodded his head in approval. Bodine and Sam were giving the young men every opportunity to back away with some dignity. Much more so than other gunslicks he'd seen in his time.

Take the offer, boys! he silently urged the trio. Take it and walk away or tomorrow I'll be listening to your weeping mothers as we bury all three of you.

But his silent plea was ignored, as he knew it would be.

"I think they're afraid of us, boys!" the Kid yelled, a wide grin on his face. "I tell you what, Bodine: you beg some and we'll let you live."

"Fools," Sam muttered. "Cocky fools."

"Maybe the Injun could do a war dance for us," Red suggested. "That'd be fun to see, wouldn't it? Dance for us, Breed!"

But Sam and Bodine had taken enough from these loud-mouthed punks. The sheriff tensed as Bodine said, "Shut your damn flapping mouths and make your play!"

"You ready, Bodine?" the Santa Ana Kid yelled, his voice suddenly high-pitched. The faces of his friends were drawn and pale.

"I've been ready, Kid."

"Then die, damn you!"

The trio dragged iron.

Bodine's hands were suddenly filled with roaring Colts. His draw had been as lightning-quick as a striking rattlesnake.

And ten times as deadly.

Sam's right hand was filled almost as quickly, the Colt roaring and bucking in his hand.

The Santa Ana Kid was the first one down, two bullet holes in the center of his belly, several inches above his belt buckle, one just above the other. The Kid was down in the street, his guns still in leather.

Sandy was on his knees, screaming in pain, both hands clutching his shattered belly from the twin .44 slugs from Sam's Colt.

Red was lying on his back in the dust. He had taken two .44 slugs in his face. One going in at nose level, the other two inches above that, in the center of his forehead. His fancy guns lay beside his body, unfired.

"Help me, Mommy!" the Santa Ana Kid cried out. "It hurts!"

Bodine and Sam were punching out empties, reloading. Their faces were impassive.

Several kids ran out into the street, to snatch up the empty brass for souvenirs.

"I never even seen Bodine draw," came the whisper from

the crowd. "And the breed is nearabouts as fast. I never seen nothin' like it."

"Oh, God, Mommy!" The Santa Ana Kid screamed. "Please help me. I can't stand the pain."

Bodine holstered his guns.

"Get him to a doctor," the sheriff said. "And call the undertaker for Red."

Bodine and Sam wheeled about in the street and returned to the boardwalk in front of the hotel and sat down, relighting their cigars.

The sheriff looked down as a piece of paper was pressed into his hand.

"Telegram for Matt Bodine," the station operator said. "It just come in. I missed the shootin' because of the damn thing."

"Deliver it," the sheriff said.

"*You* deliver it!"

The sheriff walked across the wide street, past the still-hollering Santa Ana Kid and the moaning Sandy. He glanced at the young man. Sandy, he guessed accurately, would be dead before morning. And so would the Kid, he figured. Anytime a man goes up against the house, he silently wrote the would-be toughs' epitaphs, he's bucking bad odds.

"This just came in for you, Bodine." He held out the telegram. "For whatever it's worth, boys, you tried to talk them out of it. I'll give you both that much. But I still want you gone in the morning."

Bodine took the telegram without any comment and opened it.

GIRLS SAFE. FOUND THEM OUTSIDE TIJUANA. MORGAN GOT AWAY. BELIEVED HE JOINED LAKE AND PORTER SOMEWHERE IN SOUTHERN CALIFORNIA. GOOD HUNTING.

It was signed Luis de Carrillo.

"We'll be gone at first light," Bodine said, handing the telegram to Sam.

* * *

They rode out of San Diego before dawn, heading north. The sheriff was standing in front of his office, watching them leave. He lifted a hand in farewell and the young men returned the salute.

The sheriff walked back into his office. He had three funerals to attend that day.

Sam and Bodine rode about five miles outside of town and found a creek. There they made camp and cooked breakfast. They would stay there for a couple of days, giving their horses the rest they had planned on them having in San Diego. They both had put the gunfight out of their minds. They hadn't started it, so it wasn't their fault. In the West, if a boy strapped on a gun, he became a man, and that was that.

When they left the camp, they rode for a day and then turned west, toward the ocean. When they came upon it, it was as Vasco had said it would be: the vastness and the seemingly endless beauty of it took their breaths away. They camped on the bluffs above the ocean, and for several days did nothing but relax and walk the lonely, windswept beaches, picking up and admiring shells they found along the way.

But because of the monsters therein that Benito and Vasco had talked about, they did not go for a swim. They did taste the water and found it unpalatable.

The constantly moving waters soothed them for a time, but then it began to bring out the restlessness in both of them.

They packed up and pulled out, heading north, following the coastline. They both knew that Los Angeles had been taken by U.S. forces back in 1846, and they knew, too, that the wearing of guns was frowned upon in these rapidly changing times. Los Angeles was becoming a very modern city, with gas streetlamps and indoor water closets and a police force that walked their beats with billyclubs and would brook no nonsense for troublemakers.

"It sounds like it's going to be just too damn civilized for me, brother," Bodine said. "What do you think?"

"I think it might be a good place for us to visit and listen for the whereabouts of Morgan, Lake, and Porter." He smiled. "And you might be at last exposed to some civility. Lord knows, your poor mother did her best to make you a gentleman. She used to tell me she wondered where she went wrong."

Bodine muttered under his breath and turned his horse's head toward the west, and Los Angeles.

"You best get shut of them guns," the stableman told them. "Or if you don't want to do that, stick one down behind your belt and tote it thataway when you hit the street."

They were making ready for Christmas in Los Angeles, and while Sam's people had never celebrated it, Sam had spent many a Christmas day at the Bodine ranch. The gayness of it all, here in Los Angeles, hundreds of miles from home country, laid a touch of sadness on the young men. But a couple of young ladies who came sashaying by, walking in that way that ladies do, all giggling and batting of eyelashes drove the lonelies from the young men and made them realize how trail-weary and dusty they were. They hightailed out, looking for a fancy hotel and a shave, a bath, and a haircut while they had their suits cleaned and pressed.

The desk clerk at the fancy hotel looked at their dusty clothing and arched one eyebrow in distaste. His expression was that of a man who'd been chewing on a persimmon that wasn't ripe.

He brightened up considerably when both Sam and Bodine pulled out pokes of gold coin and tried to pay for their rooms in advance. He waved that offer away.

The desk clerk stiffened when he heard Bodine ask where the roughest part of town might be.

"Sir, that would be the Calle de los Negros section. But no decent man and *certainly* no decent woman would ever go there."

"Why not?" Sam asked, his expression bland.

The desk, looking to be a rather fussy man, got even more flustered. "Sir, ladies of the evening and scoundrels and brigands and the like frequent the . . . ah, establishments there."

"Sounds like just the place for us," Bodine said.

The desk clerk looked like a man about ready to keel over.

All duded up, neither Bodine nor Sam felt inclined to wear their guns in any way other than how they normally did. They checked the loads, strapped them on, tied them down and stepped out into the late afternoon of Los Angeles.

"I never seen so many people in one place," Bodine commented.

"While you were taking a bath, wallowing about like a bear in a creek," Sam said, "and singing just about as well, I met several very nice people in the lobby. The population of the city is now close to fifteen thousand."

"That's ridiculous! That's more people than in all of Wyoming Territory. What the hell do they do around here?"

"I used to wonder about that myself. But then, I have been to New York City and am therefore much more an authority on the subject than you."

"And you got lost for two days," Bodine reminded him with a grin. "I never heard of such a thing. An Indian getting lost."

"I want to be there when, and if, you ever venture to New York City, brother. Talk about a country bumpkin in the city."

"Is it bigger than this place?"

"My word, yes! There are several *hundred* thousand people living there."

"I just can't imagine that."

"Be quiet. I am attempting to enlighten you. The people who live here in the city are in business."

"What kind of business?"

"Business, Bodine! The haberdasher must buy groceries just as the grocer must buy clothing."

"Well, you've accounted for two people. What about the other fourteen thousand nine hundred and ninety-eight?"

"You're impossible, Bodine. Sometimes I wonder if you've fallen off your horse one time too many."

"Well, explain it, then, Mister Know-it-all!"

"It would take too long and besides, trying to make you understand anything makes my head hurt."

"At least I don't stand around out in the rain looking up, wondering where it comes from."

They argued all the way to a saloon's batwings. At this time in the history of Los Angeles, the saloons numbered over a hundred.

The men pushed open the batwings and stepped into the noisy and beery-smelling saloon. Some of the conversation stopped as unshaven and rough-appearing men watched them walk to the bar, all of them noting the open display of guns.

Matt and Sam sipped at their mugs of beer, listening to the hubbub of conversation going on all around them. They left after a few minutes, deciding there was nothing being said that was of interest to them.

A young boy tugged at Bodine's sleeve. "Got a message for you, mister."

Bodine looked down at the child.

"Man gimme fifty cents to tell you this: Meet me in Chester's as quickly as possible."

"Who was the man?" Bodine's silent warning bells were ringing in his head. If there ever was a set-up, this was it. He exchanged glances with Sam and could see his brother was thinking the same thing.

"I don't know. I never seen him before."

"What'd he look like?"

"Hard to tell. He was standin' in the shadows. He was big, though. Bigger than you. And he talked like he was real educated. Talked like a schoolteacher."

"Lake," Sam said.

"More than likely." Bodine gave the boy a dollar and a smile. "Where and what is a Chester?"

"It's a bad place to go," the boy said solemnly. "A real rough bar about a block and a half from here. It's located in an alley. There." He pointed the way. "You got to be careful down there. They's ladies that'll mickey-up your drink and rob you. Men who'll kill you for what's in your pockets. Men who'll pick a fight with you just 'cause they like to hurt people."

"Did you see which way this man went after he spoke with you?" Sam asked.

The boy grinned. "Sure did. He went back into the bar."

Sam returned the smile and gave the boy another dollar "It's almost dark, boy. You'd better get off the streets and get home."

"The streets is my home, mister. You two be careful. That man had friends in Chester's. They'll be layin' for you. See you." He ran off into the dusk.

"Shall we?" Sam asked, jerking a thumb in the direction of the infamous bar.

"Why not?" Bodine replied.

The two of them slipped the hammer-thongs from their Colts and walked up the street.

Chapter 27

They turned off the street and stepped into the gloom of an alley. A man was lying next to a wall, in the dirt, face down. He might have been drunk, he might have been dead. They did not stop to investigate. It was not that either man was unfeeling. Their philosophy was that anyone who ventured into places such as this did so of their own free will, and if they got knocked in the head or served a drugged drink, they were grown men, they knew what they were getting into from the start.

A drunk staggered out of Chester's and slammed into the wall across the alley. He sat down hard, mumbling to himself. He reeked of cheap whiskey and vomit.

"This place certainly caters to a lovely clientele," Sam remarked drily.

"Shall we improve this joint's image?" Bodine said with a grin.

"Oh, by all means! Things have been so dull lately."

The place didn't have a door . . . just the hinges. It had probably been ripped off years back and never replaced.

The patrons of the joint were some of the sorriest-looking

men and women either man had ever seen. The stench of booze and sweat and cheap perfume hung in the air.

The place had become silent as a tomb at their entrance.

Spurs jingling softly, Bodine and Sam walked to the bar. Neither one of them had any desire whatsoever to drink anything served up in this bar. Bodine faced the loutish-looking barkeep and Sam turned to face the men in the murky room.

"Well, now," the bartender said. "Ain't we the fine-lookin' gentlemen? Real gentry come to pay us a visit. And what might your name be—Percival?"

The men up and down the dirty bar hoo-hawed at that, the women making lewd suggestions.

They all stopped laughing when Matt said, "Matt Bodine. This is my brother, Sam Two Wolves."

The long bar was suddenly vacated, leaving Matt and Sam alone.

The barkeep's eyes narrowed. "What'll it be, boys?"

"Someone wanted to see me. So here I am."

A man stepped into the room, using a rear door. He was tall and broad-shouldered—he would have been handsome had it not been for his drooping eye, which gave him a sinister look. He was clean-shaven and smelling of expensive men's cologne, and neatly dressed in a dark suit, white shirt, and black tie. His boots were polished to a high sheen. He held his coat wide, showing Bodine he was not armed . . . at least so far as Matt could see.

"We finally meet, Mister Bodine, Mister Two Wolves," the man said.

"You'd be Lake," Bodine said.

"That is correct. I am not armed, Mister Bodine. And I will submit to a search if you feel it necessary."

"No. I'll take your word. You're not armed, but fifty others in this room are. And you could, and probably have, bought this scum for a dollar a head."

Several of the men in the room stirred at that slur, but

none of them made a move toward the guns they were openly wearing.

"You are a plain-spoken man, Mister Bodine. But, yes, you are quite correct in your assumption."

"That they're scum or that you bought them off?"

Lake smiled, showing very white teeth. "I'll keep you guessing about that."

"The first man who drags iron," Bodine said, "and I kill you, Lake."

Lake's smile faded. "Yes," he spoke the words low. "I imagine you would."

"So what do we do now?"

"Have either of you had dinner?"

"No. We haven't."

"My treat then. I know a charming place just a few blocks from here. And so we'll be meeting as equals, do you have any objections to my retrieving my guns?"

"None at all. We'll meet you out front."

Lake joined them by the street. "That is quite a disgusting place back there. But there are many disgusting people in this world and they have to have a place to congregate. Is that not correct, Bodine?"

"I suppose."

"You two have very nearly wrecked my little empire. It was quite profitable for a time."

"And you have the nerve to speak of disgusting?" Sam glanced at the man.

Lake laughed. "Don't be so naive, Sam. I took those children from a life of dreary farm work and tedious drudgery and offered them security."

"I suppose the sad thing is, you really believe that, don't you?" Bodine asked.

"But of course! What else is a woman good for? I just started the girls doing what they do best a bit earlier, that's all."

Lake rattled on while Matt and Sam were silent as they

walked out of the violent district and crossed over into the more acceptable part of the city.

"Right over there," Lake pointed. "A wonderful restaurant. You'll both enjoy it, I assure you."

"No, we won't," Bodine told him. "Because we're not eating there."

Lake took no umbrage. He laughed. "You think I would have you poisoned? You really don't trust me, do you, Bodine?"

"I really don't, Lake." Bodine stopped on the edge of the street and faced the man. "Sam and I prefer to eat alone, Lake. State your business with us or drag iron. Makes no difference to me."

"I think it does, Bodine." Lake's words were spoken more harshly now. "I think you really want to kill me. And you might be good enough to do it. But I don't think so."

"Oh, I'm going to kill you, Lake. You and Porter and Morgan, too, if I can."

"Umm," Lake said, then motioned them across the street to a small park. He sat down and the others followed suit. "Why, Bodine?" Lake questioned.

"Here we go again," Sam said. "I have this memorized."

"Because I made a promise, that's why?"

"To Dick Wellman?"

"Yes."

"But Jenny is safe."

"That's more than you can say for her parents. You killed them."

"Ahh, quite the contrary, Bodine. I did nothing of the sort. Chappo and his savages did that. And you killed Chappo. So it's even."

Bodine stood up. "The next time we meet, Lake, you best have your hand wrapped around the butt of a Colt."

"You'll never make it out of this city alive, Bodine," Lake warned him, his words cold and menacing. "Neither you nor that breed with you."

"We're both light sleepers," Sam assured the outlaw slaver.

"Are you backshooters?" Lake stood up.

"No. We leave things like that to scum like you," Bodine told him.

Lake flushed and turned his back to the men, swiftly walking out of the park.

"Now what was all that about?" Sam mused aloud. "The dinner invitation and so forth?"

"I don't know. Maybe he really thought he could talk us out of following him. Maybe the food was poisoned. I guess we'll never know."

It was that time of day when carriage traffic and pedestrians was the slowest. Most were already home, getting ready for dinner and it was still too early for the night-crawlers to be out.

The park was deserted.

A stick cracked faintly in the darkness behind the men, whirling them around. The thugs came at them in a rush, waving clubs and leather wrapped head-knockers. But no guns.

Bodine and Sam immediately shifted locations, splitting up, each giving the other ample fighting room.

Sam flung himself to the ground and rolled fast, slamming his body against the ankles and knees of several rowdies, knocking them sprawling just as Bodine gave one a knuckle sandwich to the teeth and drove his stiffened left fingers into the throat of another.

Sam jumped to his boots and kicked one assailant in the face, the toe of the boot smashing the man's nose flat against his face. The thug rolled and screamed in pain.

Bodine jerked the club away from one and laid it on the man's skullbone. The man staggered and went down, blood streaming from his torn scalp.

Sam applied some Indian wrestling to another and tossed the man over his shoulder. He landed heavily in the bushes, cussing and struggling to get free.

Bodine stood toe to toe with a hoodlum and smashed the man's face with hard left and right combinations. The man went down and Bodine kneed him in the face just as uniformed police officers came galloping up, blowing whistles and shouting. Those few thugs able to do so jumped up and ran away into the night. The others lay on the ground, bleeding and moaning, especially that one who had received a kick in the groin from Sam.

The cops took one look at the tailored suits of Sam and Bodine, and the rough dress of the moaning men and began pulling out handcuffs.

"What happened, sir?" one asked Bodine.

"We were walking through the park, discussing where to have dinner when these hooligans set upon us." He pointed to the clubs on the ground. "With those."

"Disgraceful!" a policeman said. "How many were there?"

"Oh . . . six or eight of them, I suppose," Sam said. "We thrashed them properly."

"You certainly did that, sir. May I have your names, gentlemen. For the report, nothing more." He took out a notebook and a pencil.

"I'm Sam Two Wolves." The cop broke off the point of his pencil. "And this is Matt Bodine." The cop broke the pencil.

The cop knelt down beside one handcuffed and bleeding man. "You're lucky to be alive, lad," he told the thug.

There were only a handful of people in Chester's when Bodine and Sam returned the next morning. They had packed their suits and dressed in jeans and checkered shirts, bandanas tied around their necks. They wore their guns openly and had not been challenged for doing so. But they had received some odd looks, and some inviting ones from young ladies.

"It's a shame I had to have been born so handsome," Sam said, after one young lady batted her eyes at him.

"She's probably blind," Bodine cut him down. "Or else she felt sorry for you and did it out of sympathy. Even ugly people like you need some sort of affection every now and then."

They argued and insulted each other all the way to the bar.

Bodine jerked the barkeep—it was the same one from the night before—over the bar and slapped him across the face, twice.

"Do I have your attention, now?" he asked.

"Ye . . . yes, sir!"

"Lake? Where is he?"

"Gone, Bodine. Him and his gang pulled out late last night. After you and the breed whupped them men in the park."

"Gone where?"

"I swear to the Blessed Virgin I don't know. And I ain't got no reason to lie, Bodine. Lake said he wouldn't be back no more. He was pullin' out for good."

"Why would he do that?"

"To git away from you! He said you was a jinx on him. I swear I don't know where he went."

"Who would know?"

"His gal-friend. She lives 'cross the street, and she was shore cussin' and a squallin' at him when he rode out in the middle of the night."

"What's her name?"

"Sadie. First door to the right at the top of the stairs."

Sadie was henna-headed and had a foul mouth. After she finished cussing Lake, she plopped down on the bed and said, "Why do you want to know where he went?"

"So I can find him and kill him," Bodine was honest with her.

"You're Bodine, ain't you?"

"That's right."

"He's skittish of you, all right. Says you got a hoodoo on him. Oh, what the hell?" she waved a hand. "He's gone for good and I'll never see him again. What do I owe the no-good? He's gone to San Francisco."

"Porter and Morgan?"

"Morgan's at sea. He'll meet Lake there. Porter went with Lake."

"How many men?"

"What's it worth to you?"

Bodine dug in a vest pocket and tossed a double eagle on the bed.

Sadie grabbed it up fast. "Twenty men. All good with a gun."

"Names?"

"Don Bradley, Bob Doyle, Mavern, Hog . . . they ain't none of them pushovers."

"Going back into slaving?"

She grimaced. "Probably. Or certainly something just as awful."

"If you feel that way," Sam asked, "why'd you stay with him?"

She grinned lewdly. "He paid the rent."

Out on the street, Sam said, "You check us out of the hotel. I'll be saddling up."

"All right. We need supplies."

"We'll get them on the edge of town."

Bodine held out his hand.

Sam looked at it. "What do you want now?"

"The money for your room."

Muttering in Cheyenne, which Bodine spoke and understood just as well as Sam, he forked over some coins.

It wasn't until Bodine was checking out that he realized Sam had given him Mexican pesos.

Chapter 28

After only two days on the trail, it became apparent to Bodine and Sam that tracking Lake and his gang was going to be easy. For whatever reason, the outlaws appeared to be throwing caution to the wind: they were robbing and raping their way north, subjecting those in their path to terror and the viewing of wanton destruction of property. The gang had grown, nearly tripling in size, as punks and thugs and local ne'er-do-wells rushed to join the marauders as they passed through the country.

"The only thing I can figure out," Bodine said. "Is he's building a stake from the raids and will link up with Morgan in San Francisco and take to the seas."

"To go where?"

"Who knows? South America, maybe. Perhaps some island thousands of miles away where he—and those who choose to go with him—can take over and live like kings. It's happened before."

"Then it's a race against time," Sam said, after thinking for a moment. "If they get to San Francisco and the docks before we do, we've lost the race."

"If he is heading for that city," Bodine replied. "He might have told that to Sadie just to throw us off, knowing she was sure to tell us. Right now, Lake is heading straight north. If he starts cutting to the west, we'll know that Morgan has put in somewhere along the coast and is waiting for him."

Lake and his outlaw band did not choose the easier and more populated route to the north. They chose the inland passage north where the pickings might be somewhat less, but the law was fewer in numbers and more widely scattered.

After leaving the city, Lake headed straight north, through the Los Padres, between the Tehachapi Mountains to the east, and the Sierra Madres to the west. He was heading for a sparsely populated area, mostly cattle country, with some mining, which was dotted with tiny towns with little or no law which would interfere with his plans. As they rode, Lake and his men were leaving in their wake pillaged towns, many set blazing, and shattered lives and the bodies of any who dared try to stop them.

The outlaws were taking everything and anything of value: rings, jewelry, watches, and money. Just south of the Kettleman Hills, Bodine and Sam came up on a familiar and sickening scene, one they had witnessed several times since leaving Los Angeles: a burned-out ranch with buzzards waddling about in the yard, too bloated to fly after feasting on the dead bodies in the yard.

Wetting bandanas and tying them around their faces to help block out some of the stench of death, the young men found shovels and began digging shallow graves for the dead, which included several young people.

His words muffled, Sam said, "Lake has gone insane. These men have been horribly tortured. There is no reason behind anything like this."

Neither man commented on the obvious fact that the women had been sexually abused.

"He's gone crazy, all right," Bodine agreed.

Their work was interrupted by the pounding of hooves, riding hard from the southeast. The posse circled them in a swirl of dust. The men were trail-dusty and hard-faced, riding with rifles across the saddlehorns, about twenty of them.

"State your business and your names," the leader of the posse yelled at Matt and Sam. "And you best be damn quick in doin' it."

Bodine tossed his shovel to the ground, ire welling up in him. Nothing like what they had seen riding north from Los Angeles would have been permitted to happen in Wyoming. No truly western town could have been treed by scum like Lake and his men. It was apparent to Bodine that while California was much more progressive and modern than anything he had ever seen before, some of the aggressiveness had gone from its citizens. They had let their guard down. Many of its people had taken off their guns and were living— past tense for many of them in the path of Lake—under a false sense of security.

Bodine faced the leader of the posse, a portly man with a flushed face and a belly that hung over his belt. "You best watch your mouth with me, mister. Use your eyes for a change. This happened a good day ago, maybe two days back. If we'd had anything to do with it, we damn sure wouldn't be hanging around, burying the bodies. Now why don't you get your big fat butt out of the saddle and find a shovel before I jerk you out of the saddle and slap the piss out of you."

"You can't talk to me like that, you saddle bum!" the man hollered, his jowls quivering. "Just who in the hell do you think you are?"

"Matt Bodine."

The fight went out of the man. He sat back in the saddle, breathing heavily, but keeping his mouth closed.

"We been ridin' hard for two days, Mister Bodine," a posse member said. "The outlaws hit just southwest of Bakersfield. Four ranches and one little town. It was awful. It just seems like they're killin' for no reason."

"Oh, they have a reason," Sam said. "It's called greed, ignorance, stupidity, viciousness, and contempt for the law. We've learned that Lake's home base has been Los Angeles— off and on—for several years. Why in the hell didn't you people hang him years back?"

The posse members dismounted stiffly. The portly gentleman said, "We like to think of ourselves as more civilized than that, sir. You'd be Sam Two Wolves?"

"That is correct."

"We'll help you bury the dead and we'll rest for a time; give our horses a chance to blow. Then we'll be off to catch Lake."

"What are you going to do when you catch him?" Bodine asked. "Ask him to surrender?"

"Of course."

"Then we'll be burying you somewhere up along the trail," Bodine told him. "Lake's got about sixty hardcases riding with him." He waved his hand at the carnage. "You've all seen what they are capable of doing. Circle around and come in from the north; lay out an ambush and blow them out of the saddle."

"That would not be a lawful act," a posse member said. "There may be those in the group who are along for a lark; who are taking no active part in this terror. Young people seeking thrills. They deserve a trial and to be punished, certainly. But doing what you suggest would be to lower ourselves to the level of those we pursue."

Bodine and Sam exchanged glances. Bodine then summed up their mutual opinion of such a statement. "Crap!"

* * *

They came up on what was left of the posse a day later. The remnants of the posse were riding south, toward home. They were a pathetic-looking and defeated bunch. Not a man among the seven living had escaped unscathed. All wore bloody bandages.

"They laid in ambush for us," the portly gentleman stated. There was a bloody bandage around his head and he had taken a bullet through his left shoulder. "The outlaws took several of my men prisoner and tortured them while the others kept us pinned down in the hills. It was the most awful thing I have ever seen or heard. They're worse than a bunch of damn Injuns."

"We heard back at that little town just south of us that the state militia is out in force, looking for Lake and his bunch," Bodine said.

"They're getting organized now," the portly man said. "One hundred strong. They'll bring those savages to justice, by God."

"Sure they will," Bodine said sarcastically. "All nice and legal-like, right?"

Sam and Bodine turned their horses' heads toward the north and rode off without another word.

They came up on the bodies of the tortured men the next morning. The posse members had died very hard, in various ways. Sam shook his head and grimaced as he and Bodine dismounted, getting shovels from their pack horses.

"Very inventive bunch of people," he said. "Brother, do you remember reading about something like this taking place in Utah about five years ago?"

Bodine paused in his digging. "Yeah. Come to think of it, I do. The paper said something about it also happening in Kansas, too."

"I was beginning to feel guilty about us pursuing Lake; wondering if this was our fault. Now I realize he's done this before."

"There is a word for what he is."

"Criminally insane."

"How about just no good?"

"That's two words."

"I can think of another: scum!"

In the southern edge of the San Joaquin Valley, Lake and his gang cut a violent and deadly path as they turned, not west as Bodine had suspected, but northeast, toward the Sierra Nevada mountains.

"Now what?" Bodine questioned.

"There are probably lots of small mines in there. Lake could split his gang up into five or six groups and really terrorize those people."

Bodine reined up, allowing his horse to blow. "I don't know, brother. Lake would set up an ambush for twenty posse members, but allows us to keep on coming after him. It just doesn't make any sense. And where is the state militia?"

They found the answer to that a few miles up the trail, at a small town, as yet untouched by the rampaging band of outlaws.

"They're spread out northwest of here," the old marshal—the only law in the small town—told them. "They took a chance and guessed the gang would keep on heading northwest toward San Francisco." He spat on the ground. "They guessed wrong, I reckon."

"What's the Sierra Nevadas like?" Bodine asked.

"Wild. Mountains to desert. Sagebrush country. Wagon trains is still comin' this way, too. Although each year they's less and less of them. This outlaw might have them in mind for easy pickin'." The old marshal shook his head. "I never thought he'd come this way agin."

Both Bodine and Sam perked up. "What do you mean?"

"This is the third time in twenty years he's done something like this. He come rip-roarin' through here back about '57, I reckon it was. I was runnin' a placer operation at the time. He was just a kid; no more'un nineteen or twenty years old. They'd run him clean out of Texas under threat of a hangin'. He put together a gang of no-counts and went on a rampage. After that he went overseas and joined up with the French army, so I heard. He fought in Mexico and other places. Then he come back here about ten years later and damned if he didn't do the same thing agin. Now here it is ten years later, and he's back."

"Why is he doing it?" Sam asked.

"For one thing, he's nuts!" the old man said. "He likes to kill. Likes to hurt people. He was born of good people but born bad." He looked at the young men. "You know he killed his mommy and daddy, burned the house down around them, and took off?"

"No, we didn't," Sam said. "How old was he when he did that?"

"Fourteen."

They pulled out at dawn, two young men riding into the loneliness of the Sierra Nevadas, riding after a murderous madman and his band of cutthroats, who outnumbered them thirty to one, but who were still running from the two of them. Neither of them could figure it.

It was cold in the high-up as the men huddled around the small warmth of a fire they had built under an overhang. They had eaten bacon and bread and then each enjoyed the last of the coffee. Bodine tossed out the dregs and rinsed out the pot.

"It's us he wants," Sam said, figuring out part of the puzzle. "You know that, don't you?"

"Oh, yeah. I know. It's turned personal for him now. But he's got to stop somewhere, sometime. They've been pushing it mighty hard. He's too good a soldier not to know that once his men get tired, they also get careless. They've got to hunt a hole and rest. We just have to figure out where that is and hit them."

"Just the two of us?" Sam spoke the words with a faint grin.

"We still got some dynamite. And as far as just the two of us goes, I don't see any reenforcements riding up to lend a hand."

"I don't understand this part of the country," Sam said. "Back in Wyoming or Montana, there would be five hundred men hunting Lake. And they'd never stop until they were hanging from a tree."

"It's civilized out here, brother. Not nearly so much as it is way back east, but much more so than what we're used to back home."

In the fading light of the fire, Sam studied a crude map of the Sierra Nevadas. "I figure we're here," he said, pointing. "Now all we have to do guess where Lake might be holed up."

"He's along this river somewhere," Bodine leaned over and traced the river's southward flow. "Bet on it. They've got to rest."

"Oh, wonderful! That really narrows it down. We only have about seventy miles of river to search."

"No," Bodine said. "He'll be heading for the wildest and most desolate part. Remember what that old marshal said, about the caves right along here? That'd be perfect for him and you can bet he knows about them. Add it up, brother. The last few towns he's hit, he's taken horses and supplies. Maybe he's planning on holing up for the winter, and if we can catch them in those caves, we can seal their fate forever. It's just a guess. But what else do we have to go on?"

Sam smiled. "Now, brother, you wouldn't do something like that, would you? Sealing people alive in caves? How terrible. It's like that man in the posse told us: there might be boys along, just seeking thrills." The sarcasm in his words was thick as molasses.

Bodine rolled up in his blankets. "We buried that man, remember?"

Chapter 29

It began snowing the morning they pulled out. It was an overdue snow, coming late in the season, but now it was coming down with a vengeance. They made it to the Kern River before the snow halted them. They made camp and waited out the storm. As soon as the sun came out, the snow began to melt and they could travel. They agreed to split up, Bodine going north for fifteen miles, Sam traveling downriver the same distance. If Lake and Porter were here, they would be within that range.

For two days the men and their horses struggled through the snow, inspecting the few caves they could find along the way. No sign of the outlaw gang.

The sign they did pick up made no sense to either of them. Back at the meeting point, they sat with blankets wrapped around them, in front of a fire, a large fire, for they knew that the outlaws were nowhere in this vicinity.

"So what do you make of it, Sam?"

Sam drank his coffee in silence, then studied his brother's face for a moment. "They crossed the Kern and went east. All of them."

"Well, damn, brother. I *know* that! But why? What's he trying to pull?"

"I don't know. But according to the tracks, they're a full day ahead of us by now, if they maintained direction." He angrily tossed the dregs of his coffee cup into the snow. "But why? Why abruptly change directions?"

"We'll know that when we catch up with them."

They pulled out the next morning, just as the sky was turning steel gray in the east. They crossed the icy waters of the Kern and left the Sierra Nevadas several days later, crossing just south of a dry lake bed and continued south, not wanting to cross through the center of Death Valley. With Brown Mountain in sight, they cut due east, riding through the northern tip of the Avawatz Mountains. They found a grizzled old prospector and swapped him food for information about water holes. His directions proved out and they rode hard for Las Vegas, Nevada.

At this time, Las Vegas was no more than a sleepy little desert town with water. It had been settled by the Mormons back in '55 and was abandoned by them some two years later.

They put their horses up in the stable and told the man to rub them down and give them as much corn and oats as they could eat . . . they had earned it.

"Some young hardcases in town," the stableman said. "Over to the saloon. Guns all shiny and tied down low. They're all makin' big talk about how they made fools outta Matt Bodine and Sam Two Wolves. I 'spect they wouldn't talk like that if they figured Bodine and the breed was anywheres near."

Bodine smiled thinly, as did Sam. The stableman took a closer look at the pair. "Holy Jumpin' Jehosaphat!" he yelled. "It's you!"

"Which saloon?" Sam asked.

"That one right there!" the man pointed. "They's five or six of 'em in there."

"They ride in alone?"

"Shore did. Been here two days now. Makin' a nuisance outta theyselves. They ain't caused no real trouble. But everybody would be just as happy to see them go. Tell you what though: they all got their pockets stuffed full of money."

"Anything else in their pockets?" Sam asked.

"I don't know what you . . ." The stableman paused. "Yeah. I do know what you mean. Yeah. Watches and rings and stuff they've tried to sell to folks."

"They say where they got those articles?"

The stableman smiled. "Yeah. Said they got lucky at poker."

"Not a word to anybody that we're in town," Bodine warned the man.

"You got it," he was assured.

Bodine and Sam checked their guns and walked first to the cafe, keeping out of sight as much as possible. At the cafe, they relaxed and ordered a pot of coffee and whatever the cook could dish up for a meal. Over beef and beans and potatoes, Bodine put into words what had been nagging at him for several days.

"They're heading for Utah, brother."

Sam paused in the lifting of fork to mouth. "I don't follow you."

"Laurie."

Sam laid his fork across the plate. "For pure spite."

"That's it. That's the only thing that makes any sense to me. Porter has said that he wants her. Lake, as nutty as he is, might be blaming her and Jenny for all his misfortunes."

"This bunch in town now?"

"Put here to stop us, maybe. Although that's reaching for an answer. I just don't know. Maybe they just got tired of it all and quit."

The counterman had been leaning on the counter, listening. "Your name Bodine?" he asked.

"That's right."

"Them hardcases is here to stop you from goin' on. They been in here several times, braggin' about how they was gonna make a reputation right here in this one-horse town. By killin' you."

Sam drained his coffee cup. "I guess that settles it."

Bodine stood up and hitched at his gunbelt. Sam did the same. They tossed money on the table and moved toward the door. Before leaving the stable, Sam had tucked a spare Colt behind his gunbelt and both men had loaded up the cylinders full.

They walked up the street to the saloon the outlaws had chosen. They could hear the laughter of those inside. Bodine opened the door and they stepped inside the stuffy and beery-sweat smelling warmth of the barroom. A potbellied stove was cherry red in the center of the room. The saloon was empty except for seven gunslicks and one barkeep.

The men fell silent, watching the pair walk to the bar.

Neither one of them wanted anything to drink. Bodine told the barkeep, "Hunt a hole, mister."

The barkeep vanished into the stock room located in the back of the building.

"How come you boys didn't ride on to Utah with Porter and Lake?" Bodine suddenly tossed the unexpected question at them.

By the looks on their faces, Sam and Bodine knew they had guessed right as to where the outlaw gang was heading.

"Huh?" one of the dirty and unshaven hardcases tried to cover up.

"That'd be about your speed," Sam said. "Making war on women and little girls."

The gunslicks looked at one another. This was not the way they had planned to take out Bodine and Sam. This was no good; it was too close here in the saloon. If they opened the dance in here, they were all going to get lead in them, for

Bodine and Two Wolves were going to be hard to put down. The outlaws had planned an ambush; maybe a backshooter on a building. This just wasn't working out at all.

"I don't know what you're talkin' about," a hardcase said. "I don't know no one name of Porter or Lake."

"If you don't shoot any better than you lie," Bodine told him. "You're in a hell of a mess, coyote-face."

The man flushed, but made no attempt to grab iron.

A young man stood up. He was a fancy-dan and cocksure of himself. He was dressed to the nines, with a belt made of silver dollars and wearing twin pearl-handled pistols, tied down low. He had tried to grow a mustache, but had succeeded only in growing something that looked like a deformed dead mouse under his nose. His black-gloved hands were hovering over the butts of his guns.

Bodine looked at the young dandy. "You want something, boy?"

"My name's Sundown," the young man announced. "And I think I can take you, Bodine."

Bodine sighed, wondering where in the hell these would-be gunhawks came up with their nicknames. "That's good, boy. Everybody ought to have a name so it can be cut into their headstone."

The young man sneered at him. "What do you want on your marker, Bodine: Injun lover?"

"You'll never live to see my final resting place, boy. Now why don't you sit down and shut up and maybe you'll live through what's coming here."

"I think he's afraid of me, boys!" Sundown yelled. "Hell, he's yeller."

Another gunslick stood up. "I do believe you're right, Sundown. I think maybe Bodine's reputation is bigger than he is."

Sam said, "Well, one thing about it, brother."

"What's that?"

"A few less for us to deal with in Utah."

Both men drew and fired as if on silent signal.

The fancy-dan was doubled over from a .44 slug out of Bodine's Colt and the man who had stood up to stand with him took a slug in the center of his chest from Sam's Colt.

Neither one of them had managed to clear leather.

Both Bodine and Sam hit the floor before the echo of their shots faded and crawled behind whatever cover they could find as the room exploded in gunfire. Sam rolled to his right and came up near the edge of the bar, as Bodine went to his left and did the same.

Both men filled their hands with Colts and let them bang.

The attack came so suddenly it was seconds before the remaining outlaws could react, and those seconds cost them their lives as Bodine and Sam filled the beery air with lead.

Bodine reached behind the bar and came up with an express gun, jacking back both hammers and lining the twin barrels up with two gunnies still on their feet. He pulled the triggers and the force almost tore it from his hands, the muzzle blast rattling the windows of the saloon, the double charge taking the gunnies chest-high.

Bodine and Sam slipped behind the dubious protection of the bar and quickly reloaded, just in case any might still be alive and with some fight left in them.

They stood up, hands filled with Colts.

The barkeep stuck his head out of the storeroom, looked around wide-eyed, and said, "Holy Christ!"

One of Lake's gunslicks had crashed through the big window on the street side, hanging half in and half out of the saloon. Another was dead on his boots against the back wall, his shirt collar caught on a hatrack, both hands hanging by his side. The two gunnies who had first braced Sam and Bodine were on the floor, dead or dying. The two that Bodine had let have the loads in the sawed-off were spread all over the center of the room.

"That's six," Sam said. "Where's the other one?"

A galloping horse answered his question. They ran to the door and watched the seventh gunny hightail it out of town, riding low, presenting less of a target.

"Damn!" Bodine summed up their feelings at letting one get away. It was then he noticed the left side of Sam's face was covered with blood.

"Scratch," Sam said. "What about your shoulder?"

Bodine hadn't even noticed. He took off his sheepskin-lined jacket and looked at the bullet hole. Another fraction of an inch lower and he'd have been plugged in the shoulder.

The brothers grinned at each other and turned to the bar.

"Now give us something to drink," Sam said.

The bartender placed a bottle of rye and two shot glasses on the bar. "What about them dead folks?"

"What about them?" Bodine poured both glasses full.

"Who's gonna plant 'em?"

"Damned if I know."

A deputy pushed open the door and walked in, shaking his head at the sight.

"It's about damn time you showed up, Lars!" the barkeep yelled. "Where the hell have you been for the past two days?"

"Down south of here, chasin' rustlers, that's where." He walked to the bar, picked up the bottle and gestured for a glass. He poured a shotglass full and then looked at Bodine and said, "You boys know these hombres," he waved his hand at the dead, "or do you shoot up ever' saloon you come to?"

"They're part of a gang that's been robbing and raping and killing through half of California. We've tracked them from Los Angeles."

"You boys got names?"

"Matt Bodine and Sam Two Wolves."

The deputy lifted the glass to his lips. He paused, his eyes widening at the names. He cleared his throat and then took a first a sip, then downed the rest of it.

"We got to find somebody to dig six graves, Lars," the barkeep said.

"Eight," the deputy told him, refilling his glass. "I caught up with them rustlers. Brought them back across their saddles." He looked at Bodine. "You boys is sure welcome to stay the night and refresh yourselves and rest your horses. I'd appreciate it if you was both gone come the morning."

"We were planning on leaving at first light, Deputy," Sam said.

"Good. Las Vegas is a fine town, filled with church goin' folks. I wouldn't want it to get a bad name."

Chapter 30

One of the dying men had stayed alive long enough to tell Bodine that they had left the gang on their own accord, as had others. The other bunch had drifted up toward Carson City. Lake and Porter still had about thirty men with them. And they were the worst of the lot, bad, evil men, the gunny said. The worst he'd ever seen. He asked if he could be buried with his boots on, 'cause his feet got awful cold in the winter.

"I'll see to it personal," Bodine had told him.

The outlaw had thanked him, then closed his eyes and died.

Bodine asked the deputy where Cedar City, Utah was located.

"I reckon it's a good hundred and fifty miles from here, boys."

"Damn!" Bodine cussed. "We'll never make it."

"What's the problem?" the deputy asked.

Sam laid it out for him.

The deputy thought for a moment. "I'm changin' my mind about you boys. You're not bad hombres like some people think. This is a right honorable thing you're doin'. Tell you what. Gimme a sheet of paper, Gene," he said to the barkeep. He drew a rough map, and while he drew, he said, "You boys up to pullin' out tonight?"

"Yeah," Bodine said, after looking at Sam and receiving a nod.

The deputy looked at the barkeep. "Tell the stableman to saddle four of his best horses. Transfer these men's gear. Move! Stay north of the Muddy Mountains. It's fifty miles to the Tumblin' Bar ranch. I'll give you a note explain' what you're doin'. The foreman will switch your saddles and give you some food and you can be on your way. Just south of the Pine Valley Mountains in Utah, there's a ranch run by my brother. Name is Clint. I'm writin' him a note too. It's about forty-fifty miles from there on into Cedar City. Go, boys, and good huntin'!"

They swung into the saddles and were gone at an easy, mile-eating lope. They had no way of knowing how far ahead of them Lake and Porter and what was left of the gang might be, or whether Laurie and Jenny were dead. But they had to try to reach them.

Matt Bodine and Sam Two Wolves rode on through the cold night, pausing only to change mounts and then it was back in the saddle and keep going.

They hit the front yard of the Tumbling Bar ranch and began yelling. Within seconds they were surrounded by armed cowboys, in various stages of dress, but all with guns in their hands. The foreman read the note from the deputy and began shouting orders. The fire was stoked up and coffee heated and food prepared while the fresh horses were saddled up. Tully Brown, the owner of the Tumbling Bar read the note.

"You boys can't fight no thirty men alone," he said. " 'Sides, you don't even know where Wellman's ranch is. Dick was a friend of mine—from a long time back." He turned to his crew. "I want five men armed and saddled up in ten minutes."

His whole crew stepped forward. Tully smiled and picked out five. "Get crackin', boys. Two horses apiece. We'll switch up at Clint's place and probably pick up some more men."

Now there were eight riding through the night. There was no way that Tully Brown was going to stay out of this fight.

The men who rode with Bodine and Sam that night were not gunfighters in the sense that they were known as such, or had books and songs written and sung about them. But many a man in the west was a fine gunhandler; he just didn't push his skill or his kills were never recorded visually, to be told around campfires and barrooms. What these men were were hard men in a hard land in a hard time. More often than not, they hanged rustlers and horsethieves on the spot. Horsethieves more than rustlers. The reasoning behind that was, leave a man afoot in hostile country, and he might well die. Hence the harsh punishment.

These were men who rode for the brand, for thirty a month, and many of them died for it. They were the men who made the West—hard men, yes, sometimes unfair men in the way they treated homesteaders, yes—but they came before the others, second only to the mountain men, and these men more than any others helped to tame the wild West.

None of them knew Laurie or Jenny. They knew only that a young woman and a little girl were in trouble, and they were going to help. The trial would be by gunsmoke and guts; if any of the outlaws survived, they would swing from the nearest tree.

Tully Brown hit the yard of Clint's ranch hollering like a wild man. Inside the main house and bunkhouse, lamps were lit and armed men filled the yard. Tully was brief in his explanation. Bodine and Sam could feel eyes on them momentarily, then men were running for the corral to rope, top off, and saddle horses while the women hurriedly made fresh coffee and packed up pokes of food for the last leg of the journey.

Now there were fifteen men riding hard for Dick Wellman's ranch, the men bundled up against the freezing night, with mufflers tied around their faces and their hat straps tied under their chins, each leading a spare horse, each with an extra Colt or Remington shoved down behind his belt, each with a pocket filled with spare cartridges, each with his saddle-booted Winchester filled up with .44's or .44-.40's.

Dawn split the eastern sky with hues of silver and gold and red, and it was a welcome sight as it highlighted the pockets of snow that lingered here and there on the harsh landscape of southwestern Utah.

The men rode on through the cold, grim-faced, and ready for a fight.

"We'll need fresh hosses in case we have to charge or chase!" Clint hollered from his saddle. "Right over the next ridge they's the Lazy L. We'll change there."

Now there were twenty men riding through the morning, with Tully Brown taking the lead.

"How many did you say there was in that gang of scum?" Clint yelled to Sam as they galloped along, side by side.

"At least thirty—maybe more. I'd guess more," Sam returned the shout.

"We got enough rope," a Lazy L hand said grimly. "I can't abide a man who'd molest a good woman or hurt a child."

They had reined up to switch horses when they heard the gunfire, and there was lots of it.

Bodine was back in the saddle and going, Sam right behind him before the others could react. Tully was the next to follow, then Clint, then the others. As he topped the ridge overlooking Dick's spread, Bodine uttered a low curse, put the reins between his teeth, and filled both hands with Colts.

The gunfighters, the ranchers, and the hands rode into the circling bunch of filth and trash and scum, catching them completely by surprise.

Bodine spotted a known gun for hire named Randy Walker and ended his mercenary days by putting a .44 slug through his head. Sam knocked another out of the saddle and rode his horse right over the man, the steel-shod hooves driving the life from him, staining the snow crimson.

Tully Brown rammed his horse into the horse of an outlaw, knocking the man to the ground. Tully leveled his Colt and shot the man between the eyes.

Bodine saw Porter trying to make the house. He reined up, leveled his Colt, and dusted the man, the slug entering one side and coming out the other. Porter screamed as he hit the ground, then twisted in the snow and came up firing, the slug stinging Bodine's cheek. Bodine shot the man in the chest and turned his attention elsewhere.

Four of the hands had, at Tully's orders, stationed themselves along the ridges overlooking the ranchhouse. Using rifles, they prevented any outlaw escape.

The fight was brutal and short. Halfway through it, a group of Utah ranchers and their hands rode into the fray, having heard the news from other cowboys from the Lazy L who rode through the countryside, alerting the populace to the danger.

A few of the outlaws surrendered. They were promptly taken over the ridges so the women couldn't see what was happening and hanged.

All but one of Dick's hands were down, two of them dead, sprawled in the yard. The cook had barricaded Laurie, Jenny, and himself in the house and fought like a wild man protecting the woman and the girl.

"You old goat!" Tully yelled at the grizzled cook. "I thought you was dead twenty years ago."

"Well, I ain't, Tully," the old man growled. "So hesh up and light and sit. I got fresh coffee and bear sign."

A tin cup of steaming coffee in one hand and a doughnut in the other, Bodine prowled the carnage sprawled around the house.

Lake was not among the dead.

"Brother," Sam said softly. "Up there on the north ridge."

Bodine looked. Even at that distance he could tell it was Lake, sitting his horse, looking down into the little valley.

"Some of you boys take him," Tully shouted to his men.

"No!" Bodine stopped them. "He wants me. This is a personal matter."

Bodine walked out into the road, after getting another cup of coffee and another bear sign. He stood in the road and waited, sipping and munching.

Lake had not moved. He still sat his horse and waited and watched from the ridges.

"What the hell's he waitin' on," one of Tully's younger hands asked.

Bodine stood in the road.

"He's tryin' to spook Bodine," the rancher told him. "But he's wastin' his time, I'm thinkin'."

The sheriff and a posse had ridden out from Cedar City. The sheriff had looked at the half dozen men hanging from trees; he grunted and rode on into the ranch yard, greeting Tully and Clint and the other ranchers.

Laurie explained what had happened

"Who's that out yonder?" he asked, his eyes on the tall young man standing in the rutted wagon road.

"Matt Bodine," she told him. "That fellow up yonder on the ridge is the outlaw, Lake."

"Showdown time, Sheriff," Tully said. "You goin' to try to stop them?"

"Do I look like a fool?" the sheriff said. "You got anymore of them bear sign left, ma' am?" Coffee and doughnut in hand, he turned to Sam. "You'd be Sam Two Wolves?"

"That is correct."

"Good job you boys done down on the border. I heard about it."

"Thank you. It would not have been possible without the help of Major Luis de Carrillo and his men from the Mexican Army."

"I ain't got a thing agin Mexicans," the sheriff was quick to reply. Sam Two Wolves was damn near as well known as Matt Bodine, and just as deadly with a short gun. "Here comes Lake. Gonna be right interestin' around here shortly, boys. And girls," he added.

Bodine had taken off his gloves and had his left hand shoved down into his jacket pocket, his right hand wrapped around the warmth of the tin cup.

He watched as Lake slowly rode from the ridge onto the wagon road and reined up about a hundred feet from him.

"Good morning, Bodine!" Lake called cheerfully. "Do you think it's a good day to die?"

"For you," Bodine told him.

Lake's face flushed and he began walking toward Bodine. The crowd fell silent.

Chapter 31

Bodine tossed the coffee cup to one side and brushed back his jacket, exposing both Colts. His left hand was close to the butt of the left hand Colt, his right hand hovering near the butt of the other six-shooter. No one had yet figured out how he did it, but all knew that Matt Bodine was just as fast with the left-handed, butt-forward pistol as he was with the tied down Colt on his right side.

And Matt could tell that was worrying Lake; the outlaw's eyes kept shifting from left to right as he continued walking toward Bodine.

Matt did not attempt to talk the outlaw out of dragging iron. He knew that for Lake, surrender was out of the question. He would rather go down by a bullet than be hanged. But Matt Bodine had made up his mind that Lake would not go out so easy.

"End of an era," Lake said, stopping about fifty feet from Bodine.

"Yes," Bodine agreed. "And yours has been a bloody one."

"Oh, I wasn't talking about me," Lake called.

"I was," Bodine said, then drew and shot the outlaw in his left shoulder.

The move caught Lake completely by surprise. The slug turned him around in the road and he stumbled, somehow managing to keep his balance. He jerked out a pistol with his one good arm and managed to get off a shot, the bullet furrowing up ground at Bodine's feet.

Bodine turned, presenting less of a target, took careful aim, and broke the outlaw's right arm, leaving him helpless, unable to use either arm.

"You bastard!" Lake cussed him. "You've left me to the hangman!"

"That's the general idea," Bodine told him, then holstered his Colt and walked away. He walked over to the man with a star pinned to his heavy winter coat. "He's all yours, Sheriff. Me and Sam will be here all the rest of the winter, helping Miss Laurie to get this ranch back in shape and locating beeves for the spring roundup. If you need us to testify, we'll be here."

"You should have killed him, Bodine," the sheriff said, without any admonition in the words; just stating a fact.

"I'm tired of it, Sheriff. I'm tired of me and Sam being judge and jury."

"A condition that will soon pass, I'm sure," Sam said, his voice as dry as the deserts they had ridden through chasing Lake and his band of scum.

The sheriff smiled. "We'll make it a very quick trial, Matt."

Matt and Sam Two Wolves spent the rest of the winter and part of the spring fixing up the ranch, hiring new hands, and locating cattle for roundup and branding. The cold winds changed to cool, and then to warm as spring began laying gentle hands across the land.

One pleasant spring morning Laurie looked out the kitchen window and was not surprised to see the horses of Matt and Sam saddled and tied to the hitchrail, the men leaning against the rail, smoking. She stepped out onto the porch.

"Have some coffee before you leave?" she asked.

"We drank a pot in the bunkhouse," Sam told her. "We just wanted to say goodbye."

"Jenny will be disappointed."

"She knows we're leaving," Matt said. "I think it's better this way."

"Will you be back?"

"Probably not. I like that young fellow who's sparkin' you. I keep hearing weddin' bells in the future."

"Jenny's crazy about him," she admitted that much.

"All the more reason for us to be pulling out," Sam said.

"Thank you both for everything you've done. I'll never forget you."

They swung into the saddle and each touched the brim of their hat in farewell. They pulled out of there as soon as they saw the tears begin to form in Laurie's eyes. They reached the end of the ranch road and stopped. The wagon road ran east and west.

"I seem to recall you mentioning something about Texas," Bodine said.

"Only in jest, I assure you, brother."

"Well, we have to go back to the fort to get our horses . . ."

"And the way is west?"

"It was the last time I looked."

"Then look again, it's south of us."

"Well . . . call it southwest. I'm easy to get along with."

"Since when!"

Bodine started arguing and waving the hand that wasn't holding the reins. Sam began insulting him in Cheyenne . . . as they headed southwest.

"I'm telling you, Sam, I wanna see Texas!"

"Oh . . . all right, Bodine, all right! Stop pouting."

"I'm not pouting."

"I said all right, let's go to Texas!"

Both young men laughed and let out war whoops and let their ponies run for a time . . . toward Texas.

AFTERWORD

Notes from the Old West

In the small town where I grew up, there were two movie theaters. The Pavilion was one of those old-timey movie show palaces, built in the heyday of Mary Pickford and Charlie Chaplin—the silent era of the 1920s. By the 1950s, when I was a kid, the Pavilion was a little worn around the edges, but it was still the premier theater in town. They played all those big Technicolor biblical Cecil B. DeMille epics and corny MGM musicals. In Cinemascope, of course.

On the other side of town was the Gem, a somewhat shabby and run-down grind house with sticky floors and torn seats. Admission was a quarter. The Gem booked low-budget "B" pictures (remember the Bowery Boys?), war movies, horror flicks, and Westerns. I liked the Westerns best. I could usually be found every Saturday at the Gem, along with my best friend, Newton Trout, watching Westerns from 10 A.M. until my father came looking for me around suppertime. (Sometimes Newton's dad was dispatched to come fetch us.) One time, my dad came to get me right in the middle of *Abilene Trail,* which featured the now-forgotten Whip Wilson.

My father became so engrossed in the action he sat down and watched the rest of it with us. We didn't get home until after dark, and my mother's meat loaf was a pan of gray ashes by the time we did. Though my father and I were both in the doghouse the next day, this remains one of my fondest childhood memories. There was Wild Bill Elliot, and Gene Autry, and Roy Rogers, and Tim Holt, and, a little later, Rod Cameron and Audie Murphy. Of these newcomers, I never missed an Audie Murphy Western, because Audie was sort of an antihero. Sure, he stood for law and order and was an honest man, but sometimes he had to go around the law to uphold it. If he didn't play fair, it was only because he felt hamstrung by the laws of the land. Whatever it took to get the bad guys, Audie did it. There were no finer points of law, no splitting of legal hairs. It was instant justice, devoid of long-winded lawyers, bored or biased jurors, or black-robed, often corrupt judges.

Steal a man's horse and you were the guest of honor at a necktie party.

Molest a good woman and you got a bullet in the heart or a rope around the gullet. Or at the very least, got the crap beat out of you. Rob a bank and face a hail of bullets or the hangman's noose.

Saved a lot of time and money, did frontier justice.

That's all gone now, I'm sad to say. Now you hear, "Oh, but he had a bad childhood" or "His mother didn't give him enough love" or "The homecoming queen wouldn't give him a second look and he has an inferiority complex." Or "cultural rage," as the politically correct bright boys refer to it. How many times have you heard some self-important defense attorney moan, "The poor kids were only venting their hostilities toward an uncaring society?"

Mule fritters, I say. Nowadays, you can't even call a punk a punk anymore. But don't get me started.

It was, "Howdy, ma'am" time too. The good guys, anti-hero or not, were always respectful to the ladies. They might shoot a bad guy five seconds after tipping their hat to a woman, but the code of the West demanded you be respectful to a lady.

Lots of things have changed since the heyday of the Wild West, haven't they? Some for the good, some for the bad.

I didn't have any idea at the time that I would someday write about the West. I just knew that I was captivated by the Old West.

When I first got the itch to write, back in the early 1970s, I didn't write Westerns. I started by writing horror and action adventure novels. After more than two dozen novels, I began thinking about developing a Western character. From those initial musings came the novel *The Last Mountain Man: Smoke Jensen*. That was followed by *Preacher: The First Mountain Man*. A few years later, I began developing the Last Gunfighter series. Frank Morgan is a legend in his own time, the fastest gun west of the Mississippi . . . a title and a reputation he never wanted, but can't get rid of.

For me, and for thousands—probably millions—of other people (although many will never publicly admit it), the old Wild West will always be a magic, mysterious place: a place we love to visit through the pages of books; characters we would like to know . . . from a safe distance; events we would love to take part in, again, from a safe distance. For the old Wild West was not a place for the faint of heart. It was a hard, tough, physically demanding time. There were no police to call if one faced adversity. One faced trouble alone, and handled it alone. It was rugged individualism: something that appeals to many of us.

I am certain that is something that appeals to most readers of Westerns.

I still do on-site research (whenever possible) before

starting a Western novel. I have wandered over much of the West, prowling what is left of ghost towns. Stand in the midst of the ruins of these old towns, use a little bit of imagination, and one can conjure up life as it used to be in the Wild West. The rowdy Saturday nights, the tinkling of a piano in a saloon, the laughter of cowboys and miners letting off steam after a week of hard work. Use a little more imagination and one can envision two men standing in the street, facing one another, seconds before the hook and draw of a gunfight. A moment later, one is dead and the other rides away.

The old wild untamed West.

There are still some ghost towns to visit, but they are rapidly vanishing as time and the elements take their toll. If you want to see them, make plans to do so as soon as possible, for in a few years, they will all be gone.

And so will we.

Stand in what is left of the Big Thicket country of east Texas and try to imagine how in the world the pioneers managed to get through that wild tangle. I have wondered about that many times and marveled at the courage of the men and women who slowly pushed westward, facing dangers that we can only imagine.

Let me touch briefly on a subject that is very close to me: firearms. There are some so-called historians who are now claiming that firearms played only a very insignificant part in the settlers' lives. They claim that only a few were armed. What utter, stupid nonsense! What do these so-called historians think the pioneers did for food? Do they think the early settlers rode down to the nearest supermarket and bought their meat? Or maybe they think the settlers chased down deer or buffalo on foot and beat the animals to death with a club. I have a news flash for you so-called historians: The settlers used guns to shoot their game. They used guns to defend hearth and home against Indians on the warpath. They used guns to protect themselves from outlaws. Guns are a part of Americana. And always will be.

The mountains of the West and the remains of the ghost towns that dot those areas are some of my favorite subjects to write about. I have done extensive research on the various mountain ranges of the West and go back whenever time permits. I sometimes stand surrounded by the towering mountains and wonder how in the world the pioneers ever made it through. As hard as I try and as often as I try, I simply cannot imagine the hardships those men and women endured over the hard months of their incredible journey. None of us can. It is said that on the Oregon Trail alone, there are at least two bodies in lonely, unmarked graves for every mile of that journey. Some students of the West say the number of dead is at least twice that. And nobody knows the exact number of wagons that impatiently started out alone and simply vanished on the way, along with their occupants, never to be seen or heard from again.

Just vanished.

The one-hundred-and-fifty-year-old ruts of the wagon wheels can still be seen in various places along the Oregon Trail. But if you plan to visit those places, do so quickly, for they are slowly disappearing. And when they are gone, they will be lost forever, except in the words of Western writers.

The West will live on as long as there are writers willing to write about it, and publishers willing to publish it. Writing about the West is wide open, just like the old Wild West. Characters abound, as plentiful as the wide-open spaces, as colorful as a sunset on the Painted Desert, as restless as the ever-sighing winds. All one has to do is use a bit of imagination. Take a stroll through the cemetery at Tombstone, Arizona; read the inscriptions. Then walk the main street of that once-infamous town around midnight and you might catch a glimpse of the ghosts that still wander the town. They really do. Just ask anyone who lives there. But don't be afraid of the apparitions, they won't hurt you. They're just out for a quiet stroll.

The West lives on. And as long as I am alive, it always will.

Turn the page for an exciting preview of

BLOOD BOND #3: *Gunsight Crossing*

By *USA Today* bestselling author

William W. Johnstone

Coming in March 2006

Wherever Pinnacle Books are sold

Chapter 1

"Do you have any idea at all where we might be?" Sam asked.

"Of course I do," Matt said with a smile. "We're in New Mexico Territory."

"You said that last week!"

"It's a big territory."

And it was hot. The hard-packed and rutted road upon which they traveled eastward flung the heat back at them. They had seen jackrabbits, a few eagles soaring high in the brilliant blue of the sky, and nothing else for two days.

"But I think it's time to cut south," Matt said.

"I think it's time to do something," Sam Two Wolves agreed. "We're running out of food, and if we don't find water soon, we're going to die out here in this godforsaken place."

Matt laughed at his blood brother, but he knew the truth lay like shining steel in his words. They were going to be in serious trouble if they didn't find water, and find it very quickly.

Matt Bodine and Sam August Webster Two Wolves were blood brothers, bonded by the Cheyenne ritual that made them as one. They were also Brothers of the Wolf; they were Onihomahan: Friends of the Wolf. The two men could and often did pass as having the same mother and father—which they did not. Both possessed the same broad shoulders, lean hips, and heavy musculature. Sam's eyes were black, Matt's were blue. Sam's hair was black, Bodine's was dark brown. They were the same height and very nearly the same weight. Both wore the same type of three-stone necklace around their necks, the stones-pierced by rawhide. Both were ruggedly handsome men. Both had gone through the Cheyenne Coming of Manhood; they had the scars on their chests to prove it.

"You really think God has forsaken this country?" Matt asked.

"No. Of course not. But I think that perhaps He ignores it more than other sections."

The brothers cut south.

The horses suddenly pricked their ears and became restless.

"Indians?" Matt asked.

"I hope not," Sam replied. "This is Comanche and Apache country—I think." He stood up in the stirrups and sniffed the air. It was moist. "Water," he said.

"What do you mean, 'I think'? You don't know what tribes are around here?"

"I am Northern Cheyenne, idiot! From a thousand miles north of this desolation. Am I supposed to know everything about every tribe in North America?"

A stranger would think the two disliked each other. They loved each other as brothers. The constant poking and ribbing was their way of showing the affection both felt for the other. As many trouble-hunters had learned painfully, quickly, and sometimes fatally, mess with one and you had the other with whom to deal.

"You're half Cheyenne," Bodine corrected. "And I don't

expect you to know anything. Without me, you'd have been lost two weeks ago."

"Bah!" Sam said contemptuously. "You couldn't find your way to an outhouse if you had the squirts."

Both men were excellent trackers and woodsmen, and both had the reputation of gunfighters, although neither had ever sought nor wanted that title.

The next day, the young men crossed a road that headed south by southwest. It looked well-traveled, but neither Matt nor Sam were looking for company, so they elected to go on for another day. They topped a ridge and saw another road, this one running north and south, and just beyond that, a river.

"What river is that?" Matt asked.

"I have no inkling whatsoever. Texas was your idea, not mine." Sam sat his saddle and tried to look solemn. But his dark eyes were twinkling at the thoughts of whatever adventure lay ahead of them. The two young men were full of the juices of youth and had never run from anything in their lives.

Matt called him a very vulgar name in Cheyenne and with a whoop, they went galloping their horses toward the beckoning waters of the river.

Matt stood guard while his *I-tat-an-e,* Cheyenne for *brother,* took a bath, soaping himself generously and diving under the waters several times to rinse off. He climbed out, dried and dressed, and Matt took his turn. They both needed it: it had been about ten days since they'd bathed and shaved. But a shave was going to have to wait.

It was growing late in the afternoon, and both men were weary from the long, hot, almost waterless miles and days behind them. Sam made camp while Matt rode out to shoot some rabbits for their supper. Their supplies were growing dangerously low.

Matt killed two jackrabbits, and Sam had the last of their potatoes and onions ready for stewing when his brother returned. While the stew was bubbling and thickening, the young men drank coffee and relaxed.

"You have any idea what this river is called?" Sam asked.

"I hate to say it, but it may be the Pecos."

"The Pecos!" Sam sat up. "If that's the case, we're almost out of New Mexico."

"Yeah. Want to cut south and follow the river come first light?"

"Why not?"

The two young men were wandering, entirely aimlessly, trying to get their minds settled before returning to their home range in Montana. They had witnessed the awful carnage at Little Bighorn the past year, the battle in which Sam's father, Medicine Horse, had charged Custer with a deliberately empty rifle and counted coup on Custer—striking him with his coup stick—before dying. Matt and Sam had laid on a ridge and watched through the swirling dust as the troopers of the Seventh fell.

Even though both young men were moderately wealthy in their own right—they both owned ranches and Sam's white mother had left him quite an estate for the time—Matt and Sam knew they had to drift for a time. After seeing the slaughter at Little Bighorn, neither man felt at peace with himself.

"Riders coming," Sam said, his palm to the ground. "Several of them."

"I heard them before you did," Matt lied.

"Ha! You couldn't hear a bumblebee until it stung you on the rear."

Matt and Sam got to their boots. Both men wore two guns. Matt carried both of his in leather, tied down, while Sam carried one in leather on his right side and another butt-forward on his left side, tucked in a sash he wore around his waist.

"They don't look friendly," Sam observed.

"Looking for trouble, I'd say." Bodine moved away from Sam to lessen the odds of both of them being taken out at once should shooting start.

"Slow it down!" Bodine yelled. "We don't need all that damn dust in our stew."

Instead of easing up, the four riders kicked their horses into a gallop and came charging into the camp, knocking over the stew and scattering the blankets. They made their mistake when they slowed, turned around, and came back for another go at the camp.

Bodine reached up and jerked one out of his saddle while Sam was doing the same thing to another. The men hit the ground hard, on their backs, jarring their teeth and having the wind knocked from them. One mounted cowboy made the mistake of grabbing iron. Bodine put a .44 slug in his shoulder. The last rider sat his saddle, wanting to get into action, but not in a terrible hurry to get shot.

The shoulder-shot cowboy moaned and passed out, falling from his saddle.

A big black-headed fellow got to his boots cussing. While Sam kept a .44 on the last cowboy in his saddle, Bodine hit the big fellow twice in the belly and then came up with an uppercut that stretched him on the ground.

"You want a piece of it?" Bodine asked the other cowpoke, who was getting up.

"I reckon not. But John Lee ain't gonna like this a-tall."

"I don't give a damn what John Lee likes or dislikes," Bodine told him. "But I'll tell you what you're going to do."

"Oh, yeah?"

Bodine stepped forward and knocked the man on his rear, bloodying his mouth and momentarily crossing his eyes.

"Yeah," Matt told him. "You ready to listen?"

"I reckon so. Beats gettin' my lights punched out."

"Coffeepot's smashed and the cook pot fell into the coals. Heat cracked it," Sam said.

Bodine reached down and removed the man's guns from leather. "Now listen carefully. You ride—I don't care where—and you get back here with a new coffeepot, a new cook pot, and some meat and vegetables to go in it." He pointed to the shoulder-shot puncher. "And take that punk with you. The others will stay here for insurance."

"Are you crazy, man?" Bloody-mouth asked. "Do you know who you're foolin' with?"

Matt jerked iron and jacked the hammer back, placing the muzzle of the .44 on the man's forehead. The sharp odor of urine filled the late afternoon air as Bloody-mouth peed in his long-handles.

"If I have to tell you again, I'm going to be talking to a corpse," Matt told him. "Now ride, you bastard!"

Bloody-mouth got gone. Matt boosted the shoulder-shot puncher into his saddle and slapped the horse on the rump.

Matt turned toward the kid in the saddle as the black-headed man moaned and started to rise. He looked down the muzzle of the .44 in Sam's hand and changed his mind. "You guys are crazy! Where's Val?"

"He went to get us some food," Sam told him. "After a brief altercation with my brother, he quickly realized the boorishness of your actions and felt very apologetic about it."

"What the hell did you say?"

"Shut up!"

"I understood that."

"Get off your horse," Matt told the young puncher. "Now, use your thumb and forefinger only and toss your guns over to me."

Two revolvers hit the ground.

"What's your name?" Matt asked him.

"Childress."

"What the hell was the point of coming in here and hoorahin' us?"

"Just funnin', that's all."

"You call destroying someone's camp fun?"

"You shouldna oughta told us to slow up. You don't tell Broken Lance riders to do nothin'. And you're gonna find that out the hard way damn quick."

"I doubt it," Matt told him. "Now get that coffee pot you got tied behind your saddle and make us some coffee."

"I'll be damned iffen I will!"

Bodine moved toward him. "Do it!" his cohort yelled. "We ain't got a whole lot of choice in the matter. And be sure to get that coffee sack outta your saddlebags."

Both Sam and Bodine smiled. Childress probably had a spare six-shooter in there and black head was telling him to use it.

Sam put the muzzle of his .44 against the black-haired man's ear. The sound of the hammer jacking back was very loud in the quiet. "If he comes out of there with iron in his hand instead of coffee, you're dead."

"Forget it, Childress," the man called. "Just make the damn coffee."

"Do you have a name?" Sam asked him.

"Blackie."

Childress slowly took his coffee and his pot and made coffee, using water from his canteen. The aroma of the spilled stew wafted deliciously around the camp.

"I was looking forward to that stew," Bodine remarked, sitting on a weathered log that had drifted down the river from only God knew where and how long ago.

"You ain't gonna look forward to John's visit," Blackie said. " 'Cause shortly after he gets here, you both gonna be dead men rottin' on the ground."

"You'll be right there with us," Matt told him, then his gaze cut to Childress. "And so will you."

The bullying punchers exchanged worried glances. There was something in Bodine's manner that led them both to believe he meant exactly what he said. And Sam Two Wolves had the same demeanor.

"You two related?" Blackie asked.

"Brothers," Sam told him.

"Don't see too many men wearin' necklaces," Childress said with a nasty smirk.

"They show us to be members of the Cheyenne tribe," Bodine informed him. "We've both endured the Coming of Manhood."

"Is that 'posed to mean something?" the young punk asked.

"It means something," Blackie said, the words softly spoken. "Now shut your mouth, Childress. We're in a lot more trouble here than you might think."

"Wise man," Sam told him. "You want some coffee?"

"I'd appreciate a cup."

The men drank coffee and lounged for nearly an hour. They all heard the thunder of many hooves long before the riders topped the crest of the hill and stopped, looking down at the small camp. Sam and Bodine stood up and picked up Henry rifles, chambering rounds and keeping the hammers back.

"Don't do nothin' stupid," Blackie said. "If John was comin' in hostile, he'd done been shootin'. Just relax."

"I'm very relaxed," Bodine told him. "Are you relaxed, *I-tat-an-e?*"

"I am so at ease I might fall asleep any moment."

"You guys are crazy!" Childress said. "John Lee is one of the fastest guns ever. And that's Rawhide O'Neal next to him. Down at the end there, that's Pen Masters—"

"Shut up, Childress!" Blackie told him. "Just shut your damn mouth!"

"You know somethin' I don't?" Childress asked.

"Yeah," Blackie said sourly. "I shore do. Just be quiet."

The cowhand Matt had sent for the pots, pans, and food rode beside John Lee as the men left the column and headed down the slope. Four riders fell in behind them.

"I sent you for pots and pans and food," Matt told Val. "And you bring back an army. Tell me, do you know the difference between a cow's tail and a pump handle?"

"Huh?" Val asked.

"You don't?"

"I don't understand the question."

"I'd hate to send you out for water, then," Matt grinned the words.

Sam laughed. John Lee and the others did not see the humor in it. John Lee said, "You boys need to be taught a lesson, I'm thinking."

"You're wearing a gun," Matt told him. "Why don't you get your butt and your mouth out of that saddle and let's see what you can do besides flap your gums."

John looked like he was about to have a stroke. He sputtered for a moment. Nobody talked to him like that. He'd show the young pup a thing or two.

"That's Matt Bodine, boss." Blackie tossed the words out before John could leave the saddle.

One of the riders behind John expelled air slowly. Another one grunted. All of them kept their hands in sight.

"So it figures that's got to be Sam Two Wolves with him," Blackie added.

John Lee was a man used to getting his own way. He'd come out to that part of New Mexico and Texas years back, when life on the frontier meant facing death every day. It took hard and rough men to stay. The graveyard at his ranch was filled with men who'd died riding for the Broken Lance. But John Lee was not an ignorant man. He knew that if anyone started shooting, he'd be the first one Bodine would blow out of the saddle.

Everyone in the West had heard of Matt Bodine. Killed his first man at age fourteen. A year later, the man's brothers came to avenge the killing. When the smoke drifted away, Matt was standing amid the bodies, both hands filled with Colts. When he was sixteen, rustlers hit the ranch. Matt killed two more and wounded two others. He'd lived with the Cheyenne for more than a year. Then he was a guard, riding shotgun for gold shipments. Four more men went to rest in lonely graves. He scouted for the Army and put more so-called bad men in the ground.

Sam Two Wolves was just as fast as Matt Bodine and just as quick on the temper as he was on the trigger. John had heard the stories about Sam's high education at an Eastern university and about his white mother's wealth. John quickly surmised he was in the middle of a very volatile situation there.

"We didn't bring any cookin' utensils," John said.

"That's too bad," Bodine told him. " 'Cause we're getting hungry."

"And when we get hungry our tempers get short," Sam added.

"Why didn't you bring what I asked for?" Matt's eyes met those of John Lee.

John wanted to tell him to go right straight to hell. But he wisely kept his mouth shut.

"I'll tell you why," Matt said. "Because you allow your men to ride roughshod over anything and anybody and think it's funny when other people's possessions are destroyed. You thought you were going to come out here with your pack of hyenas and leave our bodies for the buzzards and the coyotes. You think you're God Almighty. Untouchable. I don't like people like you. At all."

Pen Masters rode down the slope. "Come on, Matt," the gunfighter said. "You and me know each other from our days back on the Tongue. I don't want this to turn into no shootin'. Not over some damn pots and pans."

"It isn't about pots and pans, Pen," Matt told him. "You know that."

"Matt," the gunfighter said, "you're the fastest man with a gun I've ever seen. But you'll be shot to ribbons if you start anything here."

"And you'll all be dead," Sam spoke. "And Lord of the Manor there," his eyes touched John, "will be the first to go."

"Copper!" John said. "Go on back to the ranch and fetch a goddamn coffeepot and other crap. Bring some food. We'll wait here for you."

The puncher left at a gallop. John's eyes were hard and mean as he looked at Bodine. "I don't take water from no man," he told Bodine. "Maybe my boys were wrong in what they done. So I'll replace your gear and provisions. Then you best ride on out of this area. No man wants to die before his time, Bodine. But if you ever brace me again and talk to me like you just done, as God is my witness, one of us will die. Come on, boys. Copper don't need no nursemaid to find his way back."

He wheeled his horse and rode away. Pen stayed for a moment, looking at Bodine while Blackie and Childress mounted up and rode off.

"Back off of this one, Bodine," he warned, not in an unfriendly tone. "John Lee runs this part of the country. He owns everything and everybody. John Lee says 'frog', people jump."

"Then maybe he needs somebody to muddy up his pond," Matt replied.

Sam grinned. He had a hunch that he and Matt were going to stick around for a time.

Chapter 2

"So what's the plan?" Sam asked, as Pen rode away.

Matt shrugged his shoulders. "What plan? I just took a dislike for the man, that's all."

"He's easy to dislike," Sam agreed. "Be interesting to see if our gear is replaced."

"Oh, I think it will be. I'm sure he considers himself to be a very honorable man . . . and he might be in a very peculiar and self-serving fashion. I think as soon as our gear is replaced, we'd best pull out. That fellow back on the trail told us there was a little two-bit town about ten miles south of the New Mexico line. Half a dozen stores and a fleabag hotel. What do you think?"

"I'm game."

Within the hour, the puncher called Copper rode back in and dropped a sack on the ground. "I ain't got a thing in the world agin you fellers, so I'm gonna give you some friendly advice. Get gone. John Lee is all of a sudden hirin' hard-cases and payin' fightin' wages. And it ain't 'cause of the Comanches neither. Quanah Parker and his bunch shot their wad a couple of years back. They's still Injuns around, but not many. I don't know what's goin' on, but was I you boys, I wouldn't stick around and get caught up in the middle of it."

Copper turned his horse and rode off.

"The Southern Cheyenne rode with Quanah and his bunch for a time," Sam said. "But not many of them. Most of the others were Kiowa, Kwahadi, and Arapaho."

"What do you think about Copper's claim to know nothing about what John Lee is up to?"

Sam did a squatting motion, cupped his hands to indicate a large mound, and made a mooing sound. Cheyenne for *bullshit*.

John Lee had returned more than had been destroyed. There was a side of bacon, some flour and beans, potatoes and onions, and a skillet, cook pot, and coffeepot. Matt and Sam quickly packed up and headed south.

It was well after dark when they rode slowly into the town. A sign had proclaimed the town's name as Crossing.

"Crossing what?" Sam questioned.

"First town after crossing the territory line, I reckon," Matt replied.

"That is as good a reply as any," Sam said.

Crossing had a big general store, a bigger saloon, a blacksmith shop/livery stable, a combination saddle and gun shop, a barber shop, a café, a marshal's office, and a hotel that was over the saloon. "Bustling little place, isn't it?" Sam said.

They had seen no signs of life. The only building lit up was the saloon.

"Let's see to our horses," Matt suggested.

They swung into the livery stable and dismounted. A middle-aged man who smelled like he slept inside a barrel of whiskey walked out and greeted them sourly.

"Treat them right," Sam told the man. "All the corn they want."

"You got any money?"

They paid him in advance and the man grumbled something under his breath.

"What was that?" Matt asked, taking his saddlebags and rifle.

"I said: you boys ain't got no sense. John Lee told you to git, you oughtta git!"

"News travels fast," Sam said.

"John Lee don't just own the biggest spread in the county, he owns the county. You're not welcome here, boys."

They found that out when they tried to register at the hotel.

"Full up," the desk clerk told them.

The saloon was on the other side of a partition. No sounds came from the saloon area.

Matt spun the registry book, glanced at it, then lifted his eyes to meet the nervous eyes of the desk clerk.

"I got orders, boys," he said, his voice breaking.

Matt took the pen, dabbed it in the ink bottle, and started to register.

"I wouldn't do that, Bodine," the voice came from behind him. It was a familiar voice. John Lee.

Matt turned, surprised to see the man alone. The surprise must have been quite obvious, for John smiled.

"Did you think I have to have bodyguards around me at all times?" he questioned.

"The only thing I know about you is that I don't like you."

John's smile widened. "You don't even know me, Bodine."

Matt studied the man. A big man, wide of shoulder with hard-packed muscle and lean of hip. Big hands, thick wrists, heavily muscled arms. Matt guessed him to be in his early forties. "I know the type."

Sam had given the outside a careful once-over. "He's not alone."

"I didn't expect him to be."

This time, John's smile vanished. "The hotel is closed to you boys. But without malice. I have guests coming in, that's all there is to it."

"All right," Matt said with a shrug. "We understand that. You object to us sleeping in the stable?"

"No. Just be gone by morning."

Riders pulled up in the front of the hotel. Their horses moved like they were weary. John Lee's back was to Sam, and he didn't see the hand signal Sam gave Matt. Trouble.

"Mind if we have a drink in your saloon?" Matt asked.

"I'd deny no man a drink to cut the dust of the trail." John's smile was once more in place. "As a matter of fact, I'll buy the first one."

"Kind of you."

"Tell the barkeep."

He seemed anxious for them to leave the small lobby of the hotel, so they accommodated his silent wishes. "Thank you," Sam told him. Saddlebags and rifles in hand, the men walked into the bar. It was empty except for the barkeep.

"Evenin', gents. What'll it be?"

Neither was a hard-drinking man, so they both ordered beer. "Got some eggs and bread and cheese left from lunch," the barkeep told them. "It'll have to do for supper, seein' as how the café's closed."

"That'll be fine," Sam told him, as they sat down at a table next to a rear wall. The table was farthest away from the lanterns and in the shadows.

The barkeep brought their beer and food. Setting the mugs down on the table, he whispered, "I heard the exchange in the lobby. All hell's fixin' to bust loose around this part of the state. Ride south in the morning until you come to the Circle S spread. Ten miles south of town. They set a good breakfast and will turn no man away from a meal. Talk to Jeff Sparks."

After the barkeep had returned to his position behind the long bar, Sam whispered, "Now what was that all about?"

"I don't know. Some damn weird things going on around this place. Makes me curious."

"Me too. And I do admire a hearty breakfast."

The blood brothers grinned at each other and fell to eating, both of them conscious of the talking going on in the lobby of the hotel. A lot of voices. Hard voices, profane language. The men from the lobby began drifting into the bar in pairs. They were uncurried and uncouth, with most of them packing two guns in leather and another six-shooter tucked behind the gunbelt.

"Well, now," Bodine said softly. "Would you just look at that."

"I see it. I know a couple of them. You?"

"Yeah. Harry Street's the biggest one. Dean Waters is the one with a scar on his face. The two standing near the batwings are Carl Jergens and Dexter Campbell. That's as worthless a quartet as ever wore boots."

"That's Jack Morgan and Jim Johnson sitting at the far table. Arizona gunfighters. Pukey Stagg is the little one off by himself. He's vicious and snake-quick. I don't know the other one."

"His name is Mack. If he has a last name, I never heard it. He's out of Utah. Gunfighter."

"Any of them know you?"

"Several of them. And I'm not on their list of best-liked people."

"I can certainly understand that," Sam needled him. "You have such an abrasive personality."

"Look who's talking," Matt fired back. "Everywhere you go you start trouble."

"What are you two a-whisperin' about over yonder?" Big Harry Street bellered.

"None of your damn business," Sam told him.

"See what I mean?" Matt said.

The no-counts all stopped talking and looked at the two men sitting in the shadows.

Big Harry turned slowly from the bar, looking hard at Matt and Sam. He was a huge man, about six inches over six feet and weighing a good two hundred and fifty pounds. And he was as worthless a human being as they came. A killer for hire who would kill a baby as quickly as he would an adult. He enjoyed killing children's pets just to see the child cry.

Matt took the handles of the beer mugs in his left hand, got up, and walked slowly to the bar, his spurs jingling softly as he walked. The crowd of crud fell silent as they recognized him. The room got very silent when they heard Sam jack back the hammer on his Henry.

"Relax, people," Dean Waters said. "We ain't here to start no trouble with Bodine or his half-breed brother."

Sam laughed softly. But Bodine knew that behind that laugh was no humor.

"Nothin' meant by that, Two Wolves," Dean said. "I just called you what you is."

"If I called you what you are," Sam retorted, "I would probably be put in jail."

"Fill them up," Matt told the barkeep.

"You a long way from Wyoming, Bodine," Harry said.

"Quite a ways, Harry."

"You still rescuin' kids and dogs and cats and little old ladies, Bodine?"

"You still hiring your gun out to shoot people in the back, Harry?" Matt fired back.

Dean stepped between the two men before Harry could

think of a comeback. He needn't have hurried, for thinking was not one of Harry's strong suits.

"Stand easy, Harry," Dean told him. He turned to face Matt. "What the hell are you on the prod about, Bodine?"

"I'm not on the prod about anything. I'm just passin' through, Waters. Having a couple of beers before turning in. But I'm not going to take a lot of mouth from this buffalo here." He looked at Harry.

"Who you callin' a buffalo, Bodine?" Harry blustered.

"You. I don't see anybody else around that looks and smells like one."

The barkeep laid a sawed-off shotgun on the bar. "No trouble in here, boys. And I mean it. I just had this floor mopped and blood is hard to get up."

Dean jerked his head at a couple of gunslicks and they led Harry off to a table, the big man mumbling and cussing. He turned to Bodine. "I hope you're not buyin' into this, Bodine. This is none of your damn affair."

"I don't even know what you're talking about, Waters. But don't crowd me. Just leave me alone and everything will be jam-up and jelly."

Matt took his refilled mugs and walked back to the table.

"Whatever is going on, it's big," Sam said. "Do we want to stay in the middle of it?"

"No. Tomorrow we'll ride out to the Circle S and look it over. At first guess I'd say that John Lee is land hungry and wants to swallow up the Circle S. But he just might be finding it tough chewing."

"And you intend to put a couple of more rocks in the stew?"

Matt smiled. "Yeah. Like you and me."

"And you call me a troublemaker."

* * *

The blood brothers rode out of town before dawn began streaking the eastern skies. The lamps were lit at the café, but while both men longed for a cup of coffee, neither man wanted to push their luck. A dozen more men, hardcases all, had ridden in during the night and put up their horses, obviously thinking the stable was deserted. They had talked and confirmed what Matt and Sam had already guessed: John Lee wanted the Circle S spread and was hiring gunslicks to help him get it.

Among the newly arrived gunmen were Bam Ford, Bob Grove, Mark Hazard, and Dave Land—all Texas gunslingers from around the Big Thicket area. Jack Lightfoot and Gil Lopez had come in around midnight. They worked as a team, both of them notorious ambushers and back shooters. Leo Grand had come in alone. He was from up around the Four Corners. And the Oklahoma gunhawk, Trest, had ridden in with Lew Hagan.

"The scum are gathering," Matt said, after about a mile on the trail.

"Yes. And it's costing John Lee a good deal of money for those men. They're all top guns."

"And I'll bet there are more coming in."

"If so, then he's building an army. But why all this to take over a ranch? According to the talk, Jeff Sparks barely has enough hands to run his ranch, much less fight."

"Maybe we can find that out over breakfast."

"I hope they make good coffee."

"I hope they don't shoot us before we can find out!"

They left the road at a battered hand-painted sign that was just legible. Circle S—3 miles. An arrow pointed the way. About an eighth of a mile from the ranch house, a closed gate blocked the way.

"Now what?" Sam asked.

"We wait."

It wasn't a long wait. Less than five minutes had passed before a tall old man with a handlebar mustache that was wider than his face rode out. He did not immediately open the gate. He sat his horse and stared at the blood brothers. He gave them the once-over very slowly and very carefully, his sharp eyes not missing a thing, and Matt knew he had pegged them as gunfighters right off the bat.

"We got the reputation of gunslingers, mister," Matt told him. "But it isn't something we wanted or work at. The barkeep at the saloon in Crossing told us the Circle S set a fine breakfast."

"Did he now?"

"Yes, sir," Sam said, and the old man picked up on the "sir" and smiled.

"Them's Cheyenne necklaces."

"Yes, they are. We're blood brothers."

"You got names?"

"I'm Matt and he's Sam."

"How come you didn't grub in town? You broke?"

Matt smiled. "We still have some coins to rub together." Fact was, Bodine and Sam had quite a bit of money in belts around their waists. "We had a run-in with a bigmouth name of John Lee yesterday. After his hands trashed our camp. We shot one and unhorsed the others. . . ."

"Rather rudely," Sam added, and the old man looked like he was going to bust out laughing.

"Sent one of them back to see his boss with orders to replace our busted gear. Mr. John Lee himself came back, with a whole bunch of hands. Had a gunfighter I knew years back with him. Name of Pen Masters. John Lee talked and we listened, then we talked and he listened. He replaced our gear."

"Do tell. Come on up to the house. I can't wait to hear the rest of this tale."

He pushed open the gate and latched it securely as soon as the brothers were inside. "Name's Dodge," he told them.

"I'm the foreman." He pointed to a battered basin and a pump by what looked like the bunkhouse. "Wash there. I'll tell the boss we got two more for breakfast." He looked at Matt. "You ain't got no Injun in you, and your brother ain't got that much either."

"My mother was white," Sam said. "Their marriage was done legally and with prayers from the white man's god and from my father's gods. I was educated at a university back East."

Dodge nodded his head. "Wash up and come to grub. And watch your language. The boss's wife and daughters will be at the table. The hands has aready et and gone."

A man met them on the front porch of the large roomy and airy home. It was a long, low home, built in the Spanish hacienda style. "Jeff Sparks, boys," he said, holding out his hand. "Which one's Matt and which one's Sam?" Jeff was in his late forties or early fifties. His red hair just graying a mite.

He led them into the house and the men could see this was a home that was lived in. It had many nice furnishings for the frontier, but the chairs and couches were to sit on, not for show.

"Girls!" he hollered. "Got two mighty handsome young men in here. Come look 'em over!"

Matt and Sam exchanged glances, unaccustomed to being viewed like sides of beef. They both wished they'd shaved that morning when the girls came into the room.

"Lisa and Lia," Jeff said, obviously enjoying himself. "Matt and Sam."

The girls smiled at the boys and the boys blushed.

Lisa was a redhead and Lia was a strawberry blonde. Both of them were shapely and very, very comely. They were wearing something that neither Matt nor Sam had ever seen before. Split skirts. They weren't britches and they weren't skirts. The brothers didn't know what the hell they were.

"You boys had coffee?" Jeff asked.

"No, sir," Sam said.

"Hell's fire!" he hollered. "That ain't decent. Girls, go fetch the pot and some cups and tell your mama to come in and meet our guests. Tell Conchita to start rattlin' them pots and pans. She's got some hungry men salivating out here." He pointed to the couch. "Sit."

Matt and Sam sat. Before they could get comfortable, the girls were back with coffeepot and cups. Before they could take the first sip, a very handsome lady entered the room. No split skirt for this one. A full dress and a nice one at that.

"My wife, boys. Nancy."

Matt and Sam were already on their feet. "Pleasure, ma'am," they said.

"Sit and drink your coffee, gentlemen," Nancy said, taking a seat. "Dodge told us you had trouble with John Lee. Why should we believe you?"

"Mother . . ." Jeff said, putting out a hand.

"No, let me finish," she persisted. "We know that John has been hiring gunfighters. These young men are gunfighters. They have the stamp upon them. How do we know John didn't send them here to kill us in our own home?"

Matt's gaze cut to Dodge standing off to the side of the room, his hand on the butt of his pistol. Another man was on Sam's right, also ready for action.

"Yes," Nancy said. "You can have a good meal, then if you're here to cause trouble, you can be buried with a full stomach."

Matt grinned. "You have a right to be suspicious, but I can assure you all that we don't work for John Lee."

"Those are good questions, ma'am," Sam said. "And you're right on one count: we have used a gun a time or two. But we don't hire them out—ever!"

"Never seen that brand before," Dodge said.

"We're from up Wyoming, Montana. Both of us own

ranches up there—paying ranches. Both of us were scouting for the Army when Custer was killed at Little Bighorn. Sam's father was killed there, too. He rode in, unarmed except for a coup stick. He did not want war."

"My mother left me an inheritance," Sam said. "While I am not wealthy, I am comfortable. So is my blood brother." He smiled. "Matt Bodine."

"Hell's fire!" Jeff shouted. "Matt Bodine!" He dropped his coffee cup.